Left Side Shadow of the Sun

Ife Fyne-Nsofor

Dedication

To God.

And to Kerry Leigh Easley Brooks

Introduction

Feb 22, 2005

"... And Cali on right offense!" came my coach's voice snapping me out of my reverie. I was gone again afoot the distant noises that had acquainted itself to my reluctant mind. I turned to pay better attention to him, fixating on his movement of his lips to keep my attention on our field assignments. He continued as he did before every game, to tell us how to play the game of our lives. It was only nine months ago. Nine months. The game of my life was just between me, the ball, and an-eighteen feet net. The ball wasn't considerably bigger than a decision I had to make; the field, much like the terrains of a rather bothersome conscience, and fickle emotions; the net - the end. Nine months ago. That time is waxed now, and when my coach mentions the game of life, the game I see - the game I play is guided now by a motion picture that plays in my mind over again, never to succumb to suppression or mere memory loss.

I play with patches of memories floating in the field with me, like I never left it behind. It escorts my mind away

4

from what it knew, what it once believed; leaving only the battered old box beneath my bed, the scars about my body, the importance of my father's words, the boy in the picture taped on my dashboard, and the boy who lies in my brother's grave.

I suppose it is a tale of survival, or perhaps it is a story about tragic loss. Perhaps it is about healing, or just a love story. On the other hand, possibly it is about all of it. For I suppose it wouldn't be much of any story without all these things.

Even though I know it is all done, and we made it and survived, I still yearned for the touch and feel of my family, mostly because I knew that even one year after it was done, we had not all healed past spending large amounts of time together. Even though I now sleep in a somewhat better state of security, I even so wake up in fear, and I still see it. I still hear them; the voices that were robbed of words. I still lay, eyes wide open and fingers clamped together, waiting for it to go away. The dread; the guilt; the hate; the blood.

January 16, 2005

The truck pulls into the driveway of the Cassidy Estate; the home I lived in for six years, a happy life prior to leaving for Northern Uganda. I stand in the drive court staring at the stately home, as what it used to be jeered its memories across my face. Sydney and I had moved into the pool house after we had graduated from high school, but for these new times with their little trials, my parents requested that we stay in the house for the first few months. I did not argue, because I could scarcely yet be in a room by myself. I see Allyson's blonde hair float across my face, carrying across her laughter echoing against the breeze that blew gently across the way. Cassie is squealing with laughter because she has the giggle fits. Whenever Cassie gets the giggle fits, it's all over. There's no stopping her. I can hear shouting and music coming from the pool where the rest of my friends are playing water polo; where Emmy keeps walking across and back to where she was certain Jeremy can see her pretend that she could not care less if he was there or not. Somewhere in my wondering I come back to the realization that there is no movement from the house. Along with that oddity was that my dad picked me up from the airport without my mom, or Sydney. There was no strangeness in Rhys's absence because with Luke's company, he returned to Uganda two days after I had given him the letter ending the love we both never learned how to do without. I expected that my friends were inside of that house, hiding behind whatever would conceal their silhouettes until the time when I would be walking into those doors to be greeted by the happiest faces of the loves I was almost certain I'd never see again. I felt their warm embrace as they held me with hands I had dreamed so long and often I would be in, that I could no longer decipher if they were yet as real as they felt. My head tells me my story again, and brings me back to that moment where I have no other choice, but to believe that the merriment in the air signaled the truth that I, Calista was home.

January 20, 20005

"Cali! Cali! Hold my hand..."

The voice is faint as I try to decide from where it came. I checked the doors, and the windows. I had checked the alarm, making sure my parents had not forgotten to turn on the motion lights. I was in the house that was safe with several guns in a safe inside my parents' room, and two very protective German Shepherds. So, what was I doing here under my bed again, breathing away the dizziness in my head, and the ache that was standing with its thousand pounds atop my chest? I had yet to sleep properly since coming home to the U.S. because of the voices in my head that retold stories I cared not for. I saw them coming for us in my dreams. They are chasing me, hunting for my blood, and I cannot seem to evade them. They catch me every time, bind my hands and feet and stab repeatedly at me. So, I lay awake as late as I can so that the images penetrate my memories alone haunting the slumber away from me. When I get up in the morning and open the blinds, the sun pours the new day inside of the space illuminating the calendar where I have to mark out the day just to remember which one it was. In the bathroom, there is a cabinet with my name on it containing medications that line the shelves, all to play their own part to set me free. There are vitamins, medicines for anti anxiety, anti depression, tranquilizers, and sleep aids. There are HIV medicines that I have to take as well for the next six months while the test results were being awaited as to whether I carried a sexual disease. Mealtimes are a struggle as I force each morsel, barely chewing before I swallow to appease the worries of my parents whose concern is a constant register on their faces. When eventually the night would find me under my bed, Sydney would lie there with me waiting for my breathing to regulate while she held my hand, and told me stories of the person who I was strong enough to become.

March 9, 2005

"Calista, do you want to get better?" My therapist asks me each day before the start of each session.

"Yes."

"Why?"

"Because... because fear is an exhausting captor. Before now, before this vile shift, I never was much for dramatics. I mean, with my friends it was different. However, generally, if there was a problem, I searched for the solution. I would then implement those solutions –

problem solved – move on. If there weren't any solutions, I would just move on anyway. I found worry such a nuisance, and fear a bandit, that I never really allowed the time to entertain them."

"Do you believe that you are going to get better? That your life will ever return to the normalcy you crave?"

"It has to. There is only either of two things that I can do: fight to live, or fight to die."

"Do you feel that you might be suicidal?"

"There'd be no sense to it, counselor. I am already dead."

 I cannot tell her the knot that ties my stomach from feeling, from swallowing the lump that rests so stagnantly inside my throat. It is always the same each time that I am there. She asks me questions, and I answer them as basely as I can. She knows that I am keeping particulars from her. I know that she knows. I do not care that she knows.

She has that kind of couch that made it almost impossible for you to want to sit in a corner of it and keep your mouth shut. I tried my best, and as usual, I succeeded.

We sat there in strangling silence, my eyes to the floor, counting the squares on the carpet. Her eyes I could feel watching me intently as if my face would betray my intense desire for lack of disclosure.

"How different was this week from the last?" She asks me as she always does at the beginning of every session.

"Nothing's different… not by much anyway," I answer as I always do at the beginning of every session. She looks at me concernedly through her glasses, and I am ashamed of my resistance to her care. However, as it happens every time, I watch the clock tick by to the end of the hour while in the meantime, I occupy my mind with the ever-present film of the circle in the sand, the hut, the raffia sponge, and the determination to bring my mother's children back to her breast.

"What do you remember?"

"Everything. Everything was good. Everything was happy. Everything was safe. Everything was perfect. And then it all changed."

"What changed?"

"Everything."

Chapter 1

April 30, 2004

I already saw before boarding the plane with Sydney, her fiancé, Luke, and my fiancé, Rhys that night, my family at the airport with smiles that stretched across their faces. I saw my mother pushing through anything and everyone to hold me, spin me around, look me over, making a fuss over any unfamiliar scars. I saw my father calmly walking down toward me, trying to hold himself from grabbing me and spinning me in his arms while shouting for joy. I saw my two younger sisters waiting impatiently for my parents to take their turns before jumping all over me and screaming away. My brothers would try to be calm like my father, but soon would surrender and fuss over me as well.

Luke and Rhys were in a conversation with a woman sitting across the waiting area when Sydney came up and snapped me out of my reverie, handing me a water bottle and a pack or trail mix. They had apparently been telling the woman where we were going, which left me to surmise that she was probably waiting for the next flight scheduled after ours.

"Oh Uganda!" Came the reply from the woman surprised. "I have heard of the war going on there. It is Uganda, right?" She asked us.

"Yeah; but there is fighting everywhere. People kill each other here too." I answered defensively.

"I'm sorry" the woman apologized. "It is just that it is been on the news."

"Yeah, that's unfortunate" I shot back sulkily.

Luke, sensing my annoyance tried to shift the focus to what we would be doing when we got there.

"Before the wedding, we would be helping Cali's parents with their refugee camp that they run there, called Hosanna. We've got a lot of sponsors with a lot of money who are willing to help, as long as they know what they are helping with."

"That's great!" the woman exclaimed excitedly.

"Thanks" Sydney said with a smile.

Luke mentioned that he felt like getting a sandwich.

"Didn't you just eat?" Sydney asked him.

"I'll get it" I offered, happy for the chance to get some air, and slightly embarrassed about my outburst.

"Cali, we are boarding in like..." she checked her watch, "...five minutes."

"I know. I'll be back in a minute."

"I'll go with her." Luke offered getting up.

"Please, you two hurry. I cannot get married without my groom, and my maid of honor." She pleaded.

"Got it" Luke and I said in unison. I kissed Rhys, and promised to be back on time.

The woman said it was nice to meet us, and I greeted likewise, to her as Luke and I left.

On our way to the sub-shop, Luke pulled me to the side to apologize for the woman's comment.

"...but you know her question was innocent." He said gently.

"I know" I answered regretfully, "it's just that whenever you talk about a country in Africa, people bring up poverty, or war, or something equally daunting, and depressing. I'm from Uganda, but I don't have AIDS, or kwashiorkor, or some other series of unfortunate events that is most likely to happen to someone from a third-world country."

Luke chuckled, and then put an arm around me to say in comfort that she was just a woman who did not know much about Uganda really until she heard the news.

"That's the thing, why can't they ask how fresh the produce is? Or how well the kids actually respect their parents over there? Or how parents actually know how to raise children?" I asked still slightly annoyed.

"Now I don't know about that." Luke said adjusting the collar of his shirt. "I think my parents did a pretty good job, and I'm pretty respectful of them." He finished playfully.

"People fight here too. Just because it is not officially labeled a war, does not mean they do not de-value human life. They kill each other too, and there are the homeless, and people dying of hunger two blocks over. The difference is , we do not talk about it in our news. I finished breathlessly.

"Breathe! You're turning red…, and that's actually a hard thing for you." He said pointing to my face.

"I'm sorry. I didn't mean to get upset with her"

"It's okay. I think Syd and Rhys will explain it to her."

"Thanks Luke"

"You're welcome" he said giving me a hug, and started to lead me back toward our terminal.

"Oh!" I remembered, "what about your sandwich?"

"I didn't want a sandwich," he smiled.

"Thanks" I offered gratefully.

We were just on time much to the relief of Sydney and Rhys. We walked faster, apologized for slightly worrying them, and boarded the plane.

* * * * * * * * * * * * * * *

I was thirteen years old when I left home. I am nineteen now. Barely six years has it been since I last lived at home except for short visits, and now, I was being summoned back for longer than short. Fear told me I had not been gone long enough, and homesickness told me it was about time they summoned for me.

When Rhys and I had written telling them of our engagement, I had earnestly thought they would make their way to the U.S. to me. Their letter encouraging me to come home to celebrate, and their reassurance that we would be safe baffled me so. I had always thought when my parents said it was okay for me to come home whether in the middle of the war or at the end of it, I would be more than suited to the idea. As I put my belongings into my portmanteau, it set in - The daunting realization that I was about to go to a country I did not know if it was still the same as I had left it, or if I were going to be able to cope with the differences it was now entertaining with bound hands. It had been years since I had been home to see that much more than should be allowed had happened. When I returned home from the U.S., the very first time, four years after I had initially left, for summer holidays, my parents had already moved my family to Kenya to feel safer from the war. I had honestly not known how I was to say good-bye to my friends because I did not know whether to say, "I'll see you later" since it would not be with the same kind of assurance that accompanied the previous times I had said it, or just say good-bye and hope that it would not mean what I feared it could. When I threw the last of my clothes in the portmanteau, I also reminded myself that I was perhaps being a bit dramatic about the whole affair, and maybe the television had exaggerated with the war like it did everything, Africa. I realized that no matter what hung heavily in my mind as to what to expect when finally home, I could not be afraid of it yet.

With Rhys's hand holding firmly unto mine doing its best to quell the nervousness that hung in indissoluble lumps inside of my stomach, I watched the clouds that now bathed the airplane. I looked into my mother's face that though of course it hung not in the clouds, was still very much apparent within the billows. It took me back again to the day after the night; the night my father would tell me that they would send me away; away to a place that was to protect me from the war they were calling me back into now. I see my me and my mother in the kitchen as she grasps tightly my hands with one of hers, and with the other cups my chin. She looks into my eyes smiling a sad smile that provokes tears I did not permit, to run pitifully down my face. She counsels me:

"My daughter," she says, "Nobody where you are going knows me, and neither do they know your father. Even so, they will soon, for they will see you, and they will watch you. Some, more closely than they should; some, just close enough; and some, not closely enough. In you they will see your father, and they will see me. Be good, because you were taught that there are such things as wrong and right; evil and good; sin and righteousness. Be a servant to your elders and respectful of the homes you walk into. Do not speak out of place and do not leave your duties undone. Remember, it is not man's praise essentially that we care for. We raised you to be a decent Ugandan woman. You are not a western girl. You must continue to learn to be a good cook; even though I am not there to teach it to you, find some way to learn it. Do not leave a mess. Do not ask for much more than what you need, but always desire for dreams beyond your imaginations. Observe more, speak less, think always, and don't bring home any babies. I want you to remember all the things that your father and I have told you, and to do them. We are not there, but our words and counsels are there to remind you that when you are gone from home, that you take us with you. My daughter, I advise that you read your bible, pray at all times, and love everyone. If you find it difficult to love people because you do not like them, then love them as a service to God. Love them because you love God. Like your father told you earlier, your education is second only to your faith and all its expectations. The schooling in America is different, but intellect is the same. You were an excellent student here, and nothing short of that is expected of you in America. No Cs, no Ds, and only one B in a test per semester.

"So, F's are okay then?" I cut in jokingly.

My mother swiped my arm in jest before pulling me to her chest which its rise and fall made me burst out in tears as I suddenly was washed over with homesickness. I did not want to stop holding her, I did not want to miss her dearly, and I did not want the rhythm I heard in her heartbeat to stop. I wanted to listen forevermore to the normalcy that had bred me to where I sat at that very spot. She pushed me gently and held me at arm's length looking me over until her eyes stopped, staring deeply into mine.

"I love you my sweet, sweet baby, with all my heart and soul."

I hugged her again, professing my undying love for her. I left her, reluctantly walking into the living room dreading the next scene because I did not know where I was to find the strength to withstand any of the heartache that was to take place. Red eyes, sniffling noses, and strained coughs filled the room as each member of my family came and hugged me whispering kind, sweet, and gentle words into my ears. I wanted to stay as I listened to them, silently wishing I did not have to go. I did not want to go. Somewhere in all the goodbyes, I found myself in the front seat of my father's car, he in the driver's seat, and my siblings lined outside with my mother looking miserably unto the two of us as the car backed out of the house. I waved good-bye and dissolved once again into sobs as their outlines, my house, and the street in all its details escaped my view. I heard my father sniffle, but I would not look at his face, for I felt I would be paying him some disservice by so doing.

I quickly wipe a tear from my face as I am awoken from my musings by the friendly flight attendant who wanted to know if I could put my seatbelt back on due to turbulence on flight. Rhys asked me what I was thinking about, and I told him that I was just wondering the same thing I had been all that week. The worries I was afraid to confront; the ones his able strong square shoulders and the comfort they brought me would not appease. I was worried about going into the midst of a battleground after being away for so long. I did not know anything about the war that we were about to get into. I was wondering why it was easier for us than it was for them. I wondered what it was like to live in a place with war tearing it apart. What would I do? How would I defend myself? I did not know.

Chapter 2

It was more than I pictured it to be; my mother's smile. It was even more beautiful than I always remember, and it grew wider as we walked closer. She wrapped me up in her gentle arms, releasing me only because she had to. She moved on to Sydney, Rhys, and Luke, equally ecstatic to see them. I hugged my father telling him I was happy to see him because I had missed his tight and comforting embrace. He hugged Rhys, Sydney, Luke, and then me again. I asked him if he missed me, and he said yes; adding that my siblings were in the car, and we were at the mercy of their excitement because their excitement would most likely tackle us to the ground.

They were crazy - my siblings. They all rushed toward us at the same time, in fact, almost tripping us to the ground, save for we knew what to expect and so braced our feet to the ground. Angela, who had grown past as tall as I was, whispered to Sydney and I as we looked her over that she had gotten her period two months before our arrival. We told her we had read about it in her letter. Augustina, my immediate younger sister, was more talkative than I remembered much to my relief, because it had always worried me that her quietness would be misconstrued as weakness by bullies. She was also about four inches taller than me now, and wore eyeglasses that I remembered her telling me about over the phone that she hated.

Samuel was also taller than me, and had gotten bigger since the last time I saw him. I was happy about that because his weight had become an issue, and there had been a lot of raw eggs my mother had had him drink. I remember getting in trouble for not feeding him enough when I was taking care of my siblings. He was much more assertive now, and I was fascinated by it. Samuel was the peacemaker of the family. Whenever there was a disagreement between any members of our family, Samuel was the first who tried to fix it; the one who tried to get everyone to apologize to one another. I think he always managed even at a very young age, to resolve conflict, which garnered for him not only everybody's love and adoration, but their respect as well. Samuel was a good boy who excelled in his school and bible studies; always offering help to whomever may need it and thoughtfully caring for everyone around him.

Jacob, the last one of my parents' children was mischievous, and extremely smart. He could make you unbelievably upset with him, and absolutely love him dearly at the same time. He was the same every time I saw him, except that he had grown almost past Angela looking less like a boy, and more like a young man. I teased him about his antics, which made him smile that little coy smile of his.

I looked beyond the group of us to the figure of a little boy standing by the car; a boy whom I had never seen before who watched us with careful intimidated eyes.

"Who's that?' I whispered to my Mama.

"We were going to write you about him, but your siblings decided it would be better to surprise you," she answered.

"Who is he?" I asked again.

"He is a young boy who survived the attack that took his parents' lives, and we could not leave him there by himself, so we adopted him."

My mother motioned for him to come over, and the small boy walked uncertainly toward us.

"This is Joshua everyone..." my mother began, "...Joshua is five years old. Joshua, this is the rest of your family, well... some of the rest anyway. Calista is your eldest sister. Sydney is your god-sister. Her brother, Rhys is your god-brother. This is Sydney's fiancé, Luke. Oh, and Rhys is Calista's fiancé" She finished, laughing.

Joshua shyly said hello, and my father motioned for everyone to start heading toward the car. I felt a sick and uncomfortable feeling settle into my stomach as we got into the van, and it was about something I did not know what it was. As my father started the car to drive away from the airport, I tapped my mother's shoulder and asked her:

"What attack?"

Chapter 3

The car became eerily quiet as all my siblings one by one stopped talking and from their seats stared at the back of my father's head, waiting for him to answer. I followed their gaze and asked him what was going on, again.

"The village is gone" came a dejected reply from my father. He continued when no words came out of my hanging wide open mouth. Sydney, Rhys, and Luke had looks of complete confusion and awe registered on their faces.

"They came while everyone was sleeping; sometime before the first cock crew..."

"Who's "they"?" I interrupted.

"The rebels" he replied shaking his head sorrowfully.

"Why? Why? Why? Why? Why? Why would they do that?" Sydney sputtered.

"For the children; they come to take the children."

"So, this is still a full-out war?" I asked.

Since my family's move to Kenya, I lived in the luxury of throwing away any semblance of this war from my memory. I was not close to home, and as far I wanted to be concerned, neither was this battle.

"Cali, it is been a war. The only people we know that escaped was Joshua." My mother answered looking back and smiling at the little boy who was now sitting on my lap.

I took a deep breath and let it out loudly.

"Did any of our friends survive?" I asked nervously.

"Not that we know of" my mother answered quietly.

"Where did you find Joshua?" Rhys asked.

"When we got the news, we went to see about Cali's uncle, aunt, and cousins."

"How are they, by the way?" I asked.

The car got that eerie silence again as my siblings looked out the window; then at their shoes, then at my parents, and then, each other.

"What...? What...?" Luke asked loudly, "When it is quiet... when you guys get quiet like this... something happened."

We chuckled nervously at Luke's outburst only because it sounded almost like exhausted sarcasm; and then the car became quiet again.

"They died." My father stated miserably.

"All of them?" I asked breathlessly holding my heart.

"Yes. All of them." My father answered, as if he wished he did not have to tell me.

Our village was a small cluster of several little sub-villages, and most of our extended family lived in those little villages. My grandparents, and most of our families lived in the sub- village closest to town, and a few lived farther away. My parents' second home which we returned to on holidays, was in Gulu; a half-hour drive from my grandparents' house. I have not been to that house since two years before I left for the U.S. When the raids began, most of our families fled town. As it got worse, my father explained, the rest of the family fled to other countries. Some were in Kenya, and some in Tanzania. I remembered

Onesimus, my godfather, sending my father some money for the families fleeing to refuge. I was always aware of how bad it was, but I guess it is different when it happens to... well... me. I had never really even talked about it, relinquishing it to just a slight rift in history, and rebels just raising up dust. I was sure it was going to be over in no time at all. Now, I remembered I had made that induction thinking of the Biafra war in Nigeria that though brutally and devastatingly claimed hundreds of thousands of lives, was over in three years. It was not a war that went on for nineteen years and counting.

"How is everybody else?" I asked slumping back dejectedly as if waiting for the absolute horrible news.

"They are fine. They got out in time. You know how your uncle is. He always thinks he is a one-man army, and he alone could face a hundred men brandishing all kinds of arms. We asked him to at least send your aunt and cousins over to us because they were scared to stay. He refused!" My father finished angrily.

I asked my father if we could go to the villages so that we could see the ruins left of them. He reluctantly agreed after arguing that it would upset us, and we would probably have nightmares of it.

∗∗∗∗∗∗∗∗∗∗∗∗∗∗∗

It was pitiful— the sight. There was dried blood on the soil, and huts burned down to the ground. Not a soul was left in any place, and a light breeze cut through the deathly stillness blowing the empty cans and plastic bags across the dirt and ashes. Joshua started to cry, and remembering that he was present during one of these massacres and was very frightful of the scene before him, I held him tight to me as my mother asked my Papa to turn around and leave.

On the way back to town, we passed several people walking with mats on their heads or carrying bags, or sheets of thick cloth. Angela explained when I asked, that they were people who leave their homes at night like they had told me about whenever they had visited, to sleep at the bus park in town. The car came to a stop where my father got out and asked Rhys, Luke, Samuel, Jacob and Joshua to do the same. He untied a big load next to our suitcases from the roof of the car which I did not notice until then. He opened the load with the boys' help, which in it were supplies divided into plastic bags. In each bag was a tube of toothpaste, toothbrush, socks, soap, eye drops, pencil, pen, notepad, t-shirt, lip balm, comb, and a tract. He had the boys along with him distribute each bag. He opened the back of the van, which had several thick sheets of cloth. With each bag of supplies handed to the weary travellers, were a blanket, and a quick word of encouragement. Some of the people they gave aid to, smiled so big and joyously, it warmed all our hearts; while some cried so mournfully it broke us all apart inside. When they were all done, my father and the boys entered back into the van, and he began to drive away. The silence in the car this time burst a dam in all of us as our tearful sniffles came alongside freely falling tears that had been waiting patiently for its turn as our bowels churned so violently inside from the tragedies that lay before us.

"Papa," Samuel called from behind my father.

"Yes," he answered looking through the rearview mirror before awe registered on his face. My mother seeing his reaction looked back to see what surprised my father so. We had all organized ourselves, leaving extra seating room in the van. I was sitting on Rhys's lap, Sydney on Luke's, Jacob on Angela's, and Samuel on Augustina's.

"We have room for ten." Samuel said through sniffles "if Joshua sits up front with mother."

My father stopped to pick up five women, and five children under five. He opened the back of the van where four boys climbed in and held on as my father headed for the bus park. We stopped crying anymore when the travelers joined us, not because we did not want to, but because our company wasn't crying. They were laughing; actually laughing. They were extremely fascinated by the 'white people' in the van with them. They touched Sydney, Rhys and Luke, and played with Sydney's hair asking her if she thought that maybe if they bleached their hair, it would look like hers.

The scene at the bus park was shocking and surreal. There were thousands of people with mats lying all around the ground.

"That does not look like a camp out to me" Rhys sadly stated.

"Not unless the skeletal kids out here are anorexics, and not actually suffering from starvation." Luke said with an annoyed sarcastic tone.

We left the park and headed home, much to mine and everybody's gratefulness. It had been a long day with a lot of information that my dreams were unfortunately left to process in my slumber.

Chapter 4

As we neared my parents' house, a warmth and comfort spread through my body, bathing me with a gentle peace that drained almost all the dreadful feeling of the day from my body. I don't think I'd ever been happier to see that place in my whole life.

When my father stopped the car, my older brother Isaiah came running out of the house toward us and opened the side door before we could. He pulled me out, hugged me, and feigning annoyance, asked my father where we had been because he had been expecting us since late that afternoon. We explained what we had been up to as my brother hugged the rest of our company and helped unload our suitcases from the roof of the car. He sympathetically stated his sadness at the situation, and his disgust with the government that did barely anything to protect its people.

I wondered what he meant by that, but sufficed my thoughts to the apparent; that a government that constantly lost its children to the mercy of an army of less than three thousand at any given time, could not claim to be doing everything in its power to rescue them.

Despite my mother's preferences, and downright begging, my older brother had decided to join the UPDF to, as he put it in his letter to me, a year before, do his part. He was home to welcome us back, but would have to leave back to duty soon thereafter.

Before going in, I stood in front of my father's house and stared at its magnificence. It was a large sixteen room dwelling, with a guest house sprawling on three acres. Lights shining from the rooms upstairs brought back nostalgic feelings of when after a long day, I would see my father's house with lights shining through those windows, and I would feel safe and protected. Samuel came up and took my hand snapping my wonders away as we walked toward the house that held all the comfort I had ever cared for in the world.

It was still almost like I remember it— my house. There was new furniture because it had been five years since the old furniture was purchased, and my parents purchased new furniture every five years. There was a new ceiling fan in the bedrooms because Sydney, Rhys and I had constantly pleaded for one every year we returned home. Sydney turned its knob to the highest level, and the blades spun bringing from it wind I thought would pick us up and bounce us from wall to wall. We all loved it. My mother came up to tell us to hurry downstairs for dinner before the boys ate it all.

As I stood by the window waiting for Sydney to come out of her turn in the bathroom, I looked over the horizon two hundred miles toward my village, a place I once proudly would proclaim about in the city. I remember bragging to friends in school as the holidays came by, about how I looked forward to the simplicity of village life, and how much I could not wait to see my grandparents and friends who would make my visit so incredibly enjoyable. I looked toward that horizon back at my childhood, and I remember when I lost it.

I was still a small child - nine years of age maybe, when I remember my grandparents being upset with my parents because they would not allow us, me, and my older brother Isaiah, to come to stay with them in the village without the company of my parents. It was not something that was previously an issue; however, I remember my parents being worried about something I did not know what it was. In the years that followed, my grandparents did much of the visiting to Kampala, where my family resided. Although we visited them as well in the village, we did not really spend a lot of time, and my parents were not altogether comfortable with our stay. My parents spent a great deal of time debating on what to do with us children with the war almost taking over our country.

That is how I came to live with the Cassidy family.

I have never, not known the Cassidy family. Long before I became my parents' daughter, my father studied in Mississippi with Onesimus, Rhys and Sydney's father. They struck a friendship that stuck long after their matriculation. My father would go on to return to his home and put to good use his education as he planted the seeds for a church and a trade school. He would, in the process of finding students, meet a young beautiful woman full of grace, named Grace, who worked at an academy for the blind and deaf. That woman, he would later marry in the U.S. only months before Onesimus who in turn had met his own beautiful woman full of grace, would also marry. The pair of pairs would be separated only by waters of the seas, and nothing else. I remember I was thirteen years old when my parents called me and my siblings to the living room. I still remember looking at my mother's face and seeing this mixture of fear, hope and protection all in those almond-shaped eyes that also consoled fears from the distance of a theatre seat watching me perform on stage. I remember seeing my mother rub her hands together as her fingers clutched at something unseen inside of her hands. Was it a necessary hope that she desperately needed to enliven and hold? All I knew was that I had never seen it before, and I did not like it. My father spoke in the same low and firm tone that he used when he was going to issue an order that already showed how hard it was for him to reach that decision, but that it had been reached and was final, and all refusals or deliberations were over. My eyes followed the shadow that the flowers cast on the verandah rails outside that evening as they traced the dark petals through the railings and onto the wall. Before then, I did not know what it meant to have your beautiful world taken away from you, but literally as I watched each word drop out of my father's lips, I lost as my father spoke, the only world I had allowed myself to love.

My parents cited the impending war that was coming upon Uganda between the LRA and the Ugandan government, as the reason why they were sending me and my brother away to different places to grow up. It wasn't because they loved any of their children more, or less than the other,

It was because they had to deal with the apparent truth; that the chance of the destruction of a whole is made less likely when the whole disperses in pieces to the wind.

"Like you all know, our family in America wants to take Calista with them for a while. They have wanted that for a time now, and so we have made some decisions, especially with this war upon us. Isaiah, we are sending you to your uncle in London."

I looked at everyone's faces. My siblings were still much too young to understand anything about what was going on beyond that they were going to miss their brother and sister.

I would return home only three times since then, and never again to my village. It was not a difficult transition with my family coming to spend the summers with me and the Cassidy family every summer.

"All done! Your turn!" Sydney exclaimed coming out of the shower and waking me from my trance.

 We finished our quick showers, got dressed, and headed for the table where I met three new habitants of my father's household with uncertain faces we had never seen before. I watched a little boy timidly hide behind his mother, and peer at us unusual beings standing by the chairs. He stared curiously at Sydney, Rhys, and Luke like pieces in a museum. My Mama put a hand over my shoulder and introduced them as escapees from a rebel camp whose families and communities had now shunned. There was a young woman, the little boy, and an infant cradled in the woman's hands. Sydney, unable to comprehend the reason why, asked plaintively, the reason why.

The woman with the little boy, the woman I later found out was only twenty one, started to cry. Her son, upset for his mother, began to cry too. A quietness so numbly gripping settled over us all at the table as we listened to that helpless girl and her son wail. We joined them in silent sorrow as I prayed for tomorrow to come. Not the morrow that came at the crow of the cock, but one of peace, of solitude, of joyous dancing and songs in the streets again. I prayed for tomorrow to bring freedom to the people of Acholiland; my people, living in bondage.

* * * * * * * * * * * * * * *

After dinner on the night of our return, my father and brothers locked the doors. This included padlocking the gates that led into the compound; activating the barbed wires atop the ten-foot fence that surrounded the house; and locking the first set of burglary proof doors. Afterwards, they would lock the main doors which were just regular four inch thick wooden double doors with six deadbolts, and the inside burglary proof doors. They then would close the windows, and padlock the proofs from the inside. We would then say our prayers together in the living room; after which, it was time for everyone to start settling down before they went to bed. My parents' television rule was that children could not watch television before six p.m. and after eight p.m. Eight p.m. was devotion time, and nine p.m. was bedtime for those seventeen and under. The night of our arrival though, was different. Excitement was still ringing in everyone's hearts, and so the celebration of our homecoming, though slightly overshadowed by the unfortunate circumstances of our new family members, continued well past nine p.m. Of course, coffee kept us travelers from succumbing to the jet lag that threatened to consume us long before devotions.

When it was time for bed, Sydney and I could not sleep. It was not excitement. It was a dense fear of something uncertain that gripped us and would not let go. We knew it had something to do with the events that had transpired earlier that day, and the horrible news we had been hearing, which would not go away even for the night. We got up and went across the hall to the upstairs living room where my parents were watching television. They regarded us, and with surprised looks on their faces asked what was wrong. We told them that we were fitful due to the events that we found great difficulty processing, and were comforted by their presence. With that, we put our blankets and pillows on the floor, and tried to go to sleep in the comfort of the presence of my parents. My sisters with whom we shared a room came out to see where we had gone; and seeing us on the floor, without a word, went back in the room, and came back with blankets and pillows, heading straight for the floor with us. Angela went into the younger boys' room, where switching on the light, she announced:

"Hey! We are sleeping out here!"

They all came rushing out, and seeing the spread on the living room floor, ran back into their room to return with blankets and pillows. Joshua ran to the older boys' room and relayed the announcement from Angela. They came to the door to see what was going on in the living room. I looked at my parents - at speechless amusements I saw in their faces. When the older boys came out, my father quickly ordered them to lie at the opposite end of the room. We all laughed as we settled in for the night. I looked at my parents with beaming happiness as my mother put her feet up to snuggle closer to my father. In that comfort, the instability in my stomach rested a bit. As we grew quiet, all our eyes shifted to the news on the television as the voice of the newscaster became clearer. I never really watched the news or paid attention when anyone did. When Onesimus did in the U.S., and the war in Uganda came up, I usually watched a bit and then left the room. The newscaster was soft and sympathetic in tone, and from what I could understand, we were fighting in a circle of death. Our government was supporting the Sudanese rebels for their aid to eradicate the Ugandan LRA rebels; and it turn, the Sudanese government supported the Ugandan LRA rebels for their aid to eradicate the Sudanese rebels.

My father turned off the television and sighed heavily while grinding his teeth in frustration with his head in his hands. In the stillness of the room, and of the night beyond it, my mother's voice birthed a song, and she softly sang that praise. It was as if she was telling demons of this war, that as long as we have that song – that praise, we will never be defeated. We shall always overcome. With one voice, we all agreed with my mother. Standing firm on the promises of our Father in heaven, we joined my mother.

And we sang.

* * * * * * * * * * * * * * *

The morning after our return, Sydney and I woke up first, and in turn woke up everyone else with a kiss on their cheeks.

"That's one thing I like about you coming home." Jacob said, rubbing the sleep out of his eyes.

"What is that?" Sydney asked.

"You always wake us up with kisses." He replied smiling sheepishly, and everyone chuckled along with him.

"I think sometimes he wakes up and just leaves his eyes closed so that you can kiss him." Augustina accused playfully.

"Where is Mama?" I asked sitting by Samuel and wrapping my arms around his shoulders.

"She is getting ready to start breakfast downstairs."

Sydney and I reminded our siblings that we would be taking them to spend the day doing whatever they would like to do with us. They shout for joy as the room becomes deserted by children flying toward every exit to their rooms to get themselves together. I look about the room in the home I grew up, happy to be there in its magnificence and warmth that no other pleasure could afford me.

Chapter 5

January 16, 2005

I am on the same plane back to the U.S. almost two months since my siblings, and I came back from the bush. It seems like an eternity ago, but it was only two months. My siblings and I were sent to different parts of the world to seek mental care so that we could heal from our ordeal. I chose to return to the U.S., in that same plane which had taken me home only ten months ago. I am in the same seats. I am in the same body. Nevertheless, I wasn't the same person. In my hands, I turn the letter I had written to Rhys, the boy who just eleven months prior to that paper in my hands, I was happily engaged to marry.

Six months. Six months. That was all it took. Six months for my life as I knew it to change forever. Sitting in the same plane I was eight months ago, on my way home, I remember the letter that would bring me home in the first place.

I disliked letters. I dislike letters. In my lifetime – all twenty years – I have gotten exactly three letters. The first was left in a hut beside a dying old woman, and a small-for-her-age five year old girl who was almost dead from a bout with malaria. The dying old woman was my mother's mother. The near-dead five year old was me. After my mother died from AIDS, as I would later learn, my father took his non-boy child to her grandmother, and dropped her off with a note that said not much more than that she was to be my guardian, to note the lack of forwarding address, and to take the hint.

The second letter was given to me six months later by my grandmother, who left it tucked firmly inside my palm as she lay gently beside me, forgetting in each shallower breath to teach me how to live without her.

A letter I would take with me to Hosanna, an orphanage just outside the village. A letter that would bring me to Moses, and Grace Okello.

My mother says that every child is special; but that the day I walked into Hosanna, and into her life was a day that still has never evaded her dream. The owners of Hosanna would later adopt six children from the orphanage to be their children. Those children would be Isaiah, Augustina,

Angela, Samuel, Jacob, and me – Calista Mirembe Okello. I do not think my mother had any choice in the matter; I followed her around from the minute I walked through the gates of that orphanage, until they asked me to call them Mama and Papa. That was my first family.

My second family was my father's brother's family. My father's brother, Onesimus, was an American man whose family had sponsored my father's stay in the U.S. from high school until his college graduation. In those years, my father and his host brother grew closer than even blood relatives, attending the same college and eventually, medical school together. My father would return to Uganda to practice because he wanted to take care of his parents, and return good to the land that bred him. He had promised my grandparents that he would return when he was finished with his education because letting him go had been difficult for them. Onesimus returned with my father to Uganda to help him start Hosanna, before he returned to the U.S. to open his own practice. It was during this new venture that my father would meet Grace, my mother; and Onesimus would meet Felicia, a young woman who applied to volunteer at an orphanage. Their love for the children who clung desperately to them, would bring them often to Uganda than they had ever planned. It is there that they would also give birth to Sydney.

At first, I had a difficult time figuring out which of the families I belonged to. When I first met Sydney, she called her parents "Mom" and "Dad," and my parents "Mama" and "Papa." When I asked her why she did not just refer to my parents as "Aunt" and "Uncle," she replied that four parents were better than two. I agreed, so I followed suit.

A year passed with me forgetting rapidly the former misfortunes that had been my beginning. I was part the daughter of parents who pleasantly adored their children, the sister of siblings to whom she was loyally dedicated, including my best friend Sydney, with whom every day was spent. My siblings and I shared our time between my parents' house, and the Cassidy's just next door in a bungalow inside the orphanage. Onesimus travelled, sometimes with my Papa, often to the U.S. for various matters that mostly concerned the adults if it scaled beyond the goodies they brought back with them. It was during one of their homecomings that I met Rhys – when everyone met Rhys. Onesimus would introduce him as our cousin who was going to be spending some time in Uganda, being part of our family. Rhys fit right in with my brothers, getting into the same mischief of picking on their sisters as often as we allowed them. As we grew older, however, Sydney and I would learn that Rhys's father, my dad's cousin, had given my dad custodial rights over his son while he sorted his life out in a California jail on drug charges. Nothing changed however, because the only thing we cared about was what it was – that Rhys was with us in Uganda, at least for as long as we would be.

Five years after my adoption, the Cassidy family would return to the U.S. where Onesimus would go on to open a surgical practice. The year before I would join them, would be the most unsettling of recent times. My best friend was gone, and even though the letters and phone calls were more regular than the sun, it could not measure up to the feel, touch, and laughter that rung close to my ears. Because my birthday wasn't a date I knew myself, my parents had decided to make one up for me. Sydney and I wanted to be twins in everything, including the date of birth. This would be the first year since we became twins, that Sydney and I would spend our birthdays apart. I had never been more grateful to have siblings in my life because I am not sure I would have handled that loneliness well enough on my own. My brothers and sisters suffered the same hole left by the company that once was the usual, and stable. More than that, my parents started to become a bit more protective of us. We had long since moved from Hosanna into our home now in the town of Gulu, and were seldom allowed with my parents on their trips to the village where Hosanna was. There was a certain tension in the air that was never fully disclosed by my parents, but saved for hushed tones behind closed doors. It would be several years before I would be privy to the secrets behind the whispers. Several years before I would wish I had never as a child bothered to hold that tumbler to the door to find out what I was being protected from behind it. It would be years before the letter that would bring me home, and return unrecognizable even to me, the plans I had made. Plans I'd made with Rhys.

We made plans like all people do, to be wed, to gallivant over the entire world to distant sands, and Foreverlands.

Where are my promises now that I am sitting on a plane holding the letter I ended up speaking to Rhys instead of giving to him?

Dear Rhys,

Away from you, I longed for you. Through the leaves of the densely overgrown bush, I saw you coming for me. In every dream, I was home with you. In some, it was our wedding day, and you are wearing your suit that way that you wear it that makes me want to show the world how incredibly luckier I am over anyone else there could be. In some, we were on our honeymoon, and I do not really know why I would dream about that because I don't really know what would necessarily happen beside the actual "point," and nobody particularly wants to dream about that. In some, we are married, and I go to get the mail, and on it is written, "Mrs. McAllister," and I know it is me. When I would wake, my heart would jump into my stomach pounding against my head the sorrowful remembrance that it was not true. Every morning when I woke up from sleep I would barely surrender myself to, I wished I would die. Visions of happier times with you were much too unbearable. A girl in the bush told me to forget about you, at least for the while that I was there in the bush. She told me that it was my memories of you in the day that saved themselves amidst the chaos in my head, and later without hindrances came uninterrupted into my rest. The more I tried to think less of you, the more I thought of you. To see you; to be in your arms; to kiss you; to know you; to love you.

Seeing your face the day of our return was indescribable. If you had not caught me when you did, I am almost sure my knees would have collapsed from under me.

Rhys, I love you. I will always love you; but the more you are selflessly, and so beautifully good to me, the more shame I feel. You have lovingly assured me time and again of your unfailing devotion to me. You have assured me of the pride I should feel in my triumph over the evil that took me from you. You have assured me that it does not matter what happened to me, or what the General did with me. You have not changed in behavior toward me. Rhys, I think that is the problem. The more you try to assure me of a love I believe never went away from you, the more I feel unworthy of it. I wonder whether I will ever fully let go enough to love you as you should be; and you should be loved Rhys. You should be esteemed.

When I go to sleep now, when the visions of war and blood subside long enough to let in a little slumber, I no longer see you. I see him. I am haunted by the evils I have done. I am possessed by the souls from whom I have robbed promises and hopes. I am bound by time that seared into me a pain I wrestle with, trying to make it foreign to me, but knowing within me that it is far *too familiar now to leave. I cannot be with*

you Rhys. I cannot reconcile myself long

enough to forgive me. I cannot let you

forgive me.

March 16, 2005

My therapist turns the paper over, when I would eventually during one of our sessions show her, to see if there was more to be read. There should be more, I am aware, but I could not write much more than that.

"Was that all you wrote?"

"No. I didn't give him the letter. That is how come you are holding it."

"Why not?"

"Because, I had spoken all the other letters I gave him, so I thought this should not be different.

"Do you still love Rhys?"

"You know how people say that they love someone more than anything in the world, and then say it to someone else, and then someone else? That never made sense to me. How can you love two things or people more than anything in the world?" I got a catch in my throat, "I love Rhys more than anything in the world. My love for him surpasses any love I hold for anyone or anything else. I used to be confident in that. Now, I am terrified of it.

"Why? What are you afraid of?"

"I am afraid that Rhys will wake up one day, and the scales will fall from his eyes, and he will realize just how damaged I am. I am afraid that Rhys will get used to being under-appreciated, and learn to deal with it. He should not have to become used to anything, but to be insanely and scandalously loved. I am afraid that I will never get better, and that he will become less of himself in the process of making me more of myself."

"What did Rhys say?"

"He hugged me. He told me that he knew there was a possibility that might happen."

"A possibility that you would break up with him? He was ready for it?"

"No. He was...," I struggle for the proper word because I know Rhys did not want me to break up with him. "...aware of... the likelihood that it may happen."

"What has your relationship been like since?"

"It has been the same as it always was. We are just not together. If everything were as it should be, I would be married to Rhys within the next five minutes. He still loves me, and I still adore him. He is in Uganda, and I am here. We both think it's best."

"Do you hope that the two of you would get back together?"

"Naturally, yes. However, I am aware of reality, and the possibility that I might never get to that place where I so achingly want to be. I do not want him to stall his life waiting for me."

"If you were to fall in love with someone else, do you think it will break his heart?"

"I will never fall in love with someone else. It would be the greatest disservice I would do another human being. I will never love another like I loved him, not in the slightest bit. If I have love to give, and nothing holding me back, I am going to give it to Rhys."

"If he were to fall in love with someone else, do you think it would break your heart?"

I cannot reply. It takes me a long time to answer my therapist because I don't want to admit what I know the truth to be. I wonder whether if I could teach my heart the lie that is supposed to make it stronger, if maybe it would believe it well enough to make it the truth.

"I would be jealous. I would hate myself for not letting me be that girl. Yes, it would break my heart."

"What has got you convinced that Rhys's love for you wouldn't be enough to guide you away from your apprehensions?"

"Guilt."

"What are you feeling guilty about?"

Chapter 6

May 3, 2004

Three days after our arrival was visitation day. Sydney, my mother, and I along with my sisters would visit close family friends to pay respects and to distribute the gifts we had brought home with us. As always, we were visited by our peers and younger mates; but for adults, we made the excursion.

On that day, I was the first to rise, so I went downstairs to start some coffee. While it still brewed, I took the big family bible that rested constantly on the center table in the living room, and began to turn the pages. As I did, I saw through the curtains, David.

~ ~ ~ ~ ~ ~ ~ ~ ~ ~ ~ ~ ~ ~ ~

"Who's David?" My therapist inquires softly.

"I still get knots in my stomach when I talk about David. His parents... he never knew them. He lived with his grandparents. His uncle worked for my father as a gate man."

"What is a gate man?""

"He was like a caretaker. He guarded our compound from unwanted people."

"Kind of like a security guard," she said nodding her head in understand.

"Yes"

"Okay…"

"David visited my home every day after school so that he could wait for his uncle to finish his shift, after which, he'd escort him home. Because of that, we became close as the years went by. People teased us that we'd get married to each other, and grow old together. Right around when we were twelve, he began to take them seriously. I never did, because I at no time had those feelings for him. With the Cassidy family coming and going every year, I began to like Rhys. I mean, it wasn't like a relationship, but I would rather foster a feeling growing inside of me, than force one that isn't.

"How old were you, by the way?"

"I was thirteen, when David told me that he loved me. When I was preparing to leave for the U.S., he told me that he loved me."

"What did you say?"

"I was thirteen. I hadn't even started my period yet. My class schedule still included recess. I didn't have time to love a boy. I told him that I did not know what love was; certainly not in the magnitude he was professing it. He asked me not to fall in love with anyone else."

"But then you and Rhys got together."

"Yes, but Rhys and I didn't get together until I was eighteen. I know I said I had feelings for him, but those were more of fascination than they were romantic. For the most part, we were family."

"Did David find someone else?"

"No. Two years after I came to the U.S., he would write, for the most part to make sure I had not fallen in love with anyone else. His subsequent letters would hail me, speaking about how much he loved me, and how, and when we'd spend our lives together."

"What did you write back?"

"I didn't."

"You didn't?"

"No"

"Why not?"

"I was scared. I had no idea what he was talking about. His goal for life, and his idea of romance and love seemed entirely too bridled for me. I felt like each of his letters were pieces of a noose. It was as if he was too in love with me, and because of that, there was little fascination for him left inside of me."

~ ~ ~ ~ ~ ~ ~ ~ ~ ~ ~ ~ ~ ~ ~ ~ ~

I stood in the living room quietly looking out at David in the yard collecting some clothes that my father had left for his uncle. I put down the bible, and walking over to the window, I watched him pick up all the clothes, then finally sit down on the bench to put a mound of shoes into a large plastic bag. I unlocked the doors, stepped outside, and walked over to the bench to sit and talk with him. We stayed in a spell of uncomfortable tension, then, I looked up when I figured the cemented driveway held no answers or aid for me within its sands.

"Hi" I said first smiling sheepishly, then laughing shyly.

"Hello, old friend" he replied laughing back. "Where have you been?"

"Here" I answered gently "why haven't you come by?"

He kept quiet for a few seconds staring at the same cold ground in its unresponsiveness.

"I heard you got engaged" He finally uttered.

"Is that a reason why you have not come by, or are we starting a new conversation?"

"It is whatever you want it to be." He said with a scornful surrender in his tone. "I have always done what you wanted. It has not been enough but..."

I shook my head at how unbelievably childish my once dear childhood friend had become. When David and I were much younger, we were great friends. We laughed, we played, getting into as much mischief as the day's sun would allow us. We had an understanding so gaily uninterrupted until Rhys and I began to date. When David found out the summer Rhys and I came home not as family but, as a couple, he became distant from us. Not understanding why his behavior had changed rather drastically, I did not really do anything or talk to him. I had written David when Rhys and I started to become interested in each other that earlier in the past years, I was too young to know what it meant to totally be selfless in devotion to someone else. He wrote back saying he did not care if I was ready, and that he would give me all the qualities in him that made a good man. I wrote back telling him that perhaps down the road, I may figure in my heart what love meant. I wasn't certain what it was then, and therefore could not return his feelings; however flattering they may have been.

A spell of time later, I found out from my mother that when I began to date Rhys, David had grown bitter that when I did discover the meaning of love, I discovered it with someone else and not him. Angela wrote shortly after, telling me that following the news of my coupling with Rhys, David had begun to see several women, and drink himself to a stupor at the town bars. Seeing him that morning, a sense of guilt had flooded through me, but following his sarcastic tone was an unpleasant feeling rising within me.

"What has made you so bitter?" I asked quietly with surprising concern.

"Can I ask you something?" He inquired rather pitifully.

"Is it depressing?" I asked eyeing him suspiciously, as he smiled sheepishly back at me.

"You must have found the meaning of love right?"

"I guess."

"What is it?"

"What is what?"

"The meaning of love; why do you love him, and you could not love me?"

"Because Dave, you cannot be in love with someone just because they are in love with you; otherwise, you're just in love with the concept of the whole affair. Besides, you were jaunting around town with several girls after I told you I did not think I was ready."

"Why did you pick him? Why are you in love with him?"

"Because when Rhys and I are apart, we are fine, and we enjoy what we are doing respectively; but whenever Rhys sees me, even though he was gone for only a few minutes, his eyes... the way he looks at me, and drops his bags, or keys, or takes off his coat, it's like... his good day just all of a sudden became even more wonderful, and his bad day didn't even matter. Whenever he touches me..." I looked up to the window of the boys' room and saw Rhys standing at the window, looking down to us. "...I'm the center of his world."

Without a word else, David got up and left. I watched him leave until his figure slipped within the fog that still coated the dawn lit road. I looked up again to Rhys giving him a sigh and a pathetic smile to let him know the meeting was not exactly pleasant. I folded my legs as I saw the front door open, and my mother walk toward me with a steaming cup of coffee. She handed it to my hands that welcomed the instant warmth, as she sat down and looked down the road.

"Pleasant talk with David?" she asked mixing a slight sarcasm in her sympathetic tone.

I took a long sip and swallowed hard.

"Hmm… has he always been this bitter?" I asked.

"This war is taking everything from everyone, and the girl he used to love isn't his either."

"He wanted to know why I fell in love with Rhys and not him. He wanted to know what I found out about love."

"What do you know about love?" My mother asked me slouching back, squinting at me curiously.

I looked at her returning the squint, and the desire to play with my mother a little came over me.

"Oh you know, that feeling that you get when you've…" I lowered my voice to a whisper "… done it."

My mother's eyes glared at me as she squared her shoulders back to wordlessly warn that I had better been joking. I laughed at her.

"Really, Ma? Come on!" I resumed in mock seriousness. "No. I know what you taught me. "Love is the happiness when it is wonderful and easy, and the extra mile when it gets difficult."

We went back into the house so that I could get Sydney up with my sisters to get ready to go.

Chapter 7

To make the day go easier, my mother asked a few friends to meet at the beauty salon. After that, it would be Amelia's, which was a local diner where everyone usually was if you were looking for them. Amelia's was famous for their roast meats, and when I was a child, I would do anything along with my friends to make a few shillings, after which, straight away to Amelia's, we would go. That place would keep the most hardened runaway in town.

The next place we would go would be at my Aunt Beatrice's house. She was my favorite aunt. She was always at the salon first, but she would go everywhere else with us, then end at the church for the midweek service, and a homecoming celebration dinner afterward.

The boys would spend the day at the house with my father and brothers running some errands in town, then meet with us at church thereafter.

Sydney and I went into my parents' room to say good morning to my father since we both still working on jet-lag, could not manage to stay asleep as long as everyone. We knocked, and when beckoned from the other side, we entered. My father was already up as I deduced from the rumpled empty section supposed to be his side of the bed.

"Where is Papa?" Sydney asked climbing into the bed and cuddling next to my mother who had gone back into her room for her devotions.

"Oh, he is already packing the things he and the boys are taking to town." My mother answered putting an arm around Sydney, and one around me as I climbed onto the bed and cuddled on her other side.

"What about the hospital? I don't think he is been there since we've been back." I said.

"Well, you've only been back for three days. Actually, he spends very little time there now. We are making other plans on where to go from here."

"Go from where?" Sydney asked with a crease of wonder in her brow.

"We are not sure yet if we'd like to leave the country, or the continent."

"Mama" I started, "how many people do you think have died so far?"

My mother got a faraway look in her eyes as deep sadness filled within them. She squeezed us tightly beside her and released with a sigh.

"I don't think I know exactly my dear. Even if I did, I do not want to admit it."

"Mama," Sydney started, "when is this going to be over?"

"I don't know…, but it is not getting better. It does not look like it will for a while."

"That's what scares me." I said nervously.

"Me too" Sydney concurred in a similar tone.

"Really?" My mother asked looking at us both. "You are safe here. You should always know that." My mother answered with a strong tone, as if trying to convince us of a faith she herself wasn't too sure about.

"I feel like I do not have a home, Mama" I said

Sydney jolted up and looked at me.

"What are you talking about? This is your home; you have a home in the U.S… and not just houses, real homes of people who love you… a lot."

"It is not the same" I interjected, "before this war, before I left, this was home. No matter where I was running from, I could always escape and run home. I knew I was safe, protected, loved. I was a citizen of a country; but not anymore. When an American is mistreated in another country, and they hear about it, they get upset - all of them. They almost want revenge. I used to like coming home where there was nothing different or awkward about me but the contents of my heart. However, home has turned its back on me. Not only will they not fight for me, they thirst for my blood. So, where do you go? Where am I supposed to go?"

"It's like the only relief is to die. What kind of world have we become that the greatest relief can be the end of the most amazing gift?" Sydney sighed.

Then, my mother spoke to me and Sydney in a firm voice that forced us not only to listen, but also against any reservation, to believe her. "I don't know the whole things in your life that you have had to, and continue to put up with; but I want you both to know something: Home is here, even if we all live in a bush, on the street, or underground. Home is where you find arms to run into when you cry, laugh, or just want to. This is where there is always a shoulder that can be a pillow, or desk, or a lean-to. Home is the group of people that do not tolerate your differences, or love you in spite of them. They celebrate you because of them. That is what home is. Never confine home to the walls of a house, or the limits of a city. Let it burst out of that myopic picture that imprisons it inside the configuration of our contained minds."

Sydney and I lay there, silently welcoming the wisdom of my mother's words. A brief while after, we got up and left for our room to get dressed. We joined my mother downstairs in the dining room to eat breakfast with our family. I kissed Rhys as I sat down next to him; Jacob sat on the other side of me, and I shared an embrace with him.

"So, what are you men up to today?" Sydney asked picking up Luke's bowl, and dishing him some oatmeal.

"Oh... just some errands" Jacob answered with a sly grin spreading across his face.

The men were going to be going into town today to purchase a goat that would eventually become part of the dinner to celebrate our homecoming later in the evening.

Sydney, though a meat eater, was opposed to the animal being in distress in close proximity to her, or anywhere around where she might be. A grave lesson was learned a few years ago when my father had underestimated her seriousness in the matter, and had 'prepared' a sheep in our backyard while Sydney was still at home, who in turn witnessed the event as she was coming out of the kitchen to find out why there was an animal bleating frighteningly outside. Sydney following that incident did not talk to my father, nor did she eat for a day and a half. Only after my father promised that that atrocity would not take place anywhere near her ever again, would she forgive him; that and a vacation to where she chose, even though she had chosen for her turn the previous year.

Sydney, still to that morning as we had breakfast, figured that one of the reasons the boys did not come along on our excursions was to help my father with the preparations of the rest of the day.

I watched the home my mother had just described to us earlier that morning before my eyes, and listened to the petty arguments between my siblings about which one of my parents was the bigger boss, I felt the love that came from everyone as it became the consensus that the girls had our fathers wrapped around our little fingers.

Emotions welled up within me as I watched Joshua climb into Sydney's lap letting her hold him while he ate his breakfast. I saw home just like my mother asked me to feel it, to hear it, to see it, and to know it.

Chapter 8

May 11, 2004

It is a great many memories that I will always remember about the war; but none quite like that morning. It had only been a week since we came home, and as uncomfortable as we felt concerning the pain we saw around us, we remained joyous even as we tended to the refugees at the camp. We had gone to the village to stay at our family home while we put in some time at the refugee camp.

The night before that morning, my father stayed home with us while my mother went to stay overnight in Hosanna due to the large influx of refugees the day before. We had all decided on a movie night, and so spent the greater part of the darkness sprawled on comforters on the living room floor in scatters.

It was five o clock in the morning, and all at once the neighborhood was awoken. It was not by a gunshot or a bomb drop, but by a scream far too heart ripping to be human. With eyes wide open, I tiptoed my way past

Samuel, who was sleeping between the window and everyone else, or at least I thought he was sleeping until he grabbed at my ankle, forcing me to take him. I went to the window, and through the darkness of the living room, hesitantly shifting the curtains, I peered through the fog. The faint lights of kerosene lamps were lit up on the left side of the hill. I felt faces next to me as each member of my family came to look out the window, along with Samuel and I.

There were two possibilities of what might have happened. Thomas may have sent for his family to the States, or somebody died. These are two extremes, but then again... it is a war, an extreme all its own.

I was startled by the strike of a match that lit up the already fading darkness. My father had gotten dressed, and wanted everybody else to do so too.

Walking into Thomas' house was a guilt trip of its own. The pots were shining clean not from scrubbing with sponge and soap, but from being licked so many times by starving tongues. Wiseman, the family's last born, led us into the living room after opening the door for us. Sydney, Rhys,

Papa, Luke, and I carefully followed him into the house. As I watched Wiseman walk, I thought about when I used to chase him and my younger brothers when they were little. Where I used to see a shirtless back filled with muscle and vigor, I could now count ribs and locate the backbone without feeling for it. Where I used to see legs that ran with strength and health, I now saw thin sticks that barely could walk dangling from bony hips which could hardly carry him.

As we neared the room with the crying voices, I decided that Thomas had not called, and that only left the other extremity. The farther I walked, the harder my heart beat in sympathy. We walked into the girls' room, then the parents' room, where I noticed that neither parent was. I knew without a second's thought why Thomas's mother had screamed early that morning. Amy was lying on the floor, barely clothed, and so thin I wondered how she had survived for so long. Her head was propped up on her mother's laps who had put one of her breasts in Amy's mouth. Thomas's mother, Agnes, looked up and saw us standing miserably by the doorway. She looked haggard, with bags under her eyes, and cheeks sunken so deep one couldn't tell if she had any at all. Without a word, she shifted up Amy's head so we could see her face, which disregarding her young age, was now old, withered and dead.

"She was my only girl" Mama Thomas told us like we did not know; like she was telling a chapter of the biography of her child.

"Mama... sorry" said Papa, and so it echoed through from the rest of the company, saved for me. For that I had learned somewhere that it is rather impossible, I was almost convinced I had lost my tongue down my throat. I could not utter even a hello and for some unexplainable reason, my feet were moving closer toward the mother and her daughter.

I reached out to touch unbelief in front of me. The girl, who not so long ago sat impatiently between my legs while I braided her hair, was dead.

I recalled the last conversation I had had with her.

"What do you want to be when you grow up Amy?"

"A doctor," she replied. A doctor so that I can cure everybody, and then nobody has to die.

I was jolted back to the awful present by the words of my father. He asked where Mama Agnes wanted Amy to be buried. It was not insensitive of him, and he was not trying to rush the funeral rites and get on with life. It was just that with the war, there wasn't any money for ceremonies, and a dead body left out for long will decay, smell past the house, and foul the whole neighborhood.

Mama Agnes put her breast, which had hung from the girl's mouth back into her blouse, which was now torn from her ripping at it in agony. Calmly, she lifted herself with Amy in her hands, kissed her head and placed her in Papa's arms.

"In the backyard" she said; then she took the only kerosene lamp that had lit the room, blew it out because the light of the day was fully come, and led the way down the house to the backyard.

"Wait!" I shouted, and everyone turned to look at me. I did not know why I must have figured, but I knew Augustina should be there.

"Please. She was Aussie's best friend. Let me tell her first. Let me tell her first.

✳✳✳✳✳✳✳✳✳✳✳✳✳✳✳

I ran behind Augustina on our way back to Amy's house. Papa had let me go to get her, as long as I came back with her. Augustina thought that I had come to let them know that Thomas was taking his family with him. I think she knew the truth. I think she had known it when we had left, before my return, because as she stood there with the rest of them waiting for me to tell them the news, her face registered hopeless anticipation that made me afraid to tell her. I did not have to say what had happened while we had been gone. The look on my face affirmed her fear, and she cried. She cried many words to me, and though I may and have forgotten some of it, one statement I never will forget. Before running out of the house without changing out of her night gown, she had asked, "Why are we paying for this? Why are we, children, paying for transgressions we did not commit?"

I was relieved she had not given me time to give an answer, because I did not have one.

Chapter 9

After the death of Amy, Augustina became listless around the house. She was not sure, as she would confide in me the very few times that she did speak, what her role was supposed to be in the matter. That was the first time that she had stared death in the face, and she was not amused by it. The first four days were difficult for her and the rest of the family, for while everybody seemed to be grieved, Augustina was not quite taking it seriously. Her moods were equally unpredictable. She would have fits of laughter at certain occasions, which would be followed moments or hours later by unprecedented bouts of rage. Angela, the most patient of us all tried to spend time around Augustina, but as the days went by, it grew increasingly difficult even for her.

"You know… you are getting very thin… you are not eating." Angela waited for an answer, but not with hopeful expectation because Augustina had not had a conversation with anyone since early that morning.

"Okay…" Angela reasoned, "Maybe when you're hungry, you will eat. After all, Papa says, "never force feed a child because hunger is not pretentious." I suppose when you are hungry, you will eat."

Augustina continued to stare off into the open road beyond our gates through the downstairs verandah. Her silence would not have mattered so much if it were not for the fact that there was absolutely nothing else that signified the essence of life in her except for when she roamed gingerly around the house.

"Maybe you should get some sleep... maybe a little... before supper?" Angela continued, almost on the verge of tears. Her patience was deserting her between the impending waves of guilt, and the frustrations that were now barraging her.

"I know your best friend is dead! But you cannot just give up on everyone and everything! You have to try to..."

It was the scream that brought everyone running to the front yard. Somewhere between Angela telling Augustina that her best friend had died, and her trying to get some liveliness into her older sister, Augustina had seemed to awaken out of her usual trance into her most violent fit of rage yet. She slapped Angela so hard that she left two day finger marks on her face. She continued to box at her little sister, all the while with no sounds coming out of her; no sounds but forced breaths, and foaming at the mouth. Rhys pulled Augustina away from Angela, and took her to her room while Angela ran down the little hill toward the street on the other side of the row of houses surrounding ours almost making it past our subdivision before Sydney caught up with her. Angela cried while Sydney tried to sit down with her on the bench under the guava tree. I had gone to see what Rhys was going to do with Augustina first. He did not know what to do because she had exasperated him too. I sent all the other kids to find some firewood so that we could roast yams later on that day, also that they could be out of the house. I was beyond tempted to give Augustina a sound flogging for assaulting her sister, but Rhys would not let me, reasoning that Augustina was too absent to even realize that whatever punishment that was meted to her was meant for correcting any particular offense.

I was still trying to figure out what to do about Augustina's increasingly violent fits of rage when we all heard the faint music from a guitar growing louder as it neared the house.

I opened the front door to welcome Silas, the music man, and Sydney, with Angela holding onto her hand, standing closely behind him. They all entered bringing everyone from within the house to sit on the ground to listen to Silas entertain us with music so soft and reaching that for that moment, it stripped us of any animosity we may have had in our hearts toward anything or anyone. I heard footsteps come down the stairs, and Augustina come and stand by the doorway of the parlour. Silas smiled motioning for her to come and sit with the rest of us whom he had seized their rapt attention. She smiled back at him walking towards us, and taking a seat right next to Angela. I sighed silently in gratefulness to the Almighty for bringing Silas with his famous guitar up to our roads. I smile to Augustina, who despite herself tries a pitiful smile to me in return.

The hot beginning of the day started cooling by the threats of roaring thunder that signaled signs of heavy rain. The drops had begun to come sparsely when we heard another knock at the door before our visitor came in carrying her young son with her.

I was overjoyed to see Amy's mother, just as I was disappointed to see her, if that was possible. She was a lovely woman whose presence I had always greatly been encouraged by. However, I was disappointed because Augustina had just started to get better, even if the only sign of that hope was her rejoining us to listen to the music man, but it was still a spark. I worried that Mama Agnes was going to be a reminder of the tragic loneliness Augustina still felt since Amy's death. I was worried that it may cause my sister to abandon the attempt she had just made at trying out this happiness thing again. Joshua was happy to see Wiseman, taking him upstairs to play video games, and to find as much mischief as they could get into.

Mama Agnes sat and talked about relatively trivial things, like the wonderment that was the mechanics of an airplane, and the redemption my head desperately needed to tame its wild and nappy mane.

"Does Amy talk to you?" Augustina asked very quietly we almost did not hear her. Her question commanded silence, bringing everyone's gaze first to Augustina in pity, and then to Mama Agnes in anticipation.

"All the time… I see her all the time… especially when I'm asleep."

"What does she say?" Augustina whispers almost breathlessly.

"Do you see her?"Mama Agnes bypasses Augustina's question.

"Yes. I see her all the time. She does not say anything. Sometimes we play. Sometimes we just sit, and then she would always smile." Augustina finished with a catch in her throat.

Angela asks Mama Agnes if Amy ever spoke to her.

"No…" the woman replied, "…she just smiles."

"Do you think she's angry with me?" Augustina asks quietly, her voice shaking. I look at my sister to see two pools of tears hanging carelessly on the lower lids of her big sad brown eyes.

"My love…" Mama Agnes inches toward Augustina on her chair "… why would you say that?"

"Because I did not save her." The tears spilled down when she tightly shut her eyes. "Because, I did not stop her from dying."

"How would you have stopped her?" Mama Agnes asked, concern clouding her eyes.

"I don't know. Sometimes I feel like if I had been there, she wouldn't have died.

Mama Agnes reached for Augustina who got up and went to the kind woman to sit on her lap. Looking into her face, Mama Agnes contentedly said: "The Lord giveth, and the Lord taketh away…" Augustina joined her as they finished a part of the bible that even for a moment calmed everybody's spirits that afternoon, "blessed be the name of the Lord."

Mama Agnes, along with the music man escorting her, eventually left, after they had joined us for dinner. Augustina helped me clean up after making plates for our parents who would be arriving home later that night. Sydney made sure the non-perishables that were returned to the storeroom were completely sealed so the rats would not get to them. I went over to the window, and there I stared at the moon. It was the biggest I had ever seen it that night. Joshua, and Wiseman, who had begged to stay the night in our home, came and stood next to me. They were waiting for my parents' car headlights to come rounding the bend so my mother could tell them a folktale. They waited beside me, looking up at the moon which cast its glorious light across a brilliant sky that bore no trace it had released a torrential pour just hours before that white glass which shone in the sky guiding the waters of the sea.

Chapter 10

May 20, 2004

We were left by my parents in Gulu the day before the conference because they had a more formal affair that did not require our presence as importantly as the following day did. That morning, we all decided to give the drivers the day off and walk instead to Hosanna. The way we knew, would take us through a path that the driver before taking his leave assured us was safe to traverse, but cautioned us still to keep our eyes open, and our ears pricked to any unusualness. He told us that at the sight of any unusual activity, to run and not stop until we were home.

I walked over to the guest quarters to ask Julia if she would like to accompany us. She declined, because her infant daughter was still asleep and grew irritable if she were woken not of her own accord.

~~~~~~~~~~~~~~~~

"Now, who is Julia?" My therapist asks with an inquisitive furrow of her brow.

"She was the girl crying at the dining table with her son the night we had come back."

"You have not spoken much about her."

"I don't actually know why that is..." I answered creasing my forehead in a frown. "...I suppose I'm somewhat ashamed."

"Ashamed of what?" The therapist asks shifting in her chair as if in preparation for a juicier tale than the ones I had previously told.

"I never asked Julia about herself in all the time that I was home with her around. We went to Hosanna every day. We asked the children questions and tried to help them make sense of the confusing emotions that wrestled within them. We taught them skills, and encouraged them to open about their experiences. We were there in Hosanna, caring for those children. I never once asked Julia about her story."

"Did you speak often with her?"

"Absolutely! She was part of my family, part of our day. The separate quarters were for her dignity, and privacy; but we were together for the most part."

"You just never asked her about her experience?" The therapist asked.

"No... and I am ashamed of that because when we returned home after been gone, she had left. She lives in Tanzania now, and my parents pay for her to go to school there. I never got to ask her, and I always wonder if she might have thought that I did not care."

"Did you care?"

"Yes. I just didn't know how to ask her. We were always talking about something else, something that did not subtly allow her to tell of her experience. I guess I did not want to believe that the scars about her body came from anything other than careless childhood plays. I wish I asked; I think I'm lacking a splinter of peace for that. I feel like she was waiting for me to care."

"Maybe" The therapist nods her head, and my heart sinks to my stomach at her agreement. "Or maybe..." she continued, "...Julia looked forward to you, because you were the one person who saw that a conversation can happen with her on something else about her. You can find something to share with her, and play with her than ask her for a story concentrated on this one aspect of her life that she may feel she has had to regurgitate ad nauseam."

My heart settles within me bringing back with it in gratitude to my therapist that splinter of peace that had hovered tauntingly over me. I take my therapist back to the day we had been allowed for the first time to walk to Hosanna.

~~~~~~~~~~~~~~~~

Halfway down the dusty path, my sisters and I took off our sandals, and walked the red warm sands plucking blades of the elephant grass that grew beside the path to braid garlands for our heads. I was rubbing Joshua's blades against a tree trunk to dull away the sharp edges when I saw a truck coming behind us. I alerted my company who had already seen it, and cautiously cleared the way. I do not remember really when we started to run, or what made us run, but suddenly, my feet were clearing twigs, and jumping over vines that were growing across the fields. I looked up often and I would see bullets, countless of them sailing through the air at us. I considered cutting across and running for the other end of the path, but changed my mind when I figured that we stood a better chance in the bush because it made it harder for whoever was shooting to spot us. This was provided we ran as fast as we could because they had begun to throw bombs, and no one knew upon where or whom it would fall.

While everyone ran, I did not know where I was supposed to be going, as suddenly the figures of my companions were gone into the thicket. It was later that I found out I was going the opposite direction from everyone else. I heard footsteps approaching behind me, and it was dangerously too close. My feet grew roots into the ground, and I froze. Suddenly, I felt a hand grab mine, and I turned around to see Rhys with the most petrified look I had ever seen as he looked between me, and the relentless infantry. Then, there was a yell, and in a split second, I knew a bomb had been thrown too close. The jolt sent Rhys and I flying and hitting the ground just in front of the rest of our family. I coughed, sending a cloud of dust over my face and blinding my eyes with dirt. I understood what was going on by then; I got up as fast as I could and with my sisters' help I ran, this time in the same direction as the others.

When we reached home, we locked the doors after calling Julia and her children into the parlour with us. Luke began to look Sydney over to see if she had broken any bones, and after she assured him that she was fairly well, he shakily sat down.

That was the first time I truly understood that there was really a war, and that I was a targeted enemy of whoever wanted the dissemination of the Acholi.

Rhys got up to leave the room, his labored footsteps heavily climbing the stairs. He would be the quietest of us all most of that day, and I would be worried for him most of that day.

We all spent the rest of that day mostly clinging to each other. We searched for the funniest stories, and told them. We looked for the funniest movies, and watched them. I had not really spoken to Rhys about the incident, and so later at the night of that day, after I tucked my siblings to sleep, I went to the second story front verandah where he had been for most of that day.

~ ~ ~ ~ ~ ~ ~ ~ ~ ~ ~ ~ ~ ~ ~ ~ ~ ~ ~

I tell my therapist of my conversation with Rhys out on that verandah:

"I knew his heart. I always knew Rhys. I always knew what he was thinking. I knew he wanted to leave, but I asked him anyway. I asked him if he was going to leave."

"Why? Why did you ask? You already knew what he was going to say."

"I did not want him to, and I hoped against hopes. I knew that I wouldn't mind being wrong, this time."

"What did he say?"

"He said yes... and that he needed me to leave with him. I did not know what to say. I did not know what to say at all."

"What did you eventually say?"

"I stood there and I thought about my family, looking at the man who I was engaged to be clung to; to be one with; to be my new family. I felt tugged at two ends with very considerable concerns. In my culture, being the first daughter is not just a title or a situation; it was a responsibility to my parents, and to my siblings. My return was their ray of hope. Having us all there when they woke up in the morning, sent a relief coursing through their bodies as they waited for us to call their names, as if to make sure it was true. My siblings could heal past that day because we were there with them. I could not leave them, because it seemed selfish, and it seemed like an abandonment of my duties as my siblings' sister, and as my parents' first daughter. I agreed with Rhys that that day was tempestuous, but I also knew we could pray past it, and lean on one another to heal.

~~~~~~~~~~~~~~~~

"I cannot leave you here Cali!" he started with growing frustration. "What if you run again until you cannot run? What if it wasn't my hand that grabbed yours? What if it had been much worse?"

"God apparently wanted me out of that thicket today. If your hand didn't grab mine, someone else's would have; and if God ran out of people, an angel would have carried me out of that bush if God wanted to save me. I would rather die here and have died for something, than to leave and regret forever that I did; which I will. Rhys, I love you but I cannot leave with you. I will not leave with you."

"I cannot keep worrying about you. If I lost you when I'm not here, I don't know how I'm going to live."

I went to sit next to him next to him against the wall facing the street. I took his hand in mine, gently raised it to my lips, softly kissing him. I search for some tiny absence of fear in his eyes, but I see none, and suddenly I was afraid. I feared what scars this incident could leave for Rhys if he left with that fear. I worried there would not be any space in his soul anymore for the power of hope.

"I'm sorry, Rhys. I cannot go with you."

"Why not?"

"Because I don't think it is even right for you to leave, so I know it is definitely not right for me to leave right now."

"So, you think it is wrong for me to leave?"

"I don't know if it is wrong, but I know it isn't right."

"It is either good to leave, or it is bad to leave…" Rhys argued.

I just stood there wrestling with the better judgment, knowing what it is, but not sure I wanted to allow what it was, to be. This was my home. This was half of me. If I got chased out of the rest of the world, this was where I had to come back to. This was it. In my heart, I had always imagined that as long as I had Rhys, there was nothing I could not do, or be, or try to be. With him I would go anywhere; I would endure anything, and be the absolute best. I told Rhys that it was not wrong to leave, but that it was dishonorable if I left. He heaved a heavy sigh, which in no certain words, asked me what I wanted him to do.

Chapter 11

Rhys and I came back into the house a bit before three a.m., and he went off to bed in the boys' room. I went downstairs to my father's office to talk to him. I slowly opened his door, and there on his seat, I could see him. Of course, my head knew he was not there, and that I would not see him until much later that day; however, there in the desperation of my mind, I could see him. He was smiling at me and motioning for me to come and sit on his lap so that he could wipe the tears from off my eyes, and tell me the exact words that made the world of unfortunate fate evaporate from my mind. With tears clouding my vision, I walked over to the chair to sit on it. I put my legs up holding it close to me as I cuddled into my father's lap wishing that he was there instead of the empty cold leather seat. I felt awful about the decision I had to make, and it pained my heart to think of what could come out of either. I loved Rhys more than anything or anyone in the world. I also knew that this decision on my lap to make was far greater than the selfish question that we had let it be succumbed to. Wanting to be with my family, and knowing that it was important especially at this time did not mean that I loved Rhys any less. Did it? Couldn't whether or not I loved Rhys be completely outside of the decision my heart was surrendering my emotions to deal with; not exceedingly well might I add. I snuggled deeper into the chair turning my ring around my finger regarding it with every ounce of earnest passion I ever felt for the boy I desperately loved, remembering when Rhys had asked me to marry him.

* * * * * * * * * * * * * * *

Rhys had decided to take a jewelry class at the University he was attending for reasons he never wanted to explain while so doing. It would ordinarily not have raised any cause for wonder, except his major was Pre-Law and therefore, did not have anything to do with jewelry. Two days after his college graduation, he took me back to my room after we had had dinner with his parents. We sat in a cuddle as we watched the stars my darling had made for me two years before by pasting cubic zirconia onto dark sheets on the ceiling on the far right corner of my bedroom. Rhys had been acting very nervously since the beginning of that day when I went into his room to help him get dressed. He watched me so closely and lovingly, which was absolutely not unusual, but there was something about the way he was looking at me this time. While I sat on his dresser helping him with his tie, he grabbed my face between his hands, and kissed me like I was going on a long trip which would take me away from him for another decade or so. I smiled at him with a somewhat awkward slight raise of the eyebrow. He told me he knew that once this whole graduation day got underway, there probably would not be any time to spend alone together away from all the family, and other company around. There was something he wanted to talk to me about before the end of the day, so he asked me to save time after dinner just to spend with him. I promised to.

Now in my room, Rhys looked at me again with those eyes that rendered me absolutely breathless, with the kisses that accompanied it again the same way he did that morning. I gave him the look again, that I had given him earlier that day, but this time asked him why he was acting so weird. He turned my back to him pulling me closer as he wrapped his arms around me. I looked up at him, and smiled a smile I hoped would soothe whatever it was that may have been troubling him so. He took out of his pocket a small black box that caused a gasp out of me when he handed it to me, and asked me to open it. I did. Inside was the most perfect silver band with a crest that should have encased a gem of some sort. This one, however, had none and I did not know how to react. Fortunately, he didn't give me much time to. He took the ring out of the box, and turned me again wrapping his arms around me, and turning the ring over in his hand. He kissed my head before quite nervously beginning his speech.

"Cali, this was why I was taking that jewelry class you all made fun of me for taking. I remember you asking me where it was, and I wouldn't show it to you; partly, because it wasn't done. I think my life has been very privileged with great parents, great siblings and an incredibly amazing girlfriend. I graduated from college two days ago, and will be starting this new life for myself with a good job that I actually like, and the support of my friends and family. For the most part, I have got everything most people would ever desire. But I want something else that no one else has, or will ever deserve; certainly not me. I want the promise of forever with you. The promise that as long as stars remain in the sky, and even after that, love will still find you and me in each other's arms. So, maybe if you do not mind... a whole lot... I want to spend the rest of my life with you.

Somewhere in the middle of the ceiling, one of those stars, with the moon shining brighter on it than the rest of them up there, began to fall. Slowly, it made its way down in front of my face where my mouth hung open in absolute awe as it rested ever so obediently in Rhys's palm. He took it and shifted to look me in the eye with both knees on the floor. He started to fit the gem into the crest of the ring before tightening the sides. He continued:

"...and maybe just as this gem is made just for this ring and just as perfectly as it fits, my life can be made whole if you made me the happiest man in the world. Calista Mirembe Okello, will you marry me?

I looked at that beautiful ring that my baby had made for me, and in that moment, and every one after it, I did not just see the silver or the diamond; I saw the time and passion that went into creating that wonder only for me. I wrapped my arms around him, kissing him with a love meant only to promise him that life with him was an experience I never wanted to stop having, and a passion I never want to stop creating.

I said yes.

* * * * * * * * * * * * * *

I watched the sun slowly rise to expose the night into day as it always does. Uncertainty growing within me due to all that had been happening, had kept me from realizing that whether or not I would be running, or hiding, or scared, there were things that were constant, like the sun. I did not know what to do with the helplessness I felt inside. On one hand, I wanted to stay home and be with the family whose plight I knew would not be any more different with or without me, but who I knew somehow needed me to be there whether the help I had to give would be great, or small. On the other hand, Rhys was the man I was about to promise the rest of my life to, to be with him where he was; to support his dreams; to carry along his fears, and to come upon the years loving, and fighting, and loving again, together. How was I to leave him? To tell him that I could not go with him in a time I knew my presence would ease even a bit what he was going through. How was I to leave my family? To go away from my siblings whom my homecoming brought a break in the mundane usualness of their day? How was I to tell them that I had chosen somebody else over them to follow? How was I to tell either party that one of them was more important to me than the other, by leaving or staying? Who would I let down, and at what cost? I had fought with it all night barely finding sleep as even the tears that could show the tempest in my heart eluded me.

It must have been somewhere around six a.m. when Sydney gently knocked on the office door.

"Cali? Cali, are you in there?" She called.

"Yeah Syd, come in" I answered.

"The door is locked Cali."

"Oh, hold on." I got up and dragged my feet under me to the door. I opened it to Sydney, who looked at me with a somewhat worried look on her face.

"Did you spend the night in here?" she asked me.

"Only since about three this morning; I think that was when Rhys went to bed.

"Why did not you just come into the bedroom?"

"I do not know…," I started running my hand exhaustedly through my braids, "… I just kept moving my feet, and they brought me down here."

"Okay" she decided, looking at me carefully "Why don't you go and clean up, and the girls and I will start on breakfast."

"Okay."

Chapter 12

May 21, 2004

At breakfast that morning, Rhys and I informed the rest of our family that he was considering his leave to be by the end of the week. He would be returning two weeks later with his parents to Kampala where we'd meet them to spend the rest of the summer. Sadness stole all our appetites as my siblings inquired as to how that would affect our engagement to be married. We explained our unwavering love for one another was certainly going to try the differing priorities, but that we were devoted to it, and would resume our wedding plans when I returned to the U.S. My siblings found it hard to make sense of how to celebrate an engagement party without the will-be groom, but tried their best to make positive the situation.

"Why don't we all just go to Kampala now?" They asked.

It was while we were discussing with my siblings, the very easy solution to the problem, that Samson came to the house to inform us that our parents had asked us to join them immediately as they had gotten word that the rebels were leading more daring attacks headed our way. Even though we were safe in our home, our parents preferred our presence with them. Before we leave, Rhys and I discuss my sibling's suggestion wondering why it never occurred to either of us.

"Because you're scared." I accused him mockingly.

"And you're stubborn" he returned.

Our car trip started out with lively conversations as the boys told jokes that made us girls laugh until our sides hurt. We talked about the weddings, and who was going to have what role. They were going to be the biggest weddings because everybody wanted to be in it, and when in Uganda, it is always a big wedding. We stopped talking when Samson looked in his rearview mirror at the car behind him. I caught unsettlement in his eyes and asked him what was bothering him about whatever he was looking at through the rearview mirror.

"Nothing Cali, but if you all don't mind keeping an eye on that truck behind us; it has been following for about twenty minutes now."

We grew quiet as Samson turned the car down a route that we knew was not the way home.

"Why are you going this way? This is not the way home." Samuel observed.

"I want to know if that van is following us." Samson stated trying to stay calm, but conveying a nervousness in his tone.

The van turned down the same route we were on, beginning to follow a bit more closely when Samson turned yet again down another unfamiliar route and asked us to put on our seatbelts. I did not think we were in immediate harm necessarily at that time, but an uneasy feeling settled in the pits of my stomach, mostly because we all grew very quiet, almost afraid even to breathe. I held Angela's hand on one side of me, and Jacob's on the other as others did the same. Joshua prayed for God's protection on us to get home safely, and perhaps not have to return to Gulu until this war was over.

Joshua's prayer would have succeeded in quelling the tumult that slowly churned my stomach if Samson had not started to drive much faster than the normal speed. Even worse, the van behind us sped up as well.

"Do you think we can outrun them?" I asked, my voice shaking.

"Do not talk like that Cali" Rhys said putting his hand on my shoulder from the backseat attempting to squeeze some relief into my tense back. "We do not know if it is bad yet."

But I know it is bad. I know that it is very bad, and I am overcome with will to grab the wheel and floor the pedals; I am aware, however, that I cannot do it any better than Samson. I hear a bump which causes the car to lurch forward sending us all jolting toward the front. Samson tries to turn into another road which the opposing van would be following too close behind to make, but the van swerves too fast and falls onto its left side, dragging almost into the gutter by the side of the road. I hit my head on the window and can feel the pounding in my head when I try to turn to see what had just happened. In the haziness of my eyes, I see Samson come out of the van. That is all I remember.

****

I woke up again to darkness around me that gave no relief to the hammer knocking around in my head as if furiously searching for its way out. I feel around me for inkling as to where I am, and what I am doing there instead anywhere else. I feel bodies around me as my hand tries to make out limbs in the dark cove with slits of light coming through the tarpaulin. We were moving, that much I knew, to a place I did not remember being aware about. I tried to remember how I came to be in this van, what we were doing before I was put in a truck with my eyes almost swelled shut. I shut my eyes, and try to play the scenes in my head that my mind allowed me to process. I remember getting in the van. I remember we were driving fast away from someone. I remember turning around just in time to feel our van flip on its side, and my head shattering the passenger-side window. I remember Samson leaving the van. A new worry settles within me aching far more than the pains that are pulsating in every part of my body that I can feel. A worry as to where the rest of my company is. I feel bodies stirring all around me, and in panic, I begin to call out as many names as I can.

"Rhys?"

"Here," he answers.

"Angela?"

"I'm here" came another feeble reply.

I call out everyone's name, and one by one, and however weakly, they answer. I call Samuel last; he does not answer. More frantically I call for him beginning to get up to feel around me as my mind convinces me that I would know it is him when I get to his of the dark figures that lay on the bed of the truck. He eventually answers me much more quietly than the others. I know he is alive. Hurt, but alive.

"Where are we?" Augustina asks, with a flood of tears stuck in her throat.

"I think we are in that truck that was pursuing us." Luke answered coughing dryly.

Rhys walked over to the back of the truck and looked through the tiny slit.

"Do you recognize anything?" Sydney asked him.

"No." He answered with a hint of panic in his voice.

"What do you see?" Augustina asked.

"Nothing... nothing... nothing...just... bush."

Chapter 13

A silence - that silence - that strangling silence we all knew too well settles over us, doing all but pressing the life out of us. We did not know where we were, but we knew one thing for certain, we were not on our way home.

"Why are we the only ones in this truck?" Angela asked, her voice still shaking.

"Yeah," Jacob agreed. "I thought everybody marched. Why are we being driven?"

Before any of us could think of an answer, the truck came to a stop. We then heard two slams of both front doors, and fear rose so very high inside me I thought I was going to vomit out my heart. We heard the clanging of chairs before the back door flung open. The light burned our eyes as we shut them quickly and squinted to see six stone-cold faces with AK-47s, and bayonets slung from their shoulders. We were ordered out of the truck quickly to line up beside one of the commanders where we were then tied to one another, and commanded to walk straight through a beaten path in the bush.

I am last in line, and I do not know why. But as we walk, my eyes adjust to the light around me settling on my family ahead. We were all bloody and had wounds and swellings all over our bodies. Our clothes had been ripped all over the place, and dust caked around the blood making it cling in clumps in our hairs and on our bodies.

We walked slowly at first from the pain and got in trouble for it. They flogged our legs with canes as we walked, while they started to count in time. We were to march in the time they were counting, and for the times we missed by walking slowly or stumbling over our feet. We got two lashes to the back of our legs. "Walk faster!" they would shout at us and laugh. "Do you think you are at your father's house?" They walked over to Sydney, Rhys, and Luke, and marched in time with them, mocking their frightened faces. They came face to face with them, where they wickedly said:

"Our beautiful white friends, you are not in Kansas anymore."

We arrived three and a half miles later, to a campground with small fires already set by other children; some washing beans and pots, and some shucking several ears of corn. When we reached the middle of the site, the commander ordered that everyone stop what they were doing, and bring themselves to where we were. Jacob in exhausted pain tried to sit down, but was beaten on the back with a panga from one of the rebel boys already at the camp. I ran to help him, but was grabbed by another rebel who slapped my face.

"You never sit when a commander is speaking!" the boy with the panga shouted at Jacob who was still writhing on the ground in pain.

I jerked up to look at the face of the voice I unmistakably could recognize anywhere. It was David's voice. He looked at me with an expression that gave away the fact that he not only appreciated the shock on my face, but was, in fact, hoping for it. He smiled at me; a sly victorious smile that told me revenge was the uttermost thing on his mind, and our brutal initiation we knew was coming was one he expected with hopeful glee. The commander ordered Jacob on his feet.

A man far better pressed than the one in charge of rounding us up while barking orders came down from a truck that careened into the rest stop. He came, looked at all of us, before his eyes rested longer at Luke, Rhys, and Sydney. He sneered at our faces and motioned for David to come before us as he himself went to sit on the boot of the truck he had arrived in.

"Alright everybody, listen to me!" David started loudly. "Our commander is going to speak now! You are to listen very carefully because he will not repeat himself at all, and you are to carry out his orders immediately. Do you understand?"

Silence.

"I said, do you understand?!"

"Yes!" Came a resounding reply from everyone.

The Commander came and stood in the middle of everyone where he started to speak. He ordered everyone who had been abducted before that day, and within the past two weeks on his right and the rest of everyone else on his left. My siblings, Sydney, Rhys, Luke, and I, did not really understand what we were supposed to be doing, but everyone around us moved so fearfully fast that we knew we must as well, or suffer a consequence – of what we were not quite sure, but had an idea about. There were about fifteen of us who were relatively new and about twenty who were not. I had always wondered, whenever I heard stories of abductions, why the abductees who seemed to be larger in number than the commanders never tried to band together to subdue their captors. I could clearly see why then. The children on the right side with us where all at the most sixteen years of age. Some looked about five, but for the most part, the most of them were approximately of age eight to thirteen. We were all also severely wounded and scarred from beatings prior to our presence at the camp. Everyone else, beside myself and family, had marched a long way to the camp in which time, the never-ending presence of the rebels' rifles, bayonets and machine guns had pierced a frightening image into the eyes and psyche of the unfortunate souls, most of whom would never again know a freedom or home they had been so mercilessly torn away from.

The Commander ordered us all to look at him and to keep our eyes on him until he finished speaking or were otherwise instructed. If anybody at anytime were to take their eyes off him without express permission to do so, they would be killed. I strained to keep my eyes on him because I realized my purse had been left in the car along with my prescription for my migraines, which had come back with a vengeance. Nevertheless, knowing that I would rather the migraine than a death that I knew would not occur painlessly, I kept my eyes on the commander.

"I know you are all wondering what you are doing here. You do not know why you run away when you hear that we are coming to town. I will tell you now. You are here because we want the government to listen. The only way that the government can listen to us is if we get them were it is painful. If you advertise for soldiers to fight, and they voluntarily come, then the government will say that any idiot who is foolish enough to join a rebel army does not deserve government protection. They will not care, and will not listen. You are here because you are innocent, and we are doing it by force so that they will come to rescue you. We will kill them all when they come to rescue you if we do not kill you first. The President does not protect the Acholi, so we are protecting the Acholi. The government is killing the Acholi and even now does not protect its people. They ask us why we abduct children, and they say we are animals that do not follow the rules of engagement. What kind of government cannot protect even its own little children? Is the President looking for you? I do not think so. Are the police looking for you? Not exactly. The government that you hoped would kill us all so that you could have your once free Acholiland, does not do anything. When they shoot, they shoot at us, and you. If you run away, they will imprison you for treason. If you make it home, your family will hate you for robbing their land. Men will never love the women because you have been somebody's wife - the enemies' wives. From here on out my friends, you are rebels. You are the enemies. Your family is us; your life giver is us, and your death sentence is us. You can never go back to the same life we took from you. If you obey, and listen, you will live to see a good destiny here and in heaven. If you disobey, or misbehave, you will neither have a good life here on in heaven. Do you hear me?"

"Yes," we all muttered.

"Do you hear me?" He bellowed at us much louder this time.

"Yes!" we shouted back.

A little boy no more than ten years of age swatted at a mosquito that landed on his shoulder, looking at it in his hand. The commander grabbed him by the neck shoving forced him on his knees.

"What did I say?" He shouted at the boy.

"You asked if we heard you." The boy frightfully stammered

"No. Before that! What did I say you must do at all times until I am finished?"

"Look at you?" The boy asked with big tear balls hanging from his lashes, and spilling over as he dissolved in a wail.

"And what did you just do?"

"I was just beating off the mosquito from my shoulder sir." He said through his tears.

The commander reached for a piece of wood with fire still burning from it, and slammed it onto the boy's face. The child screamed from the pain as he grabbed his face hurling his body to the ground. The man raised his hand to continue his vicious attack on the child even littler than the stick with which he had wounded him. My body flung itself toward the ailing boy, getting in the way of the club that headed for his knees but hit my shoulder instead. The sharp pain hit me with a power that numbed every other pain that I felt throughout my body. Between gasping for air, and screaming for my mother, I begged for the little boy who I knew that if nobody begged for him, he would die.

"Please... please..." I begged. "Let him live. Please give him another chance."

Sydney ran to my side to help plead with me for the life of the little boy. The commander watched us with an amused look on his face, and watched as all my siblings along with Luke and Rhys pleaded for the child's life. With a motion of his hand, he ordered me and Sydney to return to the place we were standing before. He then looked around the circle at the other children who had been there before us.

"What happens when someone disobeys an order?"

"They die!" the children reply in unison.

"And who kills them? I do not do the killing, do I?"

"No sir!" they replied again.

"Who does the killing?"

"We do sir!"

"And who here has done it before?"

Everybody raised their hands slowly one by one. The last person to raise his hand was a little boy I had not seen before, and he did not look anymore than six years old. His eyes gave away sadness, and fears that I felt grip my nerves forcing me to resign to the fate that awaited the little boy writhing on the camp ground. I realized in my resignation that neither my hands, nor those of my family were raised, and a dense feeling rose from the pits of my stomach. I knew the next words that would come out of the commander's mouth; in fact, I could almost speak alongside him word-for-word. The stories the children told us that still haunted their dreams included the guilt they felt from the killings they had to do. I never agreed that I would ever kill someone no matter how much I was threatened. I would rather die, I had reasoned, than take a life. However, now as I slowly lifted my face to stare at the eyes of the Commander that now pierced through me, I remembered the advice my mother had always given me, though I had been hard of hearing, and unable to practice it to the full meaning.

"Don't ever assume you would have handled a situation better than anyone unless you yourself had at some point in your life found yourself in that situation, at the same time, at the same place."

Looking into those evil eyes as they looked at mine, I felt my spirit begin to leave, and then I heard him say it:

"It seems that our newest visitors have not had the privilege of learning how we deal with disobedient little rascals like this one here" he said gesturing to the boy who now produced no sounds, but just lay there quietly with his eyes open, staring at something in the distance.

"They will kill this boy!" he shouted still looking at me, thrusting the club in his hand at me. I let it fall to the ground as my eyes left the evil that stood before me to watch the little boy who now had a smile slightly creep alongside his mouth. It was a faraway look that he had in his eyes, almost as if he had already died the death our commander thought was in his hands. The rest of my family was ordered to pick out pieces from the fire, and to beat the boy with it each person taking a turn after every hit. Jacob and Samuel began to cry as the rest of us allowed the tears that rolled down all our faces as we stood there. Three rebels came behind us with whips with which they began to flog us. We shrieked from the pain, and after a few minutes, the beatings stopped; and we were again instructed to beat the child to death. I picked up the club from the ground and watched my family each pick up a stick from the fire. I heard the sniffles of other children in that circle crying, knowing they wished they could turn away, but could not. An escapee had told us that to look away when someone was being killed was considered soft and unfit. It was an act punishable by death, or force to kill someone. I heard a thump, and then a soft cry escaped from the boy who had a trembling Jacob standing next to him. One by one, my family hit the boy, and every time they would, his cry grew quieter. When the rebels began to beat us again with their fists, I knew that my family was not ready to kill that child or anybody for that matter. I did not want to kill that boy either, but I knew that my little siblings could not stand much more beatings from those rebels. I also knew Luke, Rhys, and Sydney, especially were not going to survive any more beatings; at least not that evening. I looked over at Angela, seeing her struggle to stand. I looked at Samuel, who could barely open his eyes, which had met the fist of one of the younger rebels. Luke was bleeding from the side of his eye, and was crumpled on the ground probably unconscious. I looked at the boy whose life I had to take, not by any right, but for the salvation of my family, and for the end of his terror and turmoil, and I began to get up. As I walked slowly toward him, I silently prayed for his soul and for my forgiveness. He looked up at me smiling at me through the apple of his eye where I could see my face and the tears that fell through the dust that had caked it a lighter brown. I wanted to give him the final blow; one that would have him feel no pain, but send him to his perfect peace that no evil could ever behold. I felt my spirit leave me again as the pain in my shoulders numbed long enough to give way for the club that rose over my head and come down with great force. The sound I heard next I would always hear for as long as I lived. I looked down to see brain matter spill out of his head, silently thanking God that his pain was done.

The Commander ordered every one of the new abductees to dip their hand in his blood, and to smear it in a cross sign across their hearts. After that, we were allowed to sit down to be told that any attempt to run that night would be futile. They had eyes everywhere, and they knew we wouldn't know our way back. Besides, he said, our parents were dead, and the family left for us does not know where we were and were too busy with their own losses and pain to care about us.

Augustina replied that our parents were not dead, and were looking for us because they had gone to a social event where they were expecting us.

"Your parents are dead" the Commander replied coldly. "Your parents are Moses and Grace Okello; are they not?" He asked.

We did not answer.

"We killed them too. They were at the conference banquet for The Hosanna House were they not? We bombed the building they were in. Not a soul survived."

"So, you planned this all out?" I whispered as it was the only sound I could make without my head erupting into more pain than it already numbingly was in. "You planned to kill our parents, and then you followed us and abducted us?"

"Yes" came the cold reply.

"Why?"

"I do not have to give you a reason."

He did not have to. I knew we had not been victims of a random abduction. It all came crashing back to me in a realization that pulsated through my veins, causing my heart to beat rapidly in and out of rhythm, and in turn surrendering my head to an explosion of crippling pain. We had not been travelling on a deserted road. I knew the way to the banquet hall where that conference was to be held. We were not just any abductees; it had been a set up. I felt my spirit come back to me, and I began to drift slowly out of consciousness. It would happen several times that night.

Chapter 14

May 22, 2004

We woke up the next morning in a tent. Not everyone, however, had been roused that morning by the time the unfamiliar had returned to us still awaiting our fate. There were only seven tents that I could count through the opening of the flap that I was lying next to. All the other children who were in the circle the previous night with us, were laying outside, and the commanders were nowhere to be seen, so I assumed they were all in the tents. I looked around to see my family laying next to me. I counted to make sure that we were still the same in number. We were, and for that I whispered a grateful prayer to God. I noticed during my prayer the same feeling from the previous night creep up my nerves, accompanied by the questions that came back again with another wave of pulsating blows inside of my head. Why were we the only ones in a tent? We had not earned any type of rank; we had not even been here long enough. Why were we being spared? I knew that my attempt to deliver that little boy last night from his evil punisher was an act that could bring a death sentence upon me, but still here I was alive with as much of my family as came with me.

Augustina stirred next to me along with everybody as we inched closer to the tent opening and peered out onto the earth which was reluctantly waiting to be mercilessly beat upon by the blinding sun. I felt around my body trying not to think myself sick from being covered in blood, dirt and sweat. I made a face as I looked behind me to see everyone realizing that they were in a similar mess. Augustina stopped for a moment to look around her, and with a suspicious cock of the brow she looked outside at the kids who were obviously not in tents.

"Why are we the only ones in a tent?"

Samuel crawled over to where she was. "Yeah, what makes us so special?"

"I don't know," I replied staring off into what I supposed would be the Commanders' tent, and feeling an eerie chill creep up my spine. "Maybe we are of more value."

"More value?!" Rhys asked in shock, as if he could not believe the audacity with which his girlfriend had uttered such proud words. "I cannot believe you would think that you were more important...?"

"That's not what I mean" I interjected, "I just... I don't know... well... don't you think it is odd?" I asked almost frantically from not knowing how to explain that I did not mean to place my life at a higher value than anyone else's.

"Maybe they want something from us," Sydney said looking at the commanders' tents with the look on her face as had previously been on mine. "Maybe something bigger than fighting" she finished as she drew closer to Luke wrapping his arm around her shoulder.

I drew back closing the flap that I had been holding open, to look at the faces of my family. Rhys looked pitiful, which made me wish that I had let him go instead of having him stay and suffer this way. Luke looked as if none of the events that had transpired in the last day had registered in his mind as something other than just a dream. Sydney looked scared and excruciatingly feeble. Augustina had her knees drawn up to chin, and her arms wrapped around it rocking herself back and forth. Angela was still. She did not have any emotions on her face. She had the same look as

Luke, but it was more far away than I had ever seen it. Samuel and Jacob looked on the verge of tears, like two little boys who were lost on their way home from school with the rain pouring hard upon their backs and washing away footprints they had hoped would bring them back to where they had started, where perhaps someone would be waiting for them.

I looked around the room, and let out a deep sorrow filled sigh. I had not listened to any of them when they had asked me to drive to the conference and give Samson the day off. Of course, having the synapses of my mother and hers of her mother, one type of guilt led me through a series of others until I almost let my brain summarize that this whole war brutality was my brilliant idea.

I reached for Samuel and Jacob, and when they came beside me, I put an arm on each of them pulling them against me as tightly as I could squeeze, mindless of the tears that dropped onto my cheeks. I wiped them off and looked at my family again.

"I don't know why we are here. I don't know what to do. I don't know if we are going to make it, but I will give my life before any of you loses theirs. We are going to walk a lot. I want you to walk, and walk, and walk, until they say you must not walk anymore. You will get so tired you will want to die, but if you stop, they will kill you. Akello said that once they killed a boy because he dropped whatever it was they told him to carry. Watch out for each other. Before you eat any leaf or fruit in the bush that you have never eaten before or do not know what it is, ask me first. When it gets cool, walk bare feet and put your shoes away so that when the sands are too hot to walk on, you will have something of some form of comfort. I... I... I...." I could barely carry on as tears formed in my eyes and the words that rumbled my stomach got caught in my throat. "...I love you all so much..., and I will care for you. We are together. Together. We fight together; we walk together; we pray together. And if they kill one of us, they must kill us all."

We sat in silence for a moment before one by one everyone repeated, "I love you" to each other, and promised to be there together to go through an occurrence that we had heard of, but knew not what was to happen, or the unspeakable acts that would take place.

Holding hands, we said a prayer to God for our protection and for the salvation of our commanders. We prayed for our parents, for God's peace and consolation for them. We prayed for comfort for the mothers who have lost their children, and for the children among us who had forgotten the days of their triumphant youth.

After prayers, we all sat closely together, waiting for the day we did not want to begin, to begin.

✳✳✳✳✳✳✳✳✳✳✳✳✳✳

We heard footsteps approaching our tent until it stopped at the entrance as if to listen for our voices. Light came in a line across the floor as the entrance flaps were opened for the Commander who stood there looking at us with an expressionless face. We all drew closer together backing as far away from the entrance as we possibly could get. He told us that he knew we must feel somewhat special being driven there, and having a tent to sleep in while every other child slept outside. Rhys, scoffing at what he had just said told the Commander that there was nothing special about being kidnapped from your family and loved ones, having your parents probably killed, and being brought to a place where you constantly lived in fear.

The commander came inside the tent, his figure covering the whole entrance and casting a looming shadow over us all. He pointed to Rhys, Luke, and Sydney, telling them to follow him out. My siblings and I followed up to the door of our tent where we then watched them walk up to a truck in the middle of the square. Standing by the truck was another commander who was speaking to them in hushed tones. Slowly, as I watched, Sydney, Luke, and Rhys's faces began to grow in continued horrific stares at the Commander. Sydney's head began to shake from side to side, slowly at first, then faster. She said the word "no" repeatedly as she looked toward the tent at my me and my siblings. She began to cry, and when the commander reached for her, she screamed in defiance running as fast as she could toward me.

"What is wrong? What is going on?" I asked in rising franticness at her disposition. Fear rose intensely within me as I wondered what may have made us the next victims who had to be subjected at the square to be carried upon, the next death sentence. The real reason for her screams as I would find would be much worse and still to this day, the only thing that had managed to make me both numb and deaf and the same time. I blindly reached for her hands that grasped mine strongly and held on as if the rest of our lives depended on it.

"They are taking us back!" She screamed at me as another young soldier came pulling her away from me. "They are leaving you here, and they are taking back Rhys, Luke, and me!" She cried out. My heart dove to depths I did not know it could reach. I had wondered in my mind all the night before, how much these rebels must have thought of themselves to go too far as to abduct three young white people, and expect to cover their tracks without fear of the American people coming against them. I suppose that thought had also crossed our officers' minds as well, for now they were taking out the people that would make their efforts to keep us their captives forever all that more difficult. My siblings and I were to stay in camp with the rebels, and say good-bye to my sister, her fiancé and my love.

I glanced toward where they held Rhys, and Luke, my feet painfully dragging me on that dusty earth as the young officer took Sydney toward the truck that waited to drop them somewhere recognizable, so they could make their way home. Rhys and Luke were tied up with their hands behind them and thrown into the truck where they started to scream toward us as well trying to wriggle their arms out of their bonds, and the hands of their victors. I ran toward them grabbing Rhys to tell him nothing in particular as no words could make it past my lips to him.

Calm overcame without warning and took better control than I had in our entire ordeal, making me fall silent.

Ever since I was a child, I always knew when to cry, and when to stop; when to worry, and when to not; when to fight, and when to cease the war. I knew when to run, to hide, to take off my camouflage and confront my enemy face to face. I knew there was nothing that would make those commanders keep three of them that day, nothing that would make them release the rest of us, and nothing that would make them care for us or what became of us long after those three were gone. I looked deep into Rhys's eyes asking him wordlessly to come for me. He knew me and therefore, knew what my frightened yes were saying to me. He asked Jacob to take the cross around his neck and put them around mine. He asked me never to take it off. I wouldn't. The boys were grabbed by their collars and hoisted onto the truck. I looked at Sydney, who climbed in looking over us all standing there.

The cage guarding the inside of the truck from the rest of us came down with a great thud. Sydney grabbed onto the railings, putting one of her arms out for me to hold. I grabbed her reaching hand, and with the other holding onto those iron rods. She said to me:

"I will look for you, and I will find you; and we will laugh, and we will play, and we will get married, and we will have children, and we will rejoice and be family soon enough... again."

✶✶✶✶✶✶✶✶✶✶✶✶✶✶✶

As the dust settles and the sight of the truck begins to fade, I am made aware of the crowd of children who had roused from their slumber and gathered to witness the departure of the three Americans. I can also feel my face stiff from tears mixed with mud as the slow muggy wind started to burn my eyes as realization settles in. Taking my sisters' hand in mine, we turn around with the boys, and head toward the direction of our tent.

I was scared for my mother when she would see them, and not her children. I was afraid for the dread that would fill her soul, and the depression that will threaten her faith. I was scared for Sydney, Rhys, and Luke, and for the blame that will never release them to a far better ideal world and state of mind. Most of all, I was scared for how I was going to do everything in my power to save my siblings and myself without being killed.

Chapter 15

May 24, 2004

We were arranged according to height on the first day of training. It was three days after the Americans had left us. We were given the rest of that day to get ourselves together to observe the camp and its customs. Over the course of our training days, we were commanded to assemble ourselves into whatever order pleased the Commander to demand. Sometimes we were arranged by age, sometimes by rank, sometimes by the number of recruits we had abducted, other times by the amount of materials we had looted, or by the number of lives we had stolen.

Though I was the oldest of my siblings in the camp, I was only taller than Joshua. Augustina towered above me mercilessly. Samuel followed suit; Angela and Jacob competed over their equal size, each of them an inch taller than me. This brought me a great sense of discomfort as being able to feel my siblings or see them brought me a relative sense of relief. I was glad I could keep an eye on

Joshua at least, and silently I prayed for the helpless little boy I had just begun to know.

The newcomers, as the commander roared, were to observe the routine that was about to be performed by the former soldiers of the camp. We were to do whatever it is they were about to do because we would be doing whatever we watched them do afterwards. All around me, at the shrill blow of a whistle that came from between the Commander's fingers in his mouth, children started to run in place. Joshua, unsure of what was going on around him started to run place as well. The Commander, noticing the little boy, abruptly stopped speaking, and walked slowly to Joshua's side.

"Did you not hear what I said?" He barked at Joshua, stooping lower with his mouth booming his words next to the little child's ears. Joshua was silent, and though his back was to me, I could feel tears run down his face with mine. I silently pleaded with God to physically restrain if he had to, the lips of Augustina, and Angela from opening to emit any kind of sound in their little brother's defense.

On the previous day, I had reasoned with them to be silent until they absolutely had to speak [when and only when they were spoken to]. I told them that no matter how long we stayed here, I would do everything in my power to set them free, and anything it took, to protect them. As we sat together, we exercised our memories of our parents writing down boldly on the templates of our minds everything they had ever taught us about, love, faith, and unity. We saw our father driving into our compound and honking his horn so that we would know he was home, and run out to enter his car to ride all the way down to the back way to park.

I reminded them of their mother; of her honest smile that gave away an intense love that took hold of our fears and set them free. I told them to feel her hands, the gentleness they held within them waiting for their victim to smother with a security and care which made worries that once seemed mightier than mountains become insignificant. I told them to remember her voice, the warmth of her songs, and the peace it once bathed over us.

As the Commander before me grabbed my brother from behind his neck, I begged for my sisters' silence, my brothers' physical restraint, and for the self-control from flying toward that Commander's scrotum and tearing it to the ground.

"Why are you hopping with them when you are supposed to be watching them?" He shouted at the little boy.

"I did not understand" Joshua answered with a quivering voice and shaky knees.

"I was clear!" He stated loudly to my brother, "was I not?!" He asked this time speaking generally to the crowd of children and was now dragging Joshua alongside him before the crowd of wide-eyed subjects who either looked forward to a fix for the sight of blood which they were now so brutally addicted to, or ones who wondered fearing the fate of the little boy who now stood shaking uncontrollably before them.

My feet started to move before I realized I had begun to put them in front of each other. I walked between the stench-filled rows toward the Commander and my mother's youngest child. I did not know if he was planning to resign my brother's fate to the suit of those we had seen before him, but I was not going to be alive to watch Joshua die. I wasn't going to tell that story to my mother.

He turned around – the commander – and watched the intimidation on my face slowly approach him. A wicked smile crept along the side of his mouth to crinkle ever so slightly, his eyes.

"Would you like to do the honors?" He asked me.

I stood there quickly feeling the most intense trepidation, goose bump its way up my spine and into the nape of my neck. I felt my blood freeze despite the dry morning sun's heat.

I stopped just as soon as I had passed the first line of children. I saw the slow stain of darkness cloud the front of my brother's knickers as water trickled onto his legs. I wanted to take his fear, to spirit him away from here, even if it meant I would stay in his stead.

I saw David out of the corner of my eye come slowly to stand on the other side of the commander. I could feel his stare boring into my face, but I did not want to concern myself with him... yet.

"Let me die for him," I said through chattering teeth. "I'll die for him. You can have me."

I saw David's figure swiftly come at me. I felt something powerfully strike my head. I don't remember anymore.

~~~~~~~~~~~~~~~~

"What do you mean you don't remember anymore?" the therapist asks me.

"David beat me across the head with a club" I answered quietly. "I do not remember anything in the backyard after that."

"What happened to Joshua?"

"After David knocked me unconscious, the newer children were ordered to beat me until they were commanded to stop. They were not ordered to stop anytime soon after they started. Anyway, by the time they were done with me, the focus shifted from Joshua, and he was whipped as his warning."

May 25, 2004

When I awoke, on what I would later find out was the following afternoon, my body was screaming in pain. I tried to sit up, and realized that even though I was in excruciating agony, I could not feel my skin making contact with whatever it was I was laying on. My eyes were swollen shut and hurt when I tried to use my fingers to pry them open from the darkness they held within them. It pained me to touch any area of my body, so I let my eyelids go. I saw that I was in the tent, but I did not see my siblings. In the faint distance, I heard the chanting, and feet pounding fiercely into the ground before I crept back into the thin sheet that covered me so my mind would leave that place quietly, even if only in my mind. The rain, as if waiting for me to breathe heavily in exhaustion fell in thick clear sheets from the rather clear blue skies my eyes had rapidly made out in their blurry scan. This kind of rain happened occasionally, and would stay until the skies gave in to cloudy pillows because the rain had decided it was going to stay for a few days, whether the blue complied with the mood or not. I heard the water drums filling with the drops that trickled into them. I thought of home, how we once ran outside in the pours, fetching rain water and filling the great drum in the storeroom.

The boys would be allowed to set their traps because nobody was likely to brave the woods at that kind of downpour.

As that water thudded against the dusty earth, I felt my father's rage. I could almost see him grit his teeth, shout upon Uganda, and beat upon his heart. I somehow think I almost even heard him cry tears for a country that could not get along with its brother; for citizens who derived pleasure from their sisters' pain; for death which had maimed and robbed homes, cities and villages of its greatest and its best. Papa cried for his children who were fighting, and I knew above all, that that adorable heart wanted his children, grandchildren, and great grandchildren, to understand the predicament they were in, and handle it together with love that held absolutely no reservations.

I intended on keeping my father's hope alive. I knew this camp was likely to strip my siblings and I of the promises we had made our parents, to forever retain a love and compassion for each other and humanity at large; to never turn against one other no matter the billows, and to pray without ceasing.

Chapter 16

June 5, 2004

Two weeks after our capture, we were all awoken by a small messenger boy at approximately 4 a.m. Somehow, the Chief Commander had gotten word that the UPDF was closing in with a mass outnumbering the rebel soldiers by five to one. We were ordered to pack up as much as we could within the hour for the trek to Kitgum. We could not wait until the end of the week for the dreadful journey which had hoped for more abductees than currently had. We all formed two straight lines as ordered by two of the junior commanders after picking up some of the load that had been looted the day of our abduction. Two junior commanders walked before us, and four walked beside every tenth person. I was the first tenth, Samuel the twentieth, Augustina the thirtieth, Jacob the fortieth, Angela the fiftieth and Joshua the sixtieth. I stopped my observation after Joshua, relieved that they were within eye view. The line disappeared between the trees as children still slightly drowsy, yawned rubbing their eyes to wake up to follow commands accordingly. I looked before me at the rows of nine children before me, frightened and hopelessly casting their eyes on the gray earth while before them lay the grass that was just tall enough to hide the prisoners, that though innocent, would walk within its midst to unknown lands through desolate fields and barren grounds. The fog hung deep and only shifted by at few inches when a child coughed against it. A little boy right beside Angela began to cry and my eyes quickly darted back to where the voice came from and looked up at a terrified disposition on Angela's face. I knew that look all too well, and I prayed with all my might that the child would stop crying. If that child chose to live past five minutes after his breakdown, he needed to stop crying. I heard the Commander stomping down the beaten path until he reached the boy. He pushed away the girl standing before the boy before he stood facing him.

"What is the matter with you?" He thundered.

The crowd grew completely silent including the little boy.

"I asked: what is the matter with you?!"

"No... not... nothing" the little boy managed to stammer out.

"No; there must be something wrong because you are crying, and if you are crying, there is something wrong. So what is it?"

The boy did not answer. He could not answer; there was no answer; at least, none acceptable by our dictators. There were no allowances when it came to shedding tears, it was strongly detested by the commanders and was most likely punishable by death.

The Commander snapped his fingers, and suddenly the child was surrounded by other boys who were abducted long before we had been, and they began to beat him. His sharp outlet of screams tore at my heart and the hearts of the rest of us. I heard a tiny whimper come out of a girl closely behind me as she cringed at each blow of the fists that landed all over the little boy. I looked at Angela as her swollen eyes met mine in anguish. I had begun to turn away my head in a futile attempt to pacify the sickening feeling invading my empty stomach, when I saw Augustina dart between the legs of two of the boys beating the little child, and land on his back. My heart back flipped into my stomach, and at that point, I was amazed at how the human mind worked. Ever since our abduction, I had lived in fear of our abductors; minding them and being as far away from the edge of their machetes and the barrels of their guns as I possibly could. However, when I saw my little sister in the line of fire, a strength that I did not care to wait for its summons rose within me ready to give my life to make sure that Augustina came up from between those boys alive.

"Please!" she screamed at the commander.

He stopped and stood for a few minutes with his back still toward her. He slowly turned to look quite unbelievably at Augustina.

"I can explain." Augustina continued in a desperate plea.

"Do you have to?" I whispered silently to myself.

"Explain what?" The commander asked.

"Why he was crying." Augustina answered. When no reply came from anywhere she continued.

"He cried yesterday morning too... and the day before that... and the day before that.... When I asked him why, he said that that was how he prayed. He prays words in his heart, and cries out loud."

The Commander, I knew, did not believe her. For heaven's sake, a toddler wouldn't have believed her! But I believe he was amused, and impressed at her bravado; this conclusion reached certainly not by his exemplifying his amusement by a smirk oh his face, but by the fact that he ordered an end to the beating. Augustina stood up pulling the boy with her. She bent down to his level to face him, hissing through clenched teeth to firmly warn him:

"Never cry your prayers again."

Chapter 17

May 25, 2005

Rhys is in the therapist's office with me today, and I notice for the first time that there are fewer times than blue moons that I am ever present in the world going on around me. The others are spent chasing fears I yet desperately wish away. Every movement reminds me of the bush. I do not just see joggers on the streets; I see the fires they are running from. My parents have to remind me that a "deadline" is just a figure of speech, that dire repercussions are not always the standard. I did not hear fireworks on the fourth of July. I heard gunshots and explosions, wondering if the children beneath them would greet the morning sun. I am seldom in my therapist's office, and I take her along with me to the depths she asks of which I earnestly pray she can find her way from, and bring me up with her.

Today, I am present in her office thankfully because I notice that I am present with Rhys. When I see him, I see him. I watch his eyes dance on my face, submitting my uncertainties to nothingness. And that smile. I tell my therapist about falling in love with Rhys.

I was thirteen years old when I fell in love with Rhys. Of course, I didn't tell him. I don't think I even told myself quite yet. After all, what business did a thirteen year old have to be in love?

"What made you think that? What event brought about that feeling?" My therapist asked me. So, I tell her a tale that I had preserved in my heart, telling no one including its hero, perchance to submit it someday to accounts left only in the anthology of the legendaries.

* * * * * * * * * * * * *

By the time I was thirteen years old and living in the States with my American parents, I had known Rhys for five and half years. In all that time, never was a boy kinder, more attentive, and good to me as Rhys was. It did not go unnoticed, but again, I was a child - you don't fall in love when you're a child. One day, I stayed home from school because the adjustments were still taking their time, and my mother agreed that I needed a break. Rhys stayed home with me after quite a bit of begging, and promises that he'd make sure I would be alright.

Rhys told me about his father, the once fellow medical student with Onesimus who discovered prescription painkillers, forgetting its effect when taken without need. Perhaps there was pain, Rhys reasoned, from the burden of a young son he fathered during wild high school days he was almost certain he had abandoned. A young son, whose mother would eventually leave with his father, to go find her place in the world without a crying child on her hip. A young son, whose eventually jailed father would request that his once close friend care for. When I asked Rhys why he told me about himself in such completion, he answered that not only was he certain that everything gets better with time, experience equipped him to be there with me every step of the way. Comfort wasn't rare for me since I became the daughter of my parents and the sister of my siblings. They granted me that solace that I never knew was the ache that so obdurately sat in my heart. It was a different kind of comfort though, that Rhys gave me sitting on that couch next to me that day. He took off the cross I'd only seen him remove before every shower, and hung it around my neck. He told me to wear it as long as I remained unafraid, as long I needed it. To return it, only in that event that I no longer needed it to remind me that he was always there with me. That was the day that I fell that I fell in love with Rhys. That was the day that I knew I was going to marry him. A matter of months after that day, Rhys's father would release all parental rights of him to my American parents. Rhys tried his best to pretend that he was less than hurt by what his father had said, but I knew it pained him to be a son without parents but surrogate ones, an experience he dryly referred to as a "custodial purgatory." On one of those days, after quite a bit of begging and promises that I would catch up with school, my mom agreed that I could stay home from school with Rhys. On that day which was one of the worst ones of his depression, I sat next to Rhys on the same bridge where only a matter of months ago, he told me the same words I would say to him. I took off the cross he knew would do me good, returning it to him, promising that not only was I certain everything gets better with time, I was going to be there to with him every step of the way.

* * * * * * * * * * * * * * *

"That was the day I found that I always loved her. If I wasn't sure of it before then, if I wasn't sure of it when she promised to be there with me, I certainly was later that night. I was certain that night that I was in love with her." Rhys said smiling with that distant memory etching itself on his face.

"Why? What happened that night?" My therapist asked.

"Later that night, our parents called the family together to ask Rhys how he felt about becoming an official part of the family, although it was important for him to know that it was never a question in their minds. Before Rhys could answer, it was like I got possessed."

"Why?"

"I shouted that I did not want Rhys to be adopted; after which, I ran out of the room."

"You didn't want Rhys to be adopted?"

"No."

"How come?"

"Rhys came for me a few minutes later to make sure I was alright; after which, he asked me why I did not want him to be adopted. I told him that if were to be adopted, that would mean he would really be my brother. Rhys asked me what was so wrong about him being my brother, and I told him that if he became my brother, then I wouldn't get to marry him."

Her eyebrows rise with surprise as my therapist who shifts in her chair gives Rhys a tilt of her head hoping to elicit a reply to my confession.

"Rhys, you refer to Mr. and Mrs. Cassidy as your parents. You last name, however, remains Mr. McAllister; so I take it that you..."

"...Right. I didn't. After a tactful conversation with my parents, I chose to leave everything the way it was. My parents were my parents, whether an official document stated so or otherwise."

"And you loved Calista."

"And I loved Calista."

"Did you tell her?"

"No. Not that night."

"How come?"

"When you're sixteen years old, a girl two years younger might as well be ten years your junior."

My therapist, advised to make sure we understood that whether or not Rhys had been officially adopted, would not matter at all where our love for each other was concerned. We knew. Rhys would tell me he loved me – two years later, but I already knew long before that. I knew the night he chose to stay a McAllister just because I wanted him to.

"I wish she'd believe me..." Rhys started quietly at my therapist's bidding that he share the effects of my abduction and the subsequent demise of a love once unshakable.

"Cali is the only girl I ever loved. Everybody always talks about that one great love that happens to everyone at least once in their lifetime. But nobody tells you how it feels when it is threatened; when you are fighting to hold on to it like someone drowning in a raging sea. How you would give up anything to return to that great love. Someone who sets you free from everything you once feared. Someone who tells you that there is no tomorrow, and desperately loves you like it. Someone who if she were ever told that you weren't the best thing that ever happened to her, she sure forgot in a hurry. People talk about how complicated love can be and how many problems can come from being in love. Not ours..." Rhys's voice broke as looked tenderly to me. "... it fixed us." He turned back to the therapist.

"It fixed me."

Chapter 18

I am silent. The only thing I can feel is the waters that welled within the rims of my eyes that were to remain as they always did. Contained. Rhys is gone, leaving the silence that tugs my heart toward my own foolishness. Before she let me go, my therapist asks me a question that followed me out of her office back into the bush where like a child, I longed for home.

July 22, 2004

We prepared on a certain night for a raid to be at a village I did not know about, but knew, however, that innocent people despite our lack of formalities would be in danger. I was not exactly sure why my sisters and I were selected to come along, or why we would be going there in the middle of the night since markets would be closed, and kiosk owners had grown in smarts to transport their goods to and from their homes, or have an impenetrable barricade.

Before we left, everyone at the camp was gathered at the square by order of our commander. There would be thirteen boys and five girls going on this journey. My head throbbed at the notion of what catastrophe I knew was impending on the unfortunate unsuspecting souls whose lives we were possibly snatching without permission from them. I walked to the square and stood between my sisters who were already standing at the circle that had formed. I took their shaking hands in mine and squeezed it despite the knot that sat within my heart. I looked across the fire burning in the middle of the circle into the eyes of my brothers; the vacancy inside of them causing sympathy to well up in me. I had not always thought that I would feel guilty about the presence of my siblings in this bush. Over the course of the weeks after our capture, I had always figured that if somehow I had made a bigger fuss we go with my parents, or if we had left a little later, or if maybe, we had driven a little faster, that we would not have been in the predicament we found ourselves in. I would express these feeling several times to my siblings over the course of our capture, and they would caution me of the foolishness of such thinking.

As the truck roars through the settlements we were to reduce to ruins, I think in my mind about the terror that jumps into the hearts of children peacefully sleeping in their cots when they hear us coming. I think about the fear that paralyzes them as their blood freezes in their veins as they wonder if that night, they would escape, be overlooked, forced to join the evil ranks, or be murdered. I wonder of their mothers, and the pain that takes captive her sorrowful soul as she with remorseless fearlessness tries with all of her might to save her children. I stare expressionless at the faces of fathers who beg us in the name of God, the same God apparently in whose name his life I must take; he begs us in the that same name to take him in place of his children.

I wonder what horror must have stolen the hearts of anybody who ran to the bushes for rescue, and dropped it into their stomachs when they saw alight all around them, flames that wagged their tongues of fire hungrily for them. I see elders of our land, the same ones I once sat at their feet to imbibe their wisdom; I see them kneeling before me and offering any possession of theirs I saw fit to take. I cry rivers in my soul as I point my AK-47 and unload magazines into the frail lives in front of me, taking away an anguish I had no right to extinguish.

Every time I carry out an atrocity, I wonder how much of my soul will return home with me; to the bosom, once again, of the ones who gave me this life with all the hope that held no anticipation for the suffering we were becoming so acquainted with.

I see the little feet of the children marching to camp, not knowing that whatever evil they may just have beheld, carried no weight on the scale of what would happen along the way, and at our destination. I want to warn them that they would walk most of the night, past the day to the camp until it was time for them to go to Sudan to fight people in a land they did not know, against enemies that they did not have. I want to tell these children that a third of them will die along the way for no good reason whatsoever, except that it pleased the bloodthirsty junior commanders to order it so. I want to tell them to change their mindset concerning the loads on the heads that for some, weighed as much as a third of them. That they are expected to carry it all night and make proper use of the relief that will arrive when they are allowed to put it down for rest. I was put in command of most missions that I accompanied the soldiers to; therefore, fewer deaths occurred under my watch, and there were more frequent rest stops than abductees were generally allowed. I want to tell them that there is no food on the way to camp, and so they have to try their best to tell their stomachs whatever they have to, to convince it not to roar rapaciously within them for food. To be careful about the leaves they pluck to eat along the way because some of them would put them in an agony that though not much worse than the beatings they would most likely endure, it would not help the loads they were to carry. I want to tell them that the junior commanders are going to eat from the very food they have to carry on their weak bodies, and it will take everything in them not to stretch forth their hands to beg for even the crumbs. Nevertheless, to hold themselves back and think about anything else because those junior commanders do not need any reason to make a ruthless example of any of them. My heart goes before me to warn that some of them most likely would kill within the first hour of their abduction, and thus would lose most of the humanity they felt for anything because in that bubble of the blood of the first life they extinguished, it would vacate their spirits from them, and they will see no harm in bloodshed. They would forget that they are children, and that their innocence is the envy of even the men who took them captive.

If I could hold them while they shake, I would relieve their uncertainty by telling them that when they get to the camp, the Chief Commander would stand before their shaking bodies to tell them why they are there. He would tell them our land is corrupt; that we are trying to rid our country of the corrupt lunatics who run in office over us church rats. He would jeer at whatever efforts have been made by an ineffectual government whose aim was mostly to sweep the people's complaints under the rug for as long as their lie could run until dry.

He would tell them that they were the nightmare of the world because they were going to be stripped of whatever made them feel weaker than the guns they would have to carry. The Chief Commander would shoot one of them just to teach the others just how easy it could be, and how remorseless it was necessary for them to get. He would tell them they had to choose one of the children whom they used to know, the same ones they had played football with on the field at school, made pinkie promises with, and swore their friendship with one another. One of them now had to kill the other in exchange for their own life. They would do this by fighting until one outlasted the other, and then the victor would have to hack the loser to death with the panga. The General would grind into their brains the uncomfortable truth that they would never at this point be welcomed home. He would advise that if they obeyed, the bush would provide more home than their family and friends from whom they were stolen from. They could not go home because they would be seen as spiritless little devils walking down the street to finish the evil they had left sparsely behind.

I would remind them as they prepare for training under the devious tutelage of the General, to tell their bodies to feel no pain. To run through the wire tracks not caring the cuts the loose ends would make across their bare hands, backs, and chest. I would tell them to send their desire for liberation to any place in their spirits where they could exchange it for just enough to refuse becoming another casualty. To know that the more they ran through the tires without rest carrying AK-47 rifles, pangas, and bayonets strapped onto them, they more they would be stronger, and more resilient with each passing day. I would inform them that some of the much smaller children are going to lag behind and grow weary wishing for rest. Those children unknowingly would have unfortunately volunteered themselves as perfect examples for both a practice shooting spree, and what would become of the rest if ever they followed suit. I would tell them that the killings seldom happened with the guns that were strapped so naturally looking on their small bodies. No. They would have to step on that boy's head until they heard the brain come slowly seeping out of his cracked skull. On another, they would have to cut off all her limbs, leaving the head for the last whack to ensure that all the pain, fear and terror one could possibly feel in its highest tender was felt. I would tell them to give a thought to what name they would like to render when asked, because who they were, they were nevermore to be again, or even think of.

I would tell the girls that as the junior commanders cast themselves upon them, they were to stare deep into their eyes as they take much more than the blinding pain that will ensue in their young unready bodies. I would advise them to steal their souls as well. I would tell them the same rule I painfully gave to my sisters when they were handed to the ruthless officials: "Curse God or die? Die. Lose your virginity or die? Lose your virginity." But like most things, for an African girl, that especially is easier said than done.

I would tell them that sooner than they know, they would be ready to wreak yet another cycle of havoc; to commit the evil that they once so innocently ran from. They would do this because they did not remember; because they have no choice; because they have to live. Before they would leave, prayers would be said over them, the Chief Commander would rant once again on why they fight, and the victory they should keep as a guiding post and inspiration. Most of all, they will grow angrier with every passing day with the subconscious wonder as to why nobody was looking for them. They will kill as they had been taught was the only way to get rid of any emotion that remotely resembled the presence of a heart. They would kill to retaliate against that feeling of abandonment, of desertion. They would kill to make it all go away, and to feel better.

Chapter 19

There was a white curtain to the side of the front door, an oak table in the center of the living room. The dining room table had the familiar long scratch down the middle of it that was caused by my lugging around an art project, and then ripping it off the table without realizing the nail for hanging it was still somewhat attached. I remember it all very vividly as I storm inside the house with the soldiers seeking food, clothes, and the demise of that home and its inhabitants. I try with all of my might to escape the familiar feelings that floated my mind. With each one I push away, I seek something to destroy. The curtains were ripped apart; machetes dug in the cushions of the chair to expose the foam and wood inside them. I remembered the day I saw my uncle, when I came home from the U.S., on a visit with my aunt and cousins, beat the sanity out of my aunt. Again. I remembered when Kya and I had scratched that table, and then lived in total fear of what would happen when my uncle would arrive home. I remembered how Kya and I cried and cried, and for good reasons too. As I stood there listening to the ruckus of fellow rebels, I remember the lash from my uncle's cane whip across my

12-year-old back for the eighth time. My fingers grip my machete and bring it down with a mighty thud onto that table, and anger guides me as I effortlessly chop the wood into pieces. It was a rage I did not recognize even as it carried on. A rage I could not stop until I saw them drag the inhabitants of the house one by one to the middle of the corridor between the living room and bedroom. I dropped my machete and ran to the door suddenly torn between the necessity to be the soldier my General had trained me to be and the desire to protect the family that was mine and loved me so. Jacob, Samuel and I looked at one another with strains on our faces trying to think fast.

"Alright everyone, Get a load and get into the car!" Samuel barked pointing to the loot by the kitchen door.

"You're going to kill them?" A small boy asked with fear filled eyes.

"Take the loads and do as I told you." Samuel ordered the boy.

Quickly, Jacob and I stood side by side with guns pointed to my shaking extended family, their heads facing the ground and their arms up in total surrender. Kya cried, while James, her little brother, clung tightly to my aunt. Caroline's hands shook uncontrollably, and I knew that if we did not hurry up and rescue my family, she would faint dead away from sheer fear. With loud victorious chants with pauses to carve markings of our presence and victory into the wall, the soldiers left us.

"Turn around!" Jacob said quietly but firmly.

They all lay still not moving or making a sound, silently hoping that maybe we would go away not realizing their existence.

"I said, turn around!" Jacob commanded louder this time.

They all quickly turned over with their backs on the floor. We stood there waiting for their eyes to adjust, to get a better look at the face of their attackers. Kya jumped up first and grabbed me, embracing me close to her so tightly that I had to push her away from me so as not to let myself get acquainted with the feeling of shame that tenderness brought with such a gesture. My aunt put her hand to her mouth as gasps of unbelief and sorrowing escaped her mouth. I looked at her to see the evidence of yet another duel with an intoxicated husband who saw her fit only to descend upon her all the anger and sorrow he bore.

"My children" she cried out stretching her arms and standing up. I grabbed one of her hands and Jacob with Samuel reached for the other. We let go explaining that we could not be familiar with them as they would be killed as well as us if one of the soldiers were to walk in on us fraternizing with the "enemy."

Kya begged amidst tears for us all to take the back way and run to safety, not understanding that it was a bigger battle for us than it was for them. I tried to explain to her that it was simpler for them to run instead; that was not our opportune time to run from the terror that kept us prisoners. I looked at my uncle's face as I got down and knelt between James and Gloria. he was staunch-faced as usual, regarding us with a glare of disdain and hate glaring at me, and both of my brothers. I whispered what we were going to do in order to protect them.

"We are going to shoot five times; you all have to pretend to be dead. You cannot live here after we are done. You have to run for the backyard because we have to burn the house down in our wake. Do you understand?"

They all nodded in agreement. All, except my uncle.

"How dare you?" He started standing up, "How dare you come in here to tell me what to do in my own house?" He angrily stammered. "Get out now!" He screamed at us.

The anger like lightning flashed across my eyes bringing in that instant my machete down unto his legs cutting through into half his right knee. He screamed curses in pain, and those screams I feared would attract the attention of the rest of the soldiers. While my cousins watched in horror, I shot their father before them before I raised my gun into the air as I motioned with my hands that it was time for my family to leave the house and run behind the bushes until someday, when we would meet again. My cousins and aunt focused on something behind me, and that was when I heard the click. Slowly, I turned around to see that my uncle's screams had attracted the attention of David's servant boy who now had an AK-47 pointed right to my face, breathing hard from adrenaline and fear. In that same flash of scenes, I saw the boy's head sputter blood as he fell to the ground. I felt around my face and slid his blood down my cheek as I turned to see that Samuel had shot the boy. My cousins surrounded me in hugs and kisses, and after giving the same to my brothers, they left through the back doors, out to the backyard bushes, and into the night.

We would raid several other houses that night leaving more death, and wreaking more havoc on each one. We almost dared to go to a hospital in Gulu but one of the junior commanders silenced the madding crowd which chanted the possibilities of the fear we had created in people's minds. We had food aplenty, change of clothing for just about every child in the camp, and changes of money. There were screams in the air as the wailing and weeping of women losing their children to our guns and machetes burned into my mind with each passing sorrow. I continued in the madness that raged in all of us as my spirit continuously left to stand outside of me in wonder of who and what was left.

We were the end of happiness, the beginning of uproar and discourse. We were the takers and the looters. We were the nightmares of children and the fear of the people. We were the death that came by day. We were the horror that came by night.

When we returned, I had scarcely sat down on my mat than I had to report to the General. Halfway to his lair, I would be tackled to the ground by the same junior commanders who had been out with me on that night's rampage. The little boy Samuel had shot had not been the only one to see me set my family free. When I refused to disclose the location to which I was certain my aunt and cousins had run to, or to admit that I bore any relation to them, for that matter, they brought Joshua with a cocked gun pressed against the little boys terrorized face. I confessed the night's account in its entirety to the General, but still kept their location a secret. It was a secret I did not have much of any trouble keeping. My aunt and cousins could be with my parents in our home in Kampala, but of that I wasn't certain. It, however, was an uncertainty I was not willing to risk my family's life for. I had two options. I was either to tell them where my aunt and cousins went to, even if it may eventually be wrong, voluntarily, or have it beaten out of me. I refused to put my parents, Isaiah, Sydney, Rhys, and Luke in that jeopardy. No matter what happened to me even to the point of death, it was one life to save several. Besides, I knew to get their money, I was still a proof of life they needed.

Chapter 20

May 25, 2005

I park the car in the driveway where I sit to contemplate my therapist's question in my head.

"When you were in the bush, what did you want most in the world?"

I walk upstairs into my bedroom, where after locking the door behind me, I sit nakedly in front of the mirror willing myself to summon up the courage to keep the promises I made to time only a matter of twelve months ago. When I am nearly finished trembling at the sight I'd successfully hidden even from myself, I wrap a robe around my body and head for Rhys's room. He was laying on his bed with headphones around his ears which he promptly took off at seeing me standing at his doorway. The cross I had given back to him when I had come home, I saw hanging on the bedpost beside the shocked boy. My body resumes its trembling as one foot prompts the other to follow suit across the way to him. Rhys gets up, but stops when I raise my hands to stop him from approaching. If he were to come any closer, I imagined I would unravel before I wordlessly would tell him a story brutally written for me and my world, never to forget. I turn around to unveil the body he used to know; the body it no longer was despite former dreams.

Etched into earths of skin was the testament of my determination to protect my family.

Rhys gasped as he sat back on his bed in shock as my robe fell onto the ground. Again, I heard the screams of my siblings, who for as long as I refused to disclose my family's location were forced to watch as I was stripped naked, tied hands and foot, as new recruits armed with clubs, pangas, and whips, seared their hearts on my back and legs. Statements made in cuts and stripes messily zigzagged across skin as salt would be poured into the wounds to elicit the screams that vibrated the camp. They flogged me until I was numb to the whips. They sliced until every cut became like the hit of a drug I almost began to crave. I suffered that night with wounds that swelled so big my siblings would later tell me I looked nearly twice my size. They also told me that in retrospect perhaps, it was a good idea that I had not told even them where I supposed my aunt and cousins would run to. They would have confessed it if only to stop the sight that would steal their souls to where nothing any longer would be sacred.

The pain would eventually stop. The scars it would leave behind would, however, stay hidden to remind me I would never again be beautiful. I would never return as priceless as I once was. Who could I ever believe would love me past the scars that would brand me a rebel? Broken, abused, damaged, deflowered, disgraced. Better yet, who would I allow?

Rhys's breath on my back brings me back to his room with him standing beside me as he bring his hands to my shoulders, his touch raising every hair on my body. I inhale concentrating on the very conscious task of breathing without trembling. Rhys's fingers tangle themselves in mine as his lips graze my back resting on the scars, and kissing the pain they were meant to symbolize away. He guides me to his bed where lays me down, and proceeds to kiss every wound etched on my body like their disappearance depended on every one of those kisses. I don't remember a single word I said that night. I do not remember that I said anything, or whether Rhys ever did. I imagine, however, that I will never forget the volumes of his love Rhys would write inside of my heart as he locked his kisses across those callous strokes.

When he was finished, he covered me with his shirt, lay me back onto his bed, and put his sheets over me. He wrapped his arms around me, his lips resting softly on my forehead and his breath against my hair.

For the first time in a year, I slept without incident.

The next morning, I wake long after the morning sun had greeted the California sky. I watch Rhys get ready for work while stealing glances at me with that smile that readily prompts reckless abandon. In those moments, I am weak and strong, vulnerable and brave, a soldier and a child. I am a woman in every bit of me.

He makes his way to the bed, kneels on the ground, gently caressing my cheeks.

"Hey…" he says to me.

"Hey…" I reply back to him holding his hand and resting it on my lips.

"You slept."

"I did."

"I'll be back as soon as I can."

I nod as he tenderly kisses my forehead before heading for the door.

"Rhys…?" I start just before he is gone.

"Yeah"

"Will you help me come back?" I asked breaking down the last of the walls that tried its way up between us.

* * * * * * * * * * * * * *

"…so what'd he say?!"

Sydney is in the room exactly five seconds after Rhys is gone from it. I know it is exactly five seconds because I counted it down to her knock on the door inquiring as to if I was awake. If the transpirations of that night between Rhys and I had occurred because of anyone's prayers, the prayers would have come from Sydney Cassidy. I expected she would want to know the fruits of that labor. I tried to make room for her in the bed, but she sat in the swivel chair in the corner motioning with her hands for me to continue the story. I tell her what happened the night before up until when Rhys got up to get ready for work.

"So you didn't… you know…" She inquired with a squint of her eyes whether Rhys and I had made love.

"No… we didn't… you know…"

Sydney motioned for me to make room for her as she slid next to me on the bed.

"So what'd he say?" She asked me.

"He couldn't really say anything. I started crying because I could not believe that I actually eventually got there. He started crying. We held each other. I assume the gesture infers his answer."

"Loudly" she agreed, sitting up. "Was last night the first time you'd ever really seen them… I mean, looked at them in a mirror?"

"Yeah" I answer sitting up across from her. "I suppose you're the only one I'd ever actually shown it to."

She nods.

"Sydney?"

"Yeah"

"I'm going to get you your sister back."

Sydney smiles as she throws a pillow at me. I return a friendly cross-throw, my smile matching hers inviting the hug she subsequently wraps me in.

"It is like a comeback isn't it?" I ask her.

"Like an epic comeback." She agrees. "And you can put that in your pipe, tragedy, and smoke it!"

We laugh. Out loud.

Chapter 21

Over the course of our capture, several things unnecessary to say were abnormal. Life routines had become changed, replaced by visions of battle and bloodshed. Traditions that from birth had become part of our lives were now for the sake of keeping our lives, forgotten and neglected. We no longer could do our devotions together – my family and me. We no longer had tea and told silly stories whispering in our tent despite the chains that loomed over us. We no longer played or exchanged thoughts of our hearts in an untied togetherness. I no longer could become my brothers' sister, or my fiancé's girlfriend. I missed the most, the nights we would spend on an open landscape late in the evenings watching the bed of stars dot the brilliant sky. They would take a dark-blue night starting to send the sun on its way home, and brighten it with the reassurance that the light so calmly going home was to return again perhaps even brighter than when it first had been.

A tradition though physically taken from me, but my heart was reluctant to unhand was the Tuesday nights that I always had devoted to Rhys. I knew I could no longer be with the one I loved or even speak to him in any personal manner; even so, sitting on the railing of that verandah looking at the man I loved on the other side of the hill waiting to see my face, I knew that no commander's orders could take my promise away. So, with the moon hanging so close above his head in the hushed black night, we spoke silently to each other in the wordless way we were to succumb to. In the sounds of the crickets chirping, I went back as I always did to that night.

Actually, it was an early morning, and I was embarking on an opportunity to attend an architectural tour in L.A. Onesimus had booked me and Sydney a hotel room in the city, and Luke and Rhys took a room next to ours. This lecture was to start in the early evening and was not to stretch farther than seven p.m. It did.

I returned to the hotel having completely missed the time I looked forward to the most in my week. I ran straight upstairs to the room and was greeted by Luke and Sydney, who sat cozily on the couch by the fireplace watching a movie.

"Hi… where is Rhys?" I asked breathlessly.

"He said he was tired, so he went to bed" Sydney answered sympathetically.

"How long has he been asleep for?"

"About a half hour; he left about an hour ago," Luke answered, also with sympathy.

I stood there for a moment letting the thought swirl in my head as I tried to come up with ideas of how to show the man I love how sorry I was for missing a time so important to me and him.

"Luke, are you staying a bit longer? Can you stay a bit longer?" I asked hopefully.

"We were planning on watching movies all night. Is that alright?"

"Yeah, that's perfect, actually. Syd, could you make some coffee please. Rhys and I will be back in a couple of hours."

"Where are you going? Sydney asked with an inquisitive crinkle of her brow.

"On a date with my boyfriend; however late, I still owe him a date" I said with a sly smile before waving good-bye and quietly closing the door behind me.

I started the fire in the boys' hotel room where Rhys was sprawled on the mattress before I went to wake him.

"Rhys...? Rhys?" I called quietly.

He stirred groggily.

"Baby...? Baby it is me... wake up" I said shaking him. He opened his eyes and smiled that smile so sweet I wanted to cry.

"What are you doing here?" he asked me, rubbing his eyes.

"I owe you a date," I whispered tenderly.

"Now? Did you just get back?"

"Yes baby, I'm sorry."

"You want a date right now?"

"Yeah"

"But everything is closed; it is late and pretty dark out"

"I know. The world is quiet, which is perfect because yours is the only voice I want to hear." I smiled as he sat up leaning in for my kiss. I grabbed his comforter and laid it in front of the roaring fireplace.

"I'm going to grab some fruit and peanut butter okay?" I informed him as I left the room. I closed the door behind me and left him to get up and wait by the fire for me. I opened the door a few seconds after I'd closed it, and he looked up.

"Baby, I'm sorry I'm late" I apologized lovingly.

He looked at me adoringly and said: "Darling, when you wake me up with a kiss to a fire and a blanket in front of it to tell me how much you love me and how important I am to you, please never be on time! You can be late all you want!"

Chapter 22

August 11, 2004

I was by myself in the kitchen waiting for the other girls in the camp to join me to prepare the evening meal. Nancy had gone to the General to find out what he wanted us to prepare that evening as he and only him had a key to the storehouse. The storehouse was a shack made with sticks, oddly piled stones, and a scrap metal sheet for covering above it. The doors were two pieces of wide plywood haphazardly hinged onto the stones and then secured with a rusty padlock. I deduced two things from the possession of that key by the General, and from the absence of pilfering from the storehouse: the first was that the children did not want to incur the wrath of the "Great General" by going into the storehouse to pilfer food. The second, was that the General derived some kind of boost to his ego by being the one who held the key and kept everyone at bay; that simple things as getting food to eat, had to pass by him first. I felt disgusted by this show of an unnecessary display of a bid for power.

Through the window, I saw them; my brothers with distant looks on their faces staring at blood on their bodies, and chanting a song with their party. It was a song of victory over their foes, followed by ones recognizing the soldiers they had to leave behind. I stood partly hiding behind the curtain, wanting only to see but not be seen. I wanted to look at them as they walked and chanted monotonously, to see if they still lived within themselves, if they believed their commander, if they still remember they had a home, a father, and mother. I wondered if they remembered still that God was still watching over us.

There was a celebration dinner to be held that night of their return. Food stolen from the villages they had massacred along the way was brought to be cooked. It smelled good sending thoughts of home caressing my body with each curl of smoke that flirted across my face.

I missed my Mama as I went home in my heart again and back to the kitchen where I sat plucking leaves for soup from their long branches while listening to my mother's melodious voice carrying across the kitchen and throughout the house. There was a peace that voice brought with it – my mother's voice. I remember my most favorite times were hearing her along with my father's mother- my grandmother. Even the neighbors stopped to hear, speaking only in hushed tones if necessary.

I remembered every time my parents held a Thanksgiving dinner at our home after church. Almost everybody we knew would come to our home, wheere were ready for them; for the night before had seen us roasting a cow, cleaning, preparing all sorts of stews, soups, rice, yam porridge, meat pies, and ginger beer. The house smelled rich for a bit over a week, and no matter how many guests came and how much food we tried to give out, we always seemed to have much more than the last time we checked.

A soft thud brought me back to camp, away from my longings. I adjusted my eyes in the dim kitchen and looked toward the source of the noise at a brand new cloth. I did not touch it before I looked up at the bearer of the gift. With no clear expression on his face, David turned around to leave.

"Thank you," I said weakly. "What is it for?"

"The General says you must wear it tonight at the feast" the boy answered sorrowfully. "He will marry you while his spirits are lifted." David sighed, looking back at me with those dejected brown eyes of his. The General sent David because he knew he had once loved me; he knew it would cause us great pain, thus reminding us of his ever present power over our helpless selves.

I looked at the lone figure walking down the path, the evening becoming black night in my soul. I yearned for the fire; to crawl into it and remain there until it scorched me in its merciless insatiability. I wanted to die a thousand times. I wanted anything but to marry the General. Like a gentle peace however, the voice came back. You will get out of here; you will see your home. You will embrace your mother, and kiss your father. You will lead these children home. Just wait. Just wait.

✳✳✳✳✳✳✳✳✳✳✳✳✳✳✳

Angela and I sat near the big circle of fire out in the square along with several other girls. There was a circle of children around us chanting wedding songs and beating pangas onto the earth that cut into the dry soil as if to awaken her to let her know that her children were being taken from her, and that she must attend helplessly to their sufferings. Despite my standing only a few feet away from the big fire, I shivered cold in the thin wrapper I wore with nothing else. I looked at my sisters to see their arms wrapped tightly around them, clothed simply in wrappers almost like mine. Angela shook with quiet sobs; the big tears on her eyes falling recklessly onto her cheeks as she looked first at the ground, then slowly at me. I watched her face as I searched for the right words to say thinking back to all the movies I had ever watched where the characters in trying uncertain times had exactly the right words accompanied by the right entrance of the violin, to make everything seem better, both to the person on the television screen, and the person watching them from behind those cameras. I had no words for anyone. I had no words for myself. I summoned my spirit to vacate me as they called me up to the General in no respectable fashion. My sister, Augustina, they called to a junior commander, and Angela, to a junior official for a night as a reward for successfully overseeing the most abduction to date. I hear the children who had been at the camp longer begin a song that everybody else was expected to chant along with them as they celebrated the hitching of their General to yet another woman. Their feet come down to the sands in rhythm to the drums that they carried with their skinny arms and played with hands that moved so fast they became almost invisible. Lights flickered through the eyes in which I watched the emptiness that paraded itself without return to the purity it stole. I stand next to the General my spirit beginning to leave me standing there, hollow, unable to participate in the absence of dignity I watched transpire before me.

My spirit did not return until much later to the children dispatching to their sleeping quarters as a young boy blows on an enkwanzi, a rhythm that silenced even the reluctant crickets, as the night commanded it all to a rest; to let that little boy speak a mind that he was seldom allowed to.

Chapter 23

The other wives and I along with some of the other young girls abducted had to wake up very early in the morning after the night I was given to the General, Augustina to a junior commander and Angela for a one night trophy to an official. I woke up first, in part because I could hardly let my body rest from the night before. My body ached from the first night with the General where my body had lain underneath his unyielding weight, and my breath went forcefully away from me. I let my spirit go where it would but this time without me because I could not let whatever fond memories or any glorified futures witness the shame I felt that night, when from me was taken the only think I had to give my husband that was greater and more worthwhile than any other material I would ever have to offer him. He looked at me - the General, perhaps wanting to see if he had elicited an emotion in like to whatever it was that was registered on his face.

~~~~~~~~~~~~~~~~

My therapist gets up to get me a Kleenex as a bothersome tear made its way down my unready face. I wipe it away and stare into the rows of fiber of her carpet.

"Did you look at him?"

"How else would I know he was looking at me?"

She smiles at my smart, but keeps silent; the kind of silent with a look on her face that encourages me to continue.

"I wanted him to look me in the eyes because I wanted to haunt him for the rest of his life. I wanted the next woman he ever would do that to, one who was afraid of him, I wanted him to see me instead of her with eyes that still would haunt him. So I stared at him from the time he started to the time he expected me have felt whatever it was that he felt."

~~~~~~~~~~~~~~~~~

The General eventually climbed off, lay on the other side of the bed, and told me to call another of the girls who had been his wife far longer than me. I ran out of the room all the way to the kitchen where I grabbed a raffia sponge from the roof and began to scrub myself carelessly. No matter how much, how deep, or how quickly I scrubbed, I could still smell him. I could not stop smelling like him. I saw the other wives of the General come around me and begin to scurry around grabbing for any bucket or cup that they could find. The oldest of them took the soap, while another reached for a raffia sponge with which she began to scrub my body as I limply sat on a stool that another wife had brought for me. I felt water splash all over me repeatedly, while the oldest wife continued to scrub furiously away. When it was done, I watched the stream of red water run through the sand soaking into the earth that I was sure by now that if Abel's blood only cried out to God, this earth with all the blood in it was wailing inconsolably. I sat on that stool and watched for my sisters who I knew would come out of their own tents in no more time than I had. They walked almost robotically toward me while my vacant eyes searched their faces for any sign of the life I had hoped was not taken from them in their time with the junior commanders, but I knew better. If I did not have life within me any longer, how did I expect them to have any? I scrubbed them along with the help of those women who had helped me; this time, I scrubbed them gently as their limp bodies crashed onto the ground.

Angela lay in a foetal position holding on to the clothes that I tried blindly to rip away from her. Quietly, they sobbed, writhing slowly on the ground and mixing with the water that ran the blood like venom away from their bodies as if it knew it had no business being clung to them.

We all sat there behind the kitchen watching the sky for daybreak because we knew we had to be there early. A new fear settled inside of me as I waited to make the morning meal for the soldiers who were selected to embark on that day's mission. A group with three reluctant members I had not let out of my sight since we came to this death camp; Samuel, Jacob, and Joshua. The other wives who by now had become so used to the treatment my sisters and I endured that some of them came out of the room as if nothing had happened to them, tried to coax my sisters and I to help with the meal so that we could release our mind from playing the previous night's scenes over and over again in our heads. As we set the fires, and I pound the pepper with the mortar and pestle, I hear the square begin to fill up with children and the officials. He is standing with all his stolen importance, the Chief Commander, telling the boys whose lives he would selfishly exchange for his in the name of righteous war, that they are going to do good. He paints a cross across their chests, guiding them in a chant as their fists pump straight into the air, and their legs hit the ground in a mixture of anger and fear. I peek at the window at my brothers who are emotionless, uncertain as to why they had to commit these atrocious things which neither spoke nor taught anything about bringing peace. I pray solemnly in my heart that it is my father's words which had brought up his children that would reign supremely in my brothers. That they would believe ultimately his words which he spoke softly but firmly over the loud and insufferable bastard who stood in front of them barking contradictions. This was why, I surmised, they did not encourage that the children be educated. What educated person wouldn't see through the nonsense that was emitted out of this fool's mouth? My brothers beat the earth with panga cutting into the sand that held the sweat pouring from the children's faces from the hot early morning sun. We brought the food we had finished cooking to them so that their strength could sustain them through the battle. From the side, I looked at my brothers, and when my eyes saw them I wordlessly spoke my father's wisdom to them, telling them that I would keep watch until I see their feet darkened the entryway back into this compound. They nodded in agreement as they blinked an embrace to me. Joshua held his blink a bit longer than the older boys, and my heart ached for him in return.

Chapter 24

I do not sleep. Sometimes I close my eyes, and I can still see another life, another world; therefore, I do not sleep. When I succumb to slumber, I want to see nothing, feel nothing. I want to be dead. At night, I bathe Joshua, pray with my siblings, put them on their mats, and tell them a story. When finally, they are without sound, I take my gun and panga to the doorway of the tent, where I sit watching for the sunrise.

Sometimes I drifted off to Kampala, to the verandah of my father's house. I am sitting with Sydney, watching my siblings run after fireflies, chasing the moths that are drawn to the fluorescent light despite the restless children who hardly let them perch. Sydney is playing her violin, and I am on my flute that my grandfather had taught me how to play. I see Rhys making it rather "difficult" to play because he wouldn't stop ticking my waist and kissing my neck. My mother is dancing with my father by the doorway where I see my father's eyes looking into my mother's smiling face, her head swaying to the music. Her dress is swaying in the wind that blows through Sydney's long hair that is caressing my face behind her and tickling my nose.

I can see the scars about our bodies, and I know where they are from; but in my dreams, it is okay. The memories though they linger, seem so far away, so ineffectual against the happiness that whistles in the wind against our ears.

Sometimes I drifted off to California where I am playing volleyball with my friends at the beach laughing at the ball hitting Allison's face. Carrie is sitting under the umbrella as she always does because mom is running over her sunscreen which she had forgotten at the house, as she always does. At several intervals, I am running toward the wide open waves, letting them crash into my lanky self that tries to withstand unsuccessfully itself against the waves it lets cover my head because my knees buckle under. Sometimes I am in the mall with my Mom, Mama, Sydney, Augustina, and Angela. It is something usual, normal, a pleasant custom. Mom takes off from work one summer day, wakes her girls up to breakfast on the back patio, made by the chef she hired just for the morning. She takes us to the mall, then to lunch, then to all the things that girls do on the days off with their younger girls for whom this custom feels like the first time every time. I am laughing. I am happy. In all my dreams, I am happy. I am laughing. Always.

Have you ever gone to bed wanting to escape from whatever turmoil happened that day? Knowing that sleep even if temporary arrests that turmoil and halts it if only for a spell of time? Your dreams are happy even though your mind has recesses of pain and anguish. None of it matters because the source of it exists no longer. Have you ever woken up with your heart beating so hard, so painfully that your brain feels like a peanut swimming in a barrel of water you feel growing fuller in your head? Have you ever felt that kind of pain?

June 15, 2005

My therapist tilts her head to one side, looks at me, and purses her lips for a brief moment. She looks down at the legal pad she writes in on her lap, and shifts the papers like

211

she is trying to avoid any eye contact with me. She coughs nervously – or so I take it, before she answers me.

"Why don't we concentrate on understanding your experience...?"

"I am challenging your ability to help me." I interrupted her.

"How so?"

"I believe that the only way you can help me is to tap into your own experience. I want your compassion, not your pity."

"What is the difference... between compassion and pity?" She asked me crossing her legs.

"Compassion is wearing my shoes, while pity is... window shopping my shoes."

"Everybody has felt pain, Calista. It is all painful no matter what kind of pain it is; it is all pain."

"Have you ever felt that kind of pain? The kind I described?"

"Yes, yes I have. I have felt pain that I did not just want to sleep away from; I wanted to die from it."

I nodded my head as I felt a tendril of trust uproot itself from my heart and slide over to hers, and even if it is just a bit at that time, a release came with it.

"Do you think your dreams helped your hope and faith that you would leave?" She asks me, smiling as if she could see me unclenching for her.

"No."

"Why not?"

Chapter 25

No matter how many times I had been forced to attack the Acholi, I refused to kill. It was, however, a secret refusal. I always claimed to have killed, convincing the other children to support my lie. It did not take much convincing because there was so much going on, it was difficult to notice what did or did not happen besides the bodies that dropped around us succumbing to the bullets that flew pinging across our ears. There were times when the children did bring evidence of their killings in the forms of heads, private parts, arms, legs, ears, lips, and eyeballs. While I did bring abductees back to the camp with me, which was a very applaud worthy service, it was beginning to be apparent that I had no plans to take anybody's life, dismember them, and then bring that member walking to camp with me.

September 18, 2004

It was right after we had all retired from the day, when a small boy came to fetch me from the guard post in front of our tent for the Commander. It was unusual for the Commander to summon the presence of any particular girl soldier, so I deduced that it must have something to do with the ransom that they were expecting. I desperately hoped that it wouldn't be to tell me that my parents had been killed, and to show me proofs of it.

His back was turned to me – the Commander – he was fully suited in his military camouflage, with boots newly polished to a shiny black. I tried to control my nerves that sent shivers up my spine causing my hands to start to shake without anything but themselves to hold onto for solace. He turned around to look at me, the constant toothpick still hanging from his mouth. He slowly takes his seat, exhaling while taking the stick out of his mouth and glares at me. He motioned to his left, and a group of boys came and stood next to me. He asked how many of them had ever actually seen me take a life before, reminding them that they would be struck by lightning if anyone of them lied to him. He had such great power over those children whom I think they would have dared not raise their hands, even if they were certain they had seen me kill. The Commander continued, telling me that he did not believe that I had, in fact, proven my allegiance to the cause by bringing the evidence of my atrocities. I didn't say anything. It is widely spread in camp by the General, and Commander, that God expects us to rid ourselves of all that is unholy, after which, we were to rid our land of all that was unholy. Problem I saw was, we were neither in our land, nor did we have any proof that the lives we took were, in fact, unholy. Furthermore, I was not God; it was not my place to decide the fate of a holy or unholy person. Those children standing before that Commander did not believe him, because I had taught them not to. I had told them the truth, first by teaching them their rights as human beings, second, by teaching them of the God I knew, and how His name was being misused by radicals and noisemakers. Though the children feared the Commander because he could, in fact, take their lives, they did not trust him, and they did not respect him.

The Commander kept quiet for a spell of time before snapping his fingers toward his side again. David, who had been standing not far behind him, brought a black duffel bag, and set it on the ground in front of the Commander. He opened it to a sight that knocked the wind out of my stomach buckling my knees beneath me and landing me onto the wet earth from the light rain that had fallen earlier that afternoon.

There were stacks of dollars. It was money I knew could not possibly have come from anyone else or anywhere else than home. I tried to belt out, but no sounds other than heaving in whispers came out of me.

~~~~~~~~~~~~~~~~

"What did you feel at that time?" My therapist asks me.

"I don't remember. I do not know if... what... I do not remember. I think I went deaf, and blind, and numb, all at the same time. I remember thinking, "We might actually die in this wretched God-forsaken bush." I could not believe that my family had not succeeded in rescuing us, because I knew that they would plan this drop in a way that would help us some way, in return. When I saw the money, I knew that they obviously could not do anything."

"Was that why the Commander called you?"

"No. He informed me that the ransom had been dropped, as if somehow I had assumed that in the past three months, Uganda had switched to dollar currency with American men's heads on the bills. Anyway, he further explained that my family did not drop the full amount. They wanted some kind of proof that we were still alive before they dropped the rest."

"How did you feel after he explained that?"

"I felt my life come back to me again. It did not come back slowly though, it came in a rush, in a hurry, like it needed to tell me something quickly before my spirit decided to leave me. I knew at that moment that whatever plans my siblings and I had to escape, we needed to press play. If my parents made the first drop, the rebels would be expecting the second, and the sight of that kind of money to those vultures would catapult into measures that may be even more drastic than they had been with us. It was the kind of money that would make them confident enough to keep us alive because they actually think that our families would send the second half, or it would make them crazy enough to kill us in anger because the proceedings were not going according to their arrangement."

"So, why was he suited that night? Was it just to show you the money?" My therapist asks with a furrow of her brow.

"No. I was to go back to the tent and get my sisters and our arms. We were to get ready to leave because we would be accompanying that night's troop to fight. We were going to attack a village about ten miles from our camp with the Commander watching especially my sisters and I, to make sure that we took human lives. That we were not just covered in the blood of the other rebel soldiers' slaughters, but our own."

~ ~ ~ ~ ~ ~ ~ ~ ~ ~ ~ ~ ~ ~ ~

I gathered my siblings together, helping my sisters get up and ready to leave. When we were ready, I looked at my brothers, the terror in the eyes giving away their fear that we should die. We held hands together squeezing tightly to communicate words that seemed to elude our lips. Joshua started to cry while we whispered prayers to God asking him to keep me, and my sisters as we tried our best to stay alive. We kiss him, Samuel, and Jacob, who stay strong because they have to be, so that maybe their belief and hope may have the power to bring us back to them.

Angie grabs tightly onto my hands at the entryway stopping me from exiting toward the square.

"What is it?" I asked her gently.

"Papa once told me that my life was not more important that anyone else's. He taught us to lay down our lives for the people we loved. I am going to kill people so that I can keep my own life. Tell me Cali, where is that righteousness in that? What makes my life more save-worthy that theirs?"

I knelt down boring my gaze deep into my youngest sister's eyes. I don't know what to tell her that would be enough. I don't know how to wish my sister luck with killing somebody without associating any guilt with it.

"Angie, whether or not you kill those people, someone will kill them; especially if you refuse. They will kill you thereafter, if not first. I do not have the answer, but I am not ready to lose you. For you, I am unapologetically selfish. I need you to do it. Please Angie, do it. Please."

She nodded her compliance, and we left.

During our raid that night, my sisters and I left letters in random places. I gave notes to people running away, asking them to find a place to ask someone to find my parents, and give to them our letters in exchange for their lives. My sisters did the same knowing that if my parents weren't sure of our whereabouts, at least now they knew we were alive, camped out along the border of Sudan, although we weren't certain exactly where. Food was scarce in the bush. There was nothing to eat most of the time. Sometimes, we would eat a lot when the troops had managed to loot successfully several food stuffs, and abduct enough children to carry the loot. Some days were treacherous because there would be no food; not because there was not necessarily enough, but because the commanders and the General had to eat to their hearts' content. In the days that we had plenty to eat, I carried out experiments. I would gather leaves that I found around the camp; by the river's edge, I would scoop the finest clay. I found a rat on which I would test the leaves on. I would cook the leaves that may be new to me and feed it to the rat. If it lived until the next morning, I would find more of the leaves, and I would feed it to my siblings and myself with roasted insects. Sometimes, we just ate the soil I had collected from the river's edge."

~~~~~~~~~~~~~~~~

My therapist exhales, staring at me with a rather disbelieving look on her face. She shakes her head, looking down at the carpet, then at my face, then at the window with her mouth open like she is searching for the words to release this imprisoned thought that was building within her.

"I have a confession to make" she finally lets out in a breath. My heart skips a beat, but I ask tentatively anyway.

"What?"

"You seem unreal. I read about these things, and though I know how tragic it is, it never really hit that close to home. Here you are, on my couch, and the more you speak, the more I feel like I am in a movie... like you cannot be real."

"Why did you tell me that?" I ask her softly after a spell of silence, with me watching her face as tears she used to excuse herself to the bathroom so I wouldn't know, came coursing down her cheeks.

"Because, you need to know that… that I am a person. That I have a heart, and nerves, and emotions built inside of me to feel bad when something like this is being recanted to me. You need to know that this story is shocking, and tear jerking, and unbelievable, no matter whom you are telling it to."

"Thank you." I replied, feeling sorry for the pitiful woman sitting across from me. I grab the box of tissues sitting on the side stool and give some to her. I try to help by searching for something in my mind to tell her so that she could let go of some pity she may have felt.

"Don't cry. It really did not taste that bad."

That did not help.

~~~~~~~~~~~~~~~~

September 19, 2004

Dear Sydney,

I am in the truck on our back from the raid. We are still covered with the blood of the slaughtered from the massacre. Angela is the most absent of all of us with no emotion registered on her face. Her body is limp with her eyes staring out of the back of the truck at nothing in particular. I look at her hand still coated thickly with blood, and I take them in mine gently lifting them up to my head, rubbing the blood into my hair. I bring her hands to my lips kissing them in hopes that maybe the gesture would free my sister from the crushing blame she cannot help herself from bearing.

We reached the camp with the first cock crow waking up every sleeping soul. Samuel nudged my side to show me a present he had made for me while we had been gone. It was a flute whittled from a stick. I took it looking warmly at the holes on top and under the stick. I grazed the mouth of the wooden flute, and immediately I thought of you. On days like this, while I sat in the truck watching the dark shadows over the mountains, I could hear your violin.

I looked around at the company that arrived with me at that camp knowing that only about sixty percent of us will return home. I clutched my flute tightly against my dress on my right hand, and a satchel of six human heads on my left. I no longer dream of home.

Chapter 26

October 3, 2004

Angela had always been my best friend deep in my heart. I had loved her from the very moment that girl had come out of her mother's womb screaming out all her anger at the disturbance of an audacious doctor reaching for her to evict her from the comfort of her mother's haven just for her. I watched with amused fascination her dark-red skin fade slowly and softly. While I impatiently waited for my parents to finish signing her adoption papers, I put my finger inside of her palm, which she gripped, taking my whole heart along with it never to let go even when I had to say good-bye.

My mother's children have never really been troublesome or quick to speak in situations where we found ourselves in an uncomfortable stance. We were not unable to stand up for ourselves, but our parents were sure to have us understand that unless it was necessary, words that expressed less than our actions did, weighed very little. Angela, however, was even more so this way. She did not speak unless she was spoken to, or unless she was in her comfort zone such as, with family and very close friends. She spoke with a soft voice that always seemed like she was at a loss for breath or like she was about to cough or clear her throat. I guess it is kind of interesting to say that I was fascinated by my own sister even after several years of living with her, but I was. I looked up to her, and the little things she did that people seemed to love. Angela, in the rare instances that my mother allowed us sweets would go off on a tangent that was enjoyed by the rest of my family because she was quite animated when she did go into her, ushering us into it as well.

She was beautiful, and the part about it that made it all the more adorable and effervescent was the fact that she did not know she was beautiful. Though these characteristics were admirable and worthy of emulation sure to elicit the highest of praise from even nobility, I worried that it would do Angela no good here in this camp. I called Angie to me one night after all that was expected of the day was done save for retirement to our beds. I called her along with the rest of my siblings as we put down our mats to rest through the strangling night and a furious day in expectance. I assured all my siblings of my admiration and appreciation for every one of them in all things that made them unique and set them apart, even though it seems outwardly that we all were extremely similar. I told Angela, especially, that I did love the fact that she was unapologetic for being softhearted, and not feeling the need for confrontation. I applauded them all in the goodness and love for others they had in their ever stretching consideration to give all of themselves for everyone who needed them to. I knew, however, I told them, that their lives as horrific as it sounded was as important to me as everyone else's if not more. I did not want them giving up their lives for people, because I wasn't strong enough to imagine my life in this camp without them. Even worse, to assume or expect that I had any kind of life outside of this horror without them was to delude myself into a hellish pretense. Angela had to desist from caring so much, or at least showing it. She had to try to pray for the souls of the people that she could not save, and not attempt to give her life each time, rather than watch someone else suffer. I admitted that in some ways, I couldn't ask this of them because it was an honorable thing to want to give your life in place of someone else's suffering, but if I would die for them, then their lives were important too. To me, Angela apologized for any way she may have made our already sorry predicament even direr, and swore that she would not jeopardize it any longer.

* * * * * * * * * * * * * * * *

The day was Sunday, and though we were to report to the square to have "prayers" with the General and commanders, I still deemed it greatly important that my siblings and I say the prayers our parents had taught our infant lips. I knew I had to reinforce the work my parents had always instilled in us. Though they hoped against all hopes that we would never find ourselves in the predicament where we feel their love for us would wane due to things we could or could not control, we must always rest assured that they were our parents. Even if we ran away from home, they would pray for us, look for us and never give up until they found us. Even though with the atrocities we had already been forced to commit caused us to carry guilt and shame, we had to believe that our family's greatest desire was that we come home; however with all the mental issues we would bring home with us, but come home, they wanted us to. I looked around the room as I adjusted to the light that shone on the bodies that lay all over the room surrounding me saying a prayer for everybody on the mats, for the same count at the end of the day. Angela was the only person I usually could not see because she would always sleep under her covers even though the air was too hot, and she would wake drenched in sweat and covered in rashes. I said a prayer toward the covered mound that was always her. That day uncharacteristically, I thought of what could be the reason behind my sister's sleeping underneath all those covers but declined to ask when I realized inside that I wanted to grant her what she deemed normal and necessary for her. I did not want to interfere with however she saw fit to stay sane or disillusioned to the extent and surety of her safety.

Two hours later, "prayers" at the square was done. They were never like any prayers that my siblings or I had ever been party to. We were taught here the Ten Commandments with the General focusing on the transgressions of others against us. We were told that we had to abduct people because God called us to get people on the right path, however necessary. Those who did not agree were to die, because refusal to believe would be crucifying Jesus again, and we rebels were to prevent that from happening. I had to try with all my might to restrain myself from the smirk that constantly threatened to lift my lips in sheer mockery of the unintelligent hateful words that spewed from the General. I worried that though I was confident in the knowledge the words of the General were untrue and confounded, my siblings did not necessarily know that they were. I wanted them to know that God was not on the rebels' side, and while I honestly did not think He was on the government's side either, I knew that our present situation along with about sixty two children at this camp was abominable to him. He would care for us, watch over us, keep us in His wings and eventually lead us home.

When Augustina and I were finished preparing lunch for the General and his co-commanders, we returned to our tent to prepare the boys for a raid which was to be done to mark the arrival at our new destination, and to claim the territory by chasing the inhabitants thereof farther into the cities in fear and desolation. Deserving of mention, by the way, was that I had not seen Angela anywhere since after the gathering even though she was supposed to be in the kitchen helping her sister and I. Being the ever fragile soul she was, I resigned my worry to the possibility that she may just have confined herself to a small corner of the tent, lost in sorrow's unfair judgment. I did not see her in the tent, and so my concern grew, for she knew she was forbidden to leave out of already advised areas without permission, and having previously looked in those advised areas and not having seen her, I had expected she would be in the tent. I asked Samuel, who was waiting in the tent, and he suggested that I look in the kitchen.

"But I did..." I replied growing frantic by the second. "...She's not there."

"I think I just saw her in the backyard," he said.

I noticed he was acting sort of shifty with his second answer.

"I just came from the backyard. That is where the kitchen is," Augustina replied coming from behind him into the tent. "She's not there."

"Then look in the kitchen again, maybe she went from the bedroom to the kitchen" he said more suggestively than confidently. So with a low but much mustered sternness, I asked him where his sister was for the last time.

＊＊＊＊＊＊＊＊＊＊＊＊＊＊

As I ran to the square, knowing but not caring that I could be in trouble for even attempting to be insubordinate to a commander who may have listened to my sister and agreed that she was to be his wife to ensure the safety of the rest of her siblings.

"Please do not be upset with me, but she had left to go and make our lives easier. She said the only person who would understand that she could not be anybody but herself was you, and if that part of her would jeopardize our lives, then she was going to find a way to make it okay. Nobody would notice her when she was gone, and we were going to have enough food to eat and live." Samuel had explained.

My mind whirled, spinning my head along with it and giving me no time to think of anything but the worst of the decisions that my sister would have made in such a young life.

I told Samuel to come to the marketplace with Jacob, and Joshua looking for me as fast as he could.

I knew exactly what Angela was going to do. I would rather die of hunger and worse measures than have my sister sell her life for mine. Reaching the junior commander's tent just in time, I saw Angela being pushed onto the floor by him, and her slowly removing her dress as the General proceeded out of the junior commander's tent.

"Angela!" I ran blinded by tears as far as my legs could carry me, and I reached for her hand. She took it and looked into my eyes. On her face was the most sorrowful look I had ever seen as tears ran down from her eyes.

"What are you doing?" she asked me starting to sob.

"Angie, what have you done?" I asked her as I mustered words through my tears.

She reached into the pocket of her skirt and pulled out her supposed worth. It was a piece of paper she had somehow gotten the General to sign saying that we were to be cared for and not killed for the mere fact that we had hearts, and could not handle the blood and wickedness we were surrounded by. It was a note signed by the General stating that Angie was to remain with the junior commander, and my siblings and I were hereby free to walk into the forest and proceed through it until we reached our home. It was a lot. It was not enough. Nothing ever could be.

"Angela, you cannot do this!" I shouted again taking her in both arms. She looked at me, and she sobbed.

"You have no use for me. Everyone else has this faith and this hope. I do not have it. I keep making mistakes, forgetting to remember everything I know to be good and real."

"No, Angie. Is it whenever we cry, you give up and leave?" I asked her. With that, I turned over to the commander, and asked for the return of my sister. He refused saying that my sister had made her decision and good thing she did, because initially, we were all of no use to the camp since the reasons for our abductions were already finished. The commander pulled me from my sister's hand and threw me on the ground saying that I was wasting his time. He turned around to walk back into his tent as I tried to stand up holding on to his shirt for balance. I looked up at his face begging him to let my sister go. As Angela started to cry aloud, I looked into that boy's face, I do not know how, but I knew he was about to change his terms, and I knew what they were going to be.

From the mat on the commander's floor, I could hear my sister outside beating her head with her fists, and thrashing her legs on the dirt. Then I felt the zipper of my dress slowly go down my back ending at my waist. I noticed my sister had suddenly stopped crying so loudly and instead spoke through her sobs as if talking to somebody. As he started to pull my dress apart from the back, I heard the voices of my brothers heading for the front of the truck. Seeing that boy in that position with me must have snapped a wire because with lightning in their eyes, my brothers pulled me away from the boy. Jacob lunged at his neck and would have strangled him to death if he had not pulled out his pistol. Jacob got up from him and went to stand by the entrance door with me, Samuel and Angela.

With the gun pointed at Angie, the commander stood up.

"You can take that one" he said flicking the gun in my direction," but that one," he said indicating with a nod toward Angela "is mine. She…" he continued referring to me with a flick of his gun, "…wanted her back in return that I have my way with her."

Jacob pleaded with him to give us another offer, that we would do anything else, but the young man refused saying that our decision as quoted by my sister before our deliverance attempt was final, and he was assured of the girl, so the girl he was going to take.

The General came having been summoned by one of his little assistants of the ruckus by the junior commander's tent and inquired as to what was going on.

I told the General sorrowfully of my sister's ill decision and of the junior commander's refusal to acquiesce to my request that he return my sister. I told him of the alternative the commander had given in order that I take my sister and I back, being that he has his way with me. The General snapped his head in the direction of the junior commander who now looked very frightened, and commanded him to stand before him.

He ordered that the junior commander was going to die for overstepping the authority given to him, to accept sexual duties from anyone other than his wife; not to speak of one of those women being his – the General's wife. My heart jumped, because I did not want anyone to die for my sake, and the look on Angie's face dictated that she wanted different. The General ordered that I return to the tent with my sisters while my brothers were to beat the commander to death.

"I'll do it" my brothers replied, one by one without even a moment of the commanders words sink into me.

I froze.

"The three of you?" he asked. I stood there as the words and screams kept swirling around my head and yet somehow unable to escape my lips.

"Yes," they all replied at once.

"No!" I shouted "Please" I knelt down on the ground and blinded by tears. I begged the General to let us all go back to our tent. "What will I tell their mothers?" I sorrowed to him. "How will I explain when I see them in heaven that we lost our soul to you?"

Without many words, little assistants to the General laid clubs beside my brothers goading them to beat the junior commander who now had tears in his fear-filled eyes.

Chapter 27

As the excitement settles, and the sight of the boys carrying a dead junior commander's corpse begins to fade, I am made aware of the crowd of children who crept out of their makeshift tents to witness another vile indoctrination of three boys. I can also feel my face stiff from tears mixed with mud, and the slow muggy wind starting to burn my eyes as realization settles in. Taking my sister's hand in mine, we turn around, and head toward the direction of our tent.

As I sat by the tent entrance and watched between the blood-soaked earth next to my brothers' clothes, and listening to the sound of the water wash away the red stains on their skin, I wait for them to tell me why they had answered so quickly without even waiting for even the smallest moments that purveyed there was still some humanity that sat within even our wildest fears. When they came back in, as they stretched themselves in attempts to ravage through the nightmares that had been their fate to commit, I asked them - why.

It was enough; enough that they could take, to be the men of the house, or tent in this case, and to watch helplessly as all the time their sisters were taken advantage of. They died inside every time I went in as some prize to the General; and now Angela was going to be taken away from them without them having any option but to watch it happen - again. When they were given the chance to protect what was the most important to them even more than their very spirits, they chose to kill their sisters' enemy than have him take their spirits.

* * * * * * * * * * * * * * * *

Dear Sydney,

I want to run away – far, far away. My brothers killed a man yesterday rather than let him take Angie as his wife. Angie is putting up a straight face to show that she is better, and won't try anything drastic again. She includes herself in conversations we try to have in a trial at maintenance of some form of normalcy among us, and she does not hide any longer. But deep down, I know, especially when I see her looking into the distance, I can see the pictures she sees, of them – my brothers – and the blood that steeps into the sands that surrounded that dead commander. I know that she blames herself for what happened. We are still the six of us, and however broken and emptier by the day, we still struggle. This camp continues to override the pleasant dreams our sleep starts with, filling it with the darkness the shadow on this left side of the sun casts. It has taken away a part of the soul with every loss on these grounds.

At the news of what had happened at the camp that day while she had been away at the stream with a group of girls, the commander's sister who I had not realized had any relations to him wailed beating at her chest, knocking her head against the wall, throwing herself on the ground, and crying. "What will I tell my mother now? Who will take care of me now?"

I cried with her while trying to keep her from hurting herself. About an hour later she calmed down, laid on the floor dripping with sweat, and moaning repeatedly "...who is going to take care of me now?" I sat beside her and held her hands; after a little while, she stopped. I fixed her hair, and cleaned her face before I brushed the dirt off her clothes. She did the same to me. The rest of that day passed without incident.

That night, we did not light our lantern. We sat in the darkness and allowed the light of the moon to shine its favor into our room, hiding just enough of our pain and secrets so that we could keep it from each other. Jacob moved over toward the entrance of our tent to look at that blanket of black with stars that lit up subsequently after each other, as if to keep us hopeful as each one faded to let the other spark.

What is my mother doing? Is she crying? Is my father spending too much time in solitary? He does that in the worst of times, you know. I miss you. I miss you. I miss you so much I have to try not to think of you, which makes me think of you even more. I am hopeful I will see your face again, but I am aware of the apparent possibility that I may not.

From me,

Calista.

A few days later, as we all lay down together to sleep, Angela told me of the day she was returning home from the market with my mother. They passed by the house belonging to one of our family friends, and lying on the dirt was his wife who sorrowfully wriggled on the ground tearing at her clothes while clutching a picture of her husband. She wasn't audible enough for Angela to hear fully the words she uttered from her sobs, but Angela told me that she could never miss that part of that woman's grief as she nowadays is so unjustly unaccustomed to.

"I would take the starvation to spare his life!" She had wailed that day.

Our family friend had died in action. He had died leaving behind a wife, and twelve children, four of whom unbeknownst to him had died from kwashiorkor. We sat quietly in that room, me sitting at the door of the tent, holding the gun issued to me, while my siblings lay on the mats under God's loving care, and their sister's loaded AK-47.

Jacob's voice cut through the silence asking Augustina to tell me a story I apparently had never heard. He asked her to tell me the true story of how Joshua came to be my little brother. A story that till this day, still sends chills down my spine, and remains as unbelievable as it sounds.

Augustina began:

"The day before my fourteenth birthday, I went to the market with mummy. We had gone to buy some things for the refugee camps because they had started to run out more often due to the influx of runaway children. As we made our way past the fruit section in front of the market, I thought I saw Emmanuel. I wasn't sure since I did not see his face. I did not bother to check because the sooner one went about their business, the better; for stray hands wandered into money filled pockets and excusably so, for a woman even more so. On our way home, pushing our goods in a wheel barrow we had brought along with us, I stopped in my tracks because I thought that somebody was following us when I heard leaves rustling somewhere nearby. I looked at mummy's face following her eyes to a dead body covered with leaves lying on the side of the bush by the tall grass. It wasn't an unusual sight at this point, for reasons I care not to divulge because you already know, but this one was different. If not for the fact that she was covered with cocoyam leaves, we would have passed on by too. But I grabbed Mama's hand just after we had passed, and halted. Mummy motioned for me to be silent, gently putting her finger to her lips.

"Do you hear that?"

"Hear what?"

Mama turned around, and I with her. We looked back at the covered corpse, and - it was moving.

We both screamed, before running to hide behind a nearby tree until our heavy breathing subsided. We peeked back at the corpse, certain that it was moving, or at least, the corpse's stomach was moving.

Mummy and I walked slowly, hesitantly holding on to each other as if one was trying to keep the other from running away when we got to the body. We opened the moving stomach, only it was not a moving stomach…"

Augustina stopped, and I saw her crack. She had not cried since the day we were abducted, for I believe she had resigned herself to the fate that was ours to make peace with.

"The corpse was a pregnant woman whose stomach had been ripped open exposing a newborn baby. I think she had been dragged there, because there were scratches and dust all over her body. Inside of her abdomen…" Augustina started to heave, and I began to rub her back. She began to sob slowly at first and then heavily as she struggled between breathing, and crying out.

"The baby… the baby… it was so little… the baby had been lain back inside her stomach, and left to die. I started to hyperventilate, so Mama and I went back to the tree where we were hiding, and vomited."

I sat there rubbing Augustina's back, cradling Angela whose head was on my lap as she curled up her legs to her chest. Jacob started to cry, and Angela with him. They put their arms around each other, and I knew there was something about seeing that, and hearing about it that made all the difference. For from it came a crash from their hopes that that incident would remain just another spiced up war story.

Chapter 28

The story would later continue like this: My mother and Augustina had gotten home with the baby to tell the family what had happened. Curiously, my little cousins who were visiting at the time wanted to know how much the baby they had "bought" from the market had cost. Julia and the girls started to clean the baby while the boys and my father went back to the body to dig a grave and bury her properly. The baby had been left there for a while, and so had gotten sick. He had cried a lot and had to be fed every hour at which he only ate very little at a time. He woke up in the middle of the night running a fever every other couple of days. Everybody was getting up when the baby awoke, but the little ones had to be sent back to sleep because when they stay up late, they are a handful to organize in the morning. My mother and Angela went into the kitchen to fix a meal for the baby, while Sarah, a girl who lived with my family, changed his diapers and sang to him. In the kitchen, my mother and Augustina tried to figure a name to give the baby.

Augustina suggested that they name him Moses.

"Why?" My mother had asked.

"Because, though he wasn't drawn out of the water, he was still drawn out of a sticky situation."

When they had finished making the meal, they carried it to the living room while Augustina put the fire and kettle away. As mother was about to enter the living room, she saw Sarah holding that baby, making contented sounds to soothe the crying away. That scene brought back the story that had arrested Sarah, and put her into such despair that would never release her to the world of comfort and joy which had been so brutally taken from her.

Sarah had been born Muslim, as were her six brothers and sisters. One year after Ahmad, Sarah's youngest brother was born, Sarah converted into Christianity while listening in on a crusade at Khartoum. Before then, she had been betrothed to a Muslim man at the age of twelve, and would have married him. Her mother, however, who had also been converted shortly after, advised her against it. When Sarah's father heard that his daughter had refused to marry the man she was to, he was outraged. He beat her and her mother, threatening to kill Sarah if she did not change her mind, and reverse the shame she would bring the family were it to be that she continued in her rebellion. When he left town for a few days, news got to Sarah and her mother that the suitor and her father had heard about their conversion. With that information and fearing for their lives, Sarah's mother took her children and fled from Khartoum to the Hosanna refugee camp. With my mother's help, Sarah's mother changed the names of her children and herself, trying as best she could to stay out of public organizations and staying at least two steps ahead of her husband. Everything was going well. The last time I had been home, I had met Sarah for the first time, as my mother had taken her and her brothers to live in our home with my family. A year after I came back to the U.S., Sarah had written to tell me that she was engaged to a Christian boy named Solomon, whom she had been seeing, and whom I had met and liked as well. I sent her my felicities, wishing her a wonderful marriage. A year later, she would write to tell me she was pregnant, and my parents had given rented some quarters a bit down the road from Hosanna to her, and her growing family. I also wrote back in joy with her. News travelled fast, and so it became that Sarah's father had found out where they were, as had the suitor. Sarah's mother got word that they were coming down to Hosanna, so she told the rest of her children to go down to my parents' house as requested by my mother and stay there until everything was back to calm. She had carefully planned how she was going to beg her husband, hoping to coax him to understand why she had to leave. She resolved to tell him the children were dead, were it to be that he proved difficult. Sarah took her siblings, leaving her husband back at their house with her eldest brother, Tafawa, and Solomon's mother who was visiting at that time. Sarah's father, and former suitor stormed into the home, and without many words, tied up the boy and his mother. They made Solomon watch while they raped his mother; first the father, then Sarah's former suitor. Then they untied Solomon, and forced him to do the same. Solomon refused and was killed for defiance, and for marrying Sarah; Tafawa was killed, citing that he had aided and abetted in the rebellion against his father. And then Sarah's mother, they killed citing nothing. They had nothing.

The news sent Sarah into a withdrawal so fierce, that brought with it sorrow, and sorrow - heartache, and heartache - stress, and stress - a miscarriage. She never prayed again to the Heavenly Father, or Allah. She just walked, sometimes rather robotically ate when memories did not get the best of her.

When my mother came into that room to see Sarah holding that baby she and Augustina had found, she saw her holding her child. The child she would never know, or so mother thought; for Sarah looked up from the little boy's face, and asked if she could name him.

"Kirabo" [Gift] she said gently.

"Kirabo," my mother and Augustina repeated. They agreed there could not be a more deserving name.

"And his middle name?" Angela asked.

"Joshua," she replied looking at the child with a faraway look in her eyes.

My mother reached out and embraced Sarah, who in that instant, collapsed into my mother's arms in tears. Augustina came and took Joshua from her hands as on my mother's shoulders, Sarah let out years of injustice and grief.

"There are twelve houses in our neighborhood" Augustina said her voice breaking. "I saw faint lights of kerosene lamps go on in all of them, and I knew; twelve households had put their grief and pains on hold, and together we had cried with Sarah that night."

Silence took over again as we let Augustina's story make its mark, as we did all the stories we had been forced to familiarize ourselves with.

Angela suddenly looked up as if a spark of inspiration had been enlightened.

"We have to get out of here," she said.

We looked at her with a mix of reactions not knowing which ones to go with that would be kind to her psyche.

"Where the hell have you been?!" Augustina asked with a slight look of irritation and worry in her eyes.

"Augustina!" Jacob hissed in a reprimand.

"No," Angela replied still with a glimmer of inspired thought in her eyes. Then, she looked outside the tents at something beyond the hills.

"The shadow," she whispered more to herself as a mental note than to us.

"What about the shadow?" I asked, actually quite interested, and getting almost as excited as her voice was coaxing us to be.

"We have to get over that shadow."

"We've always been over the shadow" Augustina stated, not sure where Angela was going with her idea.

"We've never been to the end of the shadow." Angela looked at us as if she was expecting us to know what the rest of whatever her mind was cooking was actually supposed to be.

"Keep driving" Jacob said motioning with his hands for her to continue.

Samuel snapped his fingers in sudden enlightenment.

"Zion," he said with eyes wide at Angie hoping they were thinking alike.

"Zion" Angela whispered in accordance.

When we were younger, my siblings used to look over the horizon to try to pinpoint the rising of the sun. We called the shadow behind the sunrise, "The Shadow". We also called it, "The Bush", devising a plan that, were we ever to be lost, we needed to get to the right side of that shadow where the sun rose. Our home was on the right of that shadow. We knew that the sun did not rise from behind the mountain and never shine on the other side, but we also knew that the sun did not shine anywhere else like it did in the comfort of the house our parents built us. We called our plan, "Zion."

Zion was where the shadow ended. Everybody knew where Zion was, and everybody knew the plan. Everybody knew that Zion, like every plan, was easy to make; the execution of it, however, was another story. With the absence of a heightened sense of navigation, getting everyone home was now an even harder feat. To get home, we had to defeat the commanders. The most obvious way to do that lay dauntingly before us.

Augustina said it: "We have to stay away from here long enough not to care any longer whether or not we die."

My mind drifts away in sorrow once again to mourn my dear friend, Sarah. There were many things my mother had divulged to me when I was better settled in, and the travels subsided. I suppose one of them was to tell me that my little brother, Joshua came from the bush, grew up with a mother who loved him thoroughly. Sarah was killed by the rebels while I was in the U.S. She was killed while her young son watched once again, his mother, taken from him. It was difficult to hear that Sarah had passed; but being so far away, it did not affect me as much as it would have if I had been there. Now that I am here, and I inflict on others the pain that Sarah feared, I am ashamed. I was not there when Sarah was buried. That makes me die a little inside. Actually, I die a lot inside.

Chapter 29

When you are here, everything changes. Nothing anymore is the same. If you are adamant against extinction, nothing must stay the same. Sometimes when I tell people about the camp, and I say in any part of a sentence, "...on a good day...," or "...that was a good day..." their mouths hang open in astonishment as they ask me tentatively, how there could possibly be in a place so devilish, a good day.

Joy, I have come to agree, is relative. When you are here, if you are obstinate about being yet another casualty, you must let go of every other joy you used to know. The thoughts of any former happiness alone, without aid from the circumstances of your current fate, is enough to slay you. You must make new joys even in the valley of the shadow of death. You must charm the snake.

My brother Joshua was very good with this life concept. Within the first month, he had become the personal fetch-boy for the Chief Commander along with another boy of the same age whose name was Danny. Joshua and Danny became the best of friends while in the service of the Chief Commander, and were inseparable in their service. As unbelievable as it may seem, the Chief Commander was good to them, as long as they carried out their duties as they were told. I found a joy in knowing that Joshua at least was somewhat safer than the rest of us might be. The spirits of these two young boys were exceedingly contagious, so Danny's mother and I became friends as well. We were careful though, not to seem too close to the rest of the population because we did not want to be used as bait for one another. You must pretend not to love whoever you may in this camp, for fear that jealousy would arise, and one could be used to entice another to one atrocity or the other.

Danny boy, as we called him, would tell us in the confidence of the mud kitchen walls that he did not want to be here. Even though he had been born in captivity, he knew that this could not be what the rest of the world must feel like. He defined a feeling he had, like he was still in his mother's womb waiting to be born freer into the world.

The thing about the joys here, is that it is far shorter lived than the joys we had ever been familiar to.

A joy was the nights we had no sinister agenda to carry out; when it would be everyone to their tents waiting for the fires to go down to let the moon polish the starry sky. On such occasions, I would convince the children of the camp who were close to me, to go to sleep early in the evening so that they could wake up with the earliest morning light for lessons.

Danny boy who usually liked his lessons, had begun to grow disinterested in them. He asked me on one occasion, when I asked him whether he was looking forward to the next day's lessons:

"Why do we have to prepare for school?"

"Don't you want to grow up to be intelligent?" His mother asks him.

"No" all the little boys replied.

"Why?" I asked them, rather dumbfounded by their disinterest. They looked down to the ground as if they were ashamed of themselves, and even more embarrassed by whatever their reasons might be.

Then Joshua said: "Because when you go to school, you become intelligent; when you become intelligent, you know everything; when you know everything, then you can do anything; when you can do anything, you start a war."

While I pondered on what Joshua had said, Danny boy came up to me to ask if I could tell them a moon story.

"Of course I will," and taking his hand, I looked up at the moon, and began to concoct a story so convincing everyone could see movement in that little circle in the sky. A story that everyone telling a little part brought a peace in the camp that everybody so longingly was parched for.

One week later, my siblings, along with Danny boy went into the bush to teach the little boys how to set traps for small animals to roast for dinner. The girls picked leaves and stray kernels to be shelled for a snack or a holdover lunch when food was scarcer than other times. It was somewhere between picking dried fruit from the path, nuts from the ground, and trap setting, that Angela and Samuel began to shout:

"They are here, Oh! They are here, Oh!"

Like second nature, they left everything we had with them and began to run.

October 21, 2004

"Dear Sydney,

Danny boy died today. Naturally, we are supposed to be grieving and mourning his death, but we are not. His mother had him buried in the backyard along with the letter he had written to God concerning his worries for his mother, who he was leaving behind in sorrow. I had wanted to keep it as a memento, but his mother had said that Danny boy had to send it to God along with him.

We were in the kitchen that morning, Danny boy's mother and I. That morning that was supposed to be fateful but was not. Danny boy had been too close to where they UPDF soldiers had thrown the bomb while setting traps with the older boys. The explosion had picked up his small body and hurled it against a tree trunk, his head being the point of contact. Samuel took him to the stream to wash off the blood since they would pass it on their way home. After we heard the explosion, the rest of the camp went into frenzy as the General started to dispatch young men and girls armed with guns aiming for the direction in which they had heard the explosion come from. Danny boy's mother, Nancy, took my hand in hers, saying a prayer for

God's protection on the boys. After praying, she went outside toward the direction of the bush were the soldiers were going to fight, with me trailing behind. At the distant sight of her son dangling from Samuel's arms, Nancy ran off like a mad woman screaming "Not again, no! No, not again, no!!!" She grabbed her son, and took off into the direction of her tent followed closely behind by the rest of us. When we reached Danny, we discovered he was still breathing, however unconscious. Nancy, still hopelessly crying, carried her son to the bed she shared with him, searching frantically for anything to make her son better. My spirit leaves me again, and I am in my mother's room with Samuel laying on my parents' bed after he had been hit by a car just outside our compound. My mother asks me to boil a pot of water, and asks Augustina and Angela to bring a change of clothes for the near unconscious boy whose clothes she was now stripping off of him. With everybody gone, Mama began to pray for Samuel. One thing about my mother is that she tended to do first things first, and the first thing with something she had absolutely no power to right, was to pray.

I returned to Nancy and Danny boy with all my siblings still in the room with them, and nostalgia washed all over me as I saw my mother in Nancy praying loudly over Danny boy, who was now resting on her shoulder. She stopped a little later and after cleaning up her son as we stood there with tears in our eyes, she prayed, "Lord, if it is possible, do not take this child; nevertheless, let not our will, but Yours be done."

Nancy was checking on Danny boy every other minute the rest of that day. I saw my mother's figure, the same one that slept on her bed right next to Samuel years ago, when Nancy prayed with her arms around her son until she fell asleep. Joshua brought Danny boy a present every day to keep him company as he waited so impatiently for his friend to wake. David began to come even more often to check on the boy, and to bring something or the other for us to give him that may make him feel better as one folktale or other had once assured him. Nancy one day made a comment that she suspected that David might be taking a liking to me.

"Really?" Jacob asked rather sarcastically, which sent the rest of us into a fit of laughter. Laughter that had not rounded the corners of this abode for so long.

A week after the explosion that hurt Danny boy, I went into the room where he lay. I had tried for so long to avoid it, spending days and nights in thoughts of what our lives would be like without this precocious gentle life of joy in it. I decided I would go and see him, to tell him that he could not die. I walked quietly to his bed, not because I did not want to wake him. Goodness! I would have brought down the house if that would wake him. I went in slowly, so that Nancy wouldn't be aware, or she would slip back into such a withdrawal that she would cry until her throat would cough up blood. When I reached his bed, I knelt down beside him, and I told him how much I loved him. Even though Danny boy never knew me before I came here, he always trusted me in the dark when I walked in the bush with his little body carrying a gun that weighed almost as much as him. He shared his food when he wanted no more of it; he told me on several occasions, that if I weren't much older, and he weren't much younger, and we weren't here, he would never let me go until I agreed to marry him.

I prayed to God to let Danny boy live because he had to see the end of this war, and his little body should not have suffered in vain. I would tell him a moon story, and I thought he smiled when I told him that the yams were on their way from the moon.

Danny boy died two days after I had asked God to keep him alive. Nancy, who always had gone in to ask God to preserve and keep her son alive, had finally gone in the room, and looking at her little boy on the very few moments left of his life, she had said; "God, if possible, let this cup pass from me. Nevertheless, let not my will but Yours be done. I only ask that You help me handle whatever Your will turns out to be.

If he dies, take him to You. I do not know how I am going to live without him, but I will not argue with You."

We could very easily hear Nancy talk to God on behalf of her son, for though she was not screaming her heart out, there was an aching mother who did not want her son to die.

I feared for what might become of Nancy if God took Danny boy. I feared what might become of me.

After dinner, I sent Angela into Nancy's tent to bring her so that we could get her to accept even the tiniest morsel. We were just having an evening conversation where we talked mostly of the war and its destructions. When a commander or a higher standing soldier would pass by, we cursed the Ugandan government and spoke of the destruction we were getting set to ravage upon them. The children asked me about America, and when I would take them with me to that land where there are no worries, people dress their pets, and money falls like rain from the sky.

Angela came out of Nancy's room as one of the younger girls in the camp was asking me if I would forget her when next I returned to a life in America; a life I was beginning to see in a faraway past than I knew logically that it was. Angela had a sullen look on her face, and as she reached us, grabbing dizzily for the tree trunk

272

between Nancy's tent and hers. Samuel asked her what was wrong as we all inched our way towards the makeshift table where we were going to whisper our night prayers. Angela asked why this was always happening to her.

"Why what is always happening to you?" Samuel asked.

"Why am I always the one who finds out bad news first?"

"Find out what bad news?"

Unbeknownst to us, Joshua had slipped away in our curiosity and went into Nancy's tent. Before Angela could relay her news to us, Joshua slowly came to the dimly lit corner of the compound where we were sitting impatiently, with tears in his eyes almost unseen except for the shine of the lamp reflecting off his eyes, he answered Samuel's question. Danny boy was dead.

I turned immediately to look at Nancy, who was now coming out of her tent, truthfully expecting her to do just about anything, including taking her own life. As she walked over to us slowly, I wanted to run to her, hold her in an embrace, and never let her go. I wanted to tell her that God's plan was always best, and that we could not argue with it. But I was afraid. I was afraid that I was going to faint if I took an extra step; afraid that she wouldn't believe me, for barely I believed myself. The curious little ones inched behind Nancy as she sat down with us. The older girls held on to the smaller children from a very vacant Nancy. I could not move my feet after we had broken our embrace, and so I did not hear what she said when eventually she sat down. It was Angela who told me later that Nancy had gotten up in the room after she had walked in, kissed her son's head and stretched the cloth over his head. She turned to face toward the part of the compound where everybody was sitting, and solemnly she said: "Blessed be the name of the Lord. Joshua who had been standing there with uncertainty written over his face took off, his tiny feet headed straight for Danny boy, and at another sight of his lifeless friend, the little boy broke down with a voice that was already hoarse from crying over the days for his friend to come back running the byways with him again. Hearing him cry must have unplugged something in everyone because we all wailed that night. Even the makings of a man could not keep tears away from the eyes of the boys. In our mourning, each heart prayed to God silently in their own grief because for a few hours to come, we were stricken from sanity to a place of devoid of certainty, and a world we knew that the absence of calamity was to pass its way never again."

I'm still (I think),

Calista

Chapter 30

October 31, 2004

"What happens when somebody is abducted in America?"

The day is spent and we, women and girls, are sprawled on cloths we laid on the dirt to sit upon and be. My brothers in their efforts to remove any suspicions of our plans to escape fraternized with the other young boys who are listening to music and loudly laughing at the stories and jokes they were telling. The young girls sitting next to us shiver because they know all too well, that it is in this stupor that they will all be selected one by one for a ravaging of their small tender bodies. I look at the older girls - they do not shake; however dejectedly we may look, we do not shake. We know too well. We know too much. That relative joy I sneer at now when I think of, it is the one I share with most of the ladies. Being 'wifed' to only one man, though it can dehumanize you because you have been sold to him, no one else can touch you but him. Being 'unwifed', the other girls were at the mercy of any of the other boys who anxiously and frequently would become randy.

One of the younger girls came to sit on my lap. Immediately, I moved her away, sitting her down across from me and looking around to see if anybody else in the square was looking at us. I turned to the child who was now sitting with a hurt look on her face to explain:

"My siblings and I were abducted, but not like you." I tell her what happened on our way home to Kampala to join our parents at the conference for Hosanna.

With the rest of all their attention on me, I tell them a story they had never heard before.

****

I was in the General's bed laying on my back, watching the top of his tent and drawing figures in my mind across the tarp. My spirit came back to me much sooner than I cared for it to, still realizing the motions my body made beneath the weight of the General atop me. My eyes come back to his face continuing to build a hate I work hard to foster because I will need the strength of that hate to massacre him. He drips sweat onto my face as his eyes roll back into his head, and I wait for him to finally be finished with me. He lowers his face so close to mine I can smell his

278

unwashed breath which causes such a revolt in my stomach I begin to gag. Before he brings his repulsive lips to mine, I ask him a question:

"Why won't you kill me?" I ask him, summoning a look on his face that shows his lack of expectation of any speech from the girl who usually was almost lifelessly quiet, waiting for him to finish his degradation of her body. He rolls off from my stiff body and onto the other side of the mattress, while I reach for my dress on the floor on the side of me. I surmise with pleasure, that I have ruined whatever pleasure he intended to acquire from me that night. At the same time I hope he will provide me an answer I knew would be intricate to my flight from this place along with my siblings and as many people as I can convince that this camp was not life.

"Believe me, it is not because I don't want to. As soon as they keep their end of the bargain, I do not have to keep mine. If you behave the way you behave now, then woman, I will kill you."

"Who is 'they'?"

"Your parents. They are to deliver three million dollars to us in the next month, or you will all be killed."

"How? Why us? Why didn't you just abduct us like regular children? Why are we held for ransom?"

"Because your family will deliver the money to save your lives. The money will help us acquire more arms to purge Uganda of the evil that has taken it over. That is why you are here. "

"How did you pick us? Why us?"

"Because David went to kill someone who offered so much more than his life to him. That person offered you directly to us in exchange that David save his life. That is how you came to be pursued on your way home to Kampala."

"Who was it? What thing was in charge of selling us to you?"

"That is none of your business" he spat at me before sending me to bring in the next girl to him.

I walk to the doorway of the tent, moving the flap to exit the General's room but not before I turn around to I ask him:

"What happens when you get the money?"

He looks me in the eye, and with a stern raise of his eyebrow, he warned;

"Do not piss me off."

I wrap my dress around me, sympathetically tell the next girl that he is ready for her, and then make my way to the backyard after grabbing for the raffia sponge on top of the thatched kitchen roof.

I tell my siblings as soon as I can, that it was time to reason together and to put our minds exclusively on a plot to return home to the people who sorrowed for our return.

The plot was that my brothers were to participate in every single raid conducted at any chosen village as often as they could, and they were to intelligently deduce as to where they could intricately place information about where our camp was hidden. The plot was that my sisters would find some way to endure the assignments we were expected to undertake, and to stay alive long enough for our brothers to come back home to us. It was a joint worry on both ends. For them, they worried of me, asking me to be gentler and to bid my tongue to quietness so that they did not come home to mourning. For us, we prayed that those boys would come home walking on both legs, swinging their arms toward the camp beside them.

****

By the time I am finished with my explanation, the little girl is lying beside me. I bend toward her ear, and I whisper that while I cannot be killed, things can, and have been done to me to ensure that I stay within the parameters of obedience to that which has been instructed me; some of which has been to take those who were dear to me, and to mutilate, kill, or torture them before my presence. I tell her that I think they started with Samson, David's uncle, whom they took after I had seen him escape from the car to get help and never saw again. I told her I was worried for Samson, and had been hoping and praying fervently for his safety.

"Samson?" A girl not older than thirteen asks cocking her head to the side.

"Yes" I replied a little louder, thinking she could hardly hear me.

"The one they call Samba? That Samson?" She asks again with a slight rise in her voice.

"Yes" I answer again, confirming the familiar name I had never known how the man had acquired.

The girl asking me the questions regards another girl who looked much too similar to her to bear no relation. With a suspicious look in her eye, the other girl asks me:

"David's uncle? That Samson?"

Augustina, impatient from the questions that seemed to have a curious answer, asked the girls if they knew who Samson was and how they knew him.

"We know a Samson," The girl's sister answered, "but I do not think we are talking about the same Samson. The Samson we know could not possibly be a driver."

"Why do you say that?" I ask her.

"Because the Samson we know, the one they call Samba, the one who is David's uncle, is rich and quite famous for his wealth now. He has homes in both Kampala, and Kitgum. He is too wealthy to be anyone's driver. He has his own drivers.

I look at my sisters and wonder how it came to be that Samson became rich and famous in the time that we had been in this camp only the duration of three months. I see the same look of wonder in the squint in their eyes as the three of us commonly realize it could not have been a mere coincidence that Samson managed to run into van of abductors, and then vanished without a trace, leaving us at their mercy. It could not possibly be a mere coincidence that we were being held for a three million dollar ransom which I knew my parents were scrambling to pay, while Samson was not among the search parties looking faithfully for us, but was flying high in the riches that he had acquired without reason or explanation. Samson was the brains behind the affairs pertaining to our abduction, and he currently was enjoying the fruits of his labor.

The little girl turns around to lie on her back, and in the eyes with which she looks up at the starry sky, I can see the precocious twinkle in her eyes in the reflecting glint of the tiny lights that floated around the night sky. A precocious twinkle that is now diminished by the sweat of war on a body far too small to know the strength it demands of her. She heaves a great sigh before she asks me:

"What happens when someone is abducted in America?"

Chapter 31

July 5, 2005

My therapist brings me an apple today, and I take it, suspiciously staring intermittently between the apple and my therapist. I am unsure about the introduction of food and what to properly do with said introduction after its reception. She sits across from me and bites into her apple while staring at mine with a look of wonder I surmised could mean that I was supposed to follow suit. I still hold on to the apple because I do not want one. At least, not right then.

"I notice that you have not talked much about your life in America. Is there a reason for that?"

"Aren't you my therapist? Isn't that more of a question for you to answer?"

"Why do you expect that I should answer that for you?"

"Because you know why people do things that they do, even before they tell you. You just ask questions for courtesy reasons. Because you want me to feel important to have participated in my 'recovery', whatever that means."

"You don't think that I can help you?"

"In six months, I would feel just as better if I did not talk to you, as I would if I talked to you. That's what I think."

"Then why do you think you were meant to see me?"

"Because you can give me the determination to want to get better. By myself, I think I'd just wallow… or something like that."

"I do not think you'd wallow. I do not think you're a wallowing sort."

"And how do you deduce that?"

"Because, you could refuse to be here. You could tell this story with a hopelessness that you do not."

I want to agree a terrible lot with my therapist, that of course I am not hopeless. However, I shiver at the times when Sydney would wake up to find me under my bed shaking and drenched in sweat in a generously air conditioned house, flinching at the sight of her fingers raising my bed skirt to look at my desperate face. It may not be much more than hopeless that I cannot sleep without visions of blood that streams across a sky that bleeds its tears on it. I want a terrible lot to agree with my therapist, but I do not let myself, and I don't know why.

"I did not talk about America much more than the times that they asked about it. On one hand, I did not want to remember. It is a torturous thing to want heaven when you are in hell."

"Some do not consider America heaven"

"When you're in a bush hiding from bombs and bullets, eating soil while tying a string around your stomach so that you do not faint, you try not to think of anywhere else. Kampala was like the beach, and the U.S. was like, heaven."

My therapist gives me a nod I do not know if it is in agreement with what I said or an acknowledgement of it.

"What happens when a child is abducted in America?" She poses that little girl's question again to me.

"The efforts dispatched to find a missing person depends a great deal on your status in America. However, everybody has the basic package. The armed forces broadcast it among themselves in every state, there is something called an Amber alert, which tells most people who have access to informative systems, as much about an abducted person as it possibly can. If they know anything about the person who abducted you, they post that too. News stations broadcast about it as often as they can, and people form search parties that go into places they suspect the abductor may have gone. Much more than this I'm sure happens, but this is how much I know happens when someone is abducted in America."

I start to cry as I think far beyond the girl's questions to the life that now seemed too far away to have ever been real.

~ ~ ~ ~ ~ ~ ~ ~ ~ ~ ~ ~ ~ ~ ~ ~

One of the little girls who had been brought along with the five year old after the previous week's raid lay her back down on the ground and began to speak.

"We are animals. To the government, we are moles. We are a nuisance that they are waiting to slowly eradicate each other. Before they come for us, we are rats, scurrying about when they come, looking for places to hide before they close their traps over us. When the rebels catch us, we are camels and oxen, carrying their loads, being beaten. We are racehorses only good enough to do the hard work. When we grow old or tired, we are killed. Racehorses are better though; they are killed quickly. So I wait, I wait while I bore like the termite they are afraid of. Until one day, I hide securely in my castle and watch the foundations of their pride crumble to the ground."

~~~~~~~~~~~~~~~~~

"How old was that girl?" My therapist asked me.

"She was nine years old."

"Did she escape?"

~~~~~~~~~~~~~~~~~

Kelly was her name, and she was as precocious as can be. She found the joy in everyday, carefully telling us of her plan to run for Presidency because she would be good at it. She thought she would make an excellent candidate because she did not care for money, because as long as she could eat when she was hungry, and pay her rent, she did not need to continue to acquire money at the expense of forgetting the importance of paying mind to the little people. Kelly was going to travel to the U.S. to visit me and my friends, to tell us not to ask her about the evils that happened when she was nine years old; but to concentrate on the joys that have been her life since she left this place that edified nothing in a being so ethereal and delicate.

Kelly died at camp from food poisoning. She had woken up in the middle of the night not too long after that night, hunched over in pain. She vomited throughout the duration of her sickness, which did not last any longer than five hours from when it began, and I sat with her from the beginning to the end of it. I was at the end of it because she, from unbearable pain, begged me to set her free with a shot from my gun.

I remember disagreeing to do it. I remember fearing that I would no longer know Kelly. I wanted her to get better because I wanted Kelly to be President. I wanted Kelly to come to the U.S. and be my sister, to meet my friends, and for them to meet this girl who met me with this insurmountable strength that no story that I would ever tell of her could convey.

I asked Kelly how she expected me to shoot her. How she wanted me to get over that? How I was to get everyone to forget the evils I had done here?

She said to me:

"Do you remember when you taught us about what computers do, and what the internet does? Well, think about life like an internet search engine. When you do something wrong, it is going to be at the very top of the page. Do not fret about it or worry that when people search for you, they will find this person that you know in your heart you are not. Do good, and continue to do it, and the more you do good, the more they come up as well on the search engine; until one day, your evil is almost nonexistent."

I watch her dying body thinking about what Kony could possibly have been thinking when he decided this must have been the most appropriate way to bring peace to Uganda.

A prophet is not so far from mad man. They both see things that ordinarily are not apparent. They speak sometimes without understanding from the masses. They both claim to see into the future. They are both usually not the most recognized members of society to begin with. Joseph Kony is either a prophet, or he is a madman. Joseph Kony sees things that are not apparent. He speaks without understanding from the masses. He claims to see into the future. Prior to his reign of terror, he was not a recognized member of the society in the gravity in which he is today. The difference between a prophet and a madman is that a prophet works within the community; he puts his life on the line to save his people. He does not put the lives of his people in danger in claims to protect them. A prophet uses the resources that he works desperately hard to get for the benefit and harvest of his people. He does not loot, steal, and destroy people to garner their harvest for himself. A prophet gives up his own life for his people; he does not kill them. Joseph Kony is a madman.

Do you know how to turn a human being into an animal? Into a monster? Unforgiving, and unyielding? How does a man give his heart to the night wind to reap its heartless darkness? Give him intelligence without wisdom; passion, without focus; ambition, without vision; and a cause, without a heart.

How does one man control so many people that ordinarily would consider themselves rather rational and logical? How can a man garner the will of men who are greater than him both in number and in strength? I wanted to meet Kony. I wanted to kill him, even though I knew that whether or not I succeeded, my death sentence was signed at the mere thought of the plan. I wanted to spit in his face.

"You appealed to our desires. You persuaded our lust for good, fairness, and justice. Our loyalties flirted with your passions to set us free. So you took our weaknesses and made them bullets for your guns. You took our vulnerabilities and made them sharpeners for your swords. You possessed our hearts and set them on an evil fire with your bombs."

I wanted to kill Kony. If he comes back to the village, I will.

I kiss Kelly on her cheek telling her that I loved her and could not wait to see her again; which as I say, I realize that I meant it. If I did not have my therapist to give me determination, the memory of Kelly would not let me give in to my desire to wallow.

I cock my gun, and I disturb the still night air.

Chapter 32

July 12, 2005

"I waited further into our sessions to ask you this question because I needed for you to understand that I inquire for more information that the obvious."

My therapist is drawing on a piece of paper across from me. I have walked into the room to see her sitting cross-legged on the floor of her office with colored pieces of blank paper scattered all over the floor along with them were crayons with their colors even more exaggerated by the sunlight that streaked through the windows.

I sit across from her, and as if I know why those articles lay there surrounding my therapist in puerile fun, I pick up a pencil and begin to write on a blank red page.

"What was the hardest part of being abducted?"

I now know why her introduction. If I had walked into this woman's office, and she had started even our first ten sessions with that question, I would not have accredited to her, competence to care for me. By now, I am confident that there is more she wants of my answer than the apparent.

"When I was angry, threatened, or forced, I could be a soldier. To my sibling, I could be a sister; concerning their studies, I could be a teacher. To the General, with regards to the duties expected of me, I could be a wife – however reluctantly – but a wife nevertheless. To everyone, I could be a friend. I could help, love, and give my life for them if it ever was the answer to their freedom. I could be their truth that of course, God remembered them, loved them, saw them, and even then, however unbelievable, created them to be well, happy, and free.

What a child needed, what we all needed, what we all wanted was mom, and Mama; and try as I may have, I could not be a mother. The guilt alone from that, that was the hardest part, because I do not know if it ever was because I actually couldn't, or that I was too afraid to assume a role I so revered.

My mother, and my godmother – Sydney, and Rhys's mother, were the only mothers I knew too well. I know none other like them.

"What made your mother reverent?"

When I was a younger girl, I used to fixate on my mother's hands for significant amounts of time. I was fascinated by how those same hands by the end of the night would rub a generous size of Ben-gay over themselves to relieve a day long aches, almost as if they were down for the count, then would the next morning wake me up from sleep, swiftly ready her children for their days, and skillfully sort exactly the amount of spices that made each pot of food taste so divinely decadent. They were scarred from the needles that mended our clothes; sometimes, they were smooth from the creams and soaps she made, sometimes they would be rough from washing clothes, or the lines the years etched so definitively with wisdom in each mark. When I was resting, and those blessed hands gently rubbed my bare back, everything about them was almost forgotten. It was as if cottons of cloud fell softly upon me, sliding across as if only grazing the hairs that rose atop my skin.

My mother fascinates me; it is a genuine pride-filled fascination. She almost resembles the earth, like she sprang forth from it with the cassava, and the millet.

Against a sunset, with her feet moving majestically to the rhythms of an entenga, she shines like gold with the years hiding the ages in her youthful face. In her dance, she disturbs the sands with her feet gyrating under the dust that bathes over her as it mixes with the sweat from the heat of sunlight to glisten against the muscles that command her boogie.

Attributed to me by this woman, was an indomitable spirit; both to surrender to that which was greater than I, and to question that of which I was uncertain. How can the same person give me a punishment for wrong behavior in a way that made me feel like I will never speak to her again, and then confront me in a fashion that makes it all suddenly better, like blood stopped in its tracks while flowing from a wound?

One day, I walked into the kitchen where my mother was sitting by the stove grinding tomatoes with the mortar and pestle, while making sure that the pot did not boil over, while keeping an ear out to hear when any of her children should fall and shout for her healing chest to rest their head upon, and be soothed by the most familiar of music – mother's heartbeat.

That was the day my mother gave me the most unforgettable words that would, from then on, make me fearlessly proud of my people, our culture, our traditions, our land. All angers and apprehensions aside, my mother, that day, gave me pride in my identity.

She had been sick that day. Most of her time had been in bed being attended to by her husband, and one child after the other. At each mealtime however, she was found down in the kitchen preparing our meal, or overseeing my sisters and I while we attended to lunch that afternoon. My father had been in the kitchen asking her shortly before I had entered to allow him to prepare supper, while she went and got some rest. She declined his offer. When I entered, I asked her why.

"Because I am home," she answered. "When I am home, it is my responsibility to make dinner for my family."

"But Mama, times have changed; men can also cook."

"Yes, they can. But in our land, in our culture, men with wives do not cook."

"That's primitive Mama."

"Where did you learn that from?"

"Books; television…"

"What makes our ways primitive, and that of the people in the books you read, right?"

"The opposite of right isn't 'primitive', Mama."

"It isn't?" My mother asked me with a sly smile creeping up the side of her mouth.

"It is not a bad idea Mama. Maybe, if men here cooked, then they would be less controlling."

"Is your father controlling?"

"No."

"Does your father cook sometimes?"

"Yes."

My mother in not so many words, carried on to teach me that a person, a culture, a place that may do something that is not usual to me, is not better than me. It is different from me. It seems a simple enough lesson, but as I grew up remembering those words, I realized the work it took to manifest the purpose of them. My ways would be challenged several times by my American counterparts. My foods, accent, behaviors, and characteristics would be classified as "weird," "peculiar," "abnormal," and several other words that may or may not be politically correct. However, I found solace in the fact that my mother could cook; and she was there, so why wouldn't she. Why would she refuse to cook so that she could prove to my father that she should not always be expected to? Why would my mother climb a palm tree not because she particularly needed anything from atop the tree, but to prove she could do so? I found solace in the words that taught me that wrongdoing is not a cultural thing. It might be usual, it might be common, but it is not cultural. I may have been ashamed about the war, about the abuse that occurred from people against each other, but that was where it stopped. I am happy that that evening my mother was unselfish enough to teach me, that God forbid there comes a day when I am a single mother, all alone without family, with an illness that has me paralyzed, and my children are ready for dinner; my mother taught me the strength to get up long enough to feed my children. My mother taught me that our culture was right for me; it was healthy for me; it was designed for our people, and was relative to our growth. She taught me that everybody had an accent. Everybody was colored.

November 1, 2004

I sat on a bench behind our tent one evening, wondering how it had become so long ago since we had been home, since we had seen our family and loved ones. I wondered why other children seemed to be able to escape and not us. I knew that it made sense to wait until the most appropriate opportunity because I had four siblings who I refused to leave behind, and thus could not take advantage of every opportunity due to the difficulty of five people escaping and making it all the way home at the same time and as the same number. The siblings who did succeed in running from the camp never actually made it all the way home together all the time. Most of the them lost a sibling or lost each other, as most times neither would make it all the way across the border, all the way home.

I wondered about Rhys, about what was going on with him. Was he safe? Was he still in Uganda? Was he blaming me? The latter was the most angst-filled matter to contemplate. I did not know if Rhys was thinking that I should have listened and returned home with him, or if he resented me for being apart with so much uncertainty growing like the weeds along the paths that separated us. In corners of my mind, I knew he was far too sorrowful to resent me; that he was in too much pain blame me for not escaping this predicament while we had the chance.

I felt a hand on my shoulder, and flinched defensively. I turned around to see Augustina with wide white eyes frightened by my jerk, and holding her arms around her thin body. I apologized for frightening her before asking her to sit with me in the darkness both in the world around us, and in the inconsolable pits of our souls.

"What are you doing awake?" I eventually asked my immediate younger sister after we sat there wordlessly for moments, interrupted only by stifled breaths we were almost afraid to take.

"I could not sleep. I saw you when I looked out here, and so I stole away."

"That's dangerous, Aussie."

"I know. I know my sister. I just have missed you so." She said dropping her weathered face into the palms of her hands.

"I know," I reassured her "I miss you too" I finished, my throat breaking.

"You know, when we were at home, we lived under Mama and Papa's protection. I always knew that when I got in way over my head, there they'd be taking it off of me and onto themselves... well... letting me carry it for a while... maybe spanking you while you're carrying it for a while, and then taking it onto themselves."

We chuckled softly at such fond memories of our parents.

"But...," Augustina continued, "...I never really knew just how much they protected us. All their never-ending arsenals of rules, all their over-watchfulness, their butt-into-everything nature that I used to think I was too old to tolerate. I want it back," She finished looking up at me with saucer-large eyes, which were struck by the tiniest glint of the clouded moon in the sky. I saw the tears that stood just atop her lower eyelids threatening its cascade down her cheeks as I reached for my sister drawing her close to me as her body shook with silent sobs, repeating: "I want it all back. I want to be told when to be home. I want to be told when to date. I want to be told when and how to speak to my parents. I want it all back, as long as it is Mama and Papa. They'll tell me that it is all because they love me, and I'll believe them.

I continued to hold Augustina as the tears, irrespective of my will to keep them at bay, came crashing down my cheeks. I stroked my sister's hair as I silently whispered to her one of the poems my father would recite to us. It was a ritual of my father's to do this in the times when the power company cut the electricity. We would sit in the living room, bellies full from another delightful dinner made by my Mama's hands. With no complaints, we would sit and enjoy the breeze that wafted through the curtains and onto our very contented selves. My father would start to sing an old traditional song, and then he would start to recite a poem from William Shakespeare, an author he loved very much to study and read as a young boy and man. We received his voice with that breeze that brought with it secrets from the neighbor's own stove, divulging what the houses yonder had or were having for dinner.

I recited a poem that night to Augustina. A piece my father had recited to us on several occasions. One that he had recited to us two days before our truck was veered off the road. One that we mouthed along with him because we had grown accustomed to it from his frequent recitation of it.

To be, or not to be: that is the question:

Whether 'tis nobler in the mind to suffer

The slings and arrows of outrageous fortune,

Or to take arms against a sea of troubles,

And by opposing end them?

To die: to sleep;

No more; and, by a sleep to say we end

The heartache and the thousand natural shocks

That flash is heir to, tis a consummation

Devoutly to be wished.

To die, to sleep;

To sleep perchance to dream: ay, there's the rub;

For in that sleep of death what dreams may come

When we have shuffled off this mortal coil,

Must give us pause.

There's the respect

That makes calamity of so long life;

For who would bear the whips and scorns of time,

The pangs of disprized love, the law's delay,

The insolence of office, and the spurns

That patient merit of the unworthy takes,

When he himself might his quietus make

With a bare bodkin?

Who would fardels bear,

To grunt and sweat under a weary life,

But that the dread of something after death,

The undiscovered country from whose bourn

No traveller returns, puzzles the will,

And make us rather bear those ills we have

Than fly to others that we know not of?

Thus conscience does make cowards of us all;

And is sicklied o'er

With the pale cast of thought

And enterprises of great pith and moment

With this regard their currents turn away,

And lose the name of action.

Augustina grew quiet after the poem, and was for the present, consoled.

She looked up at me again, this time with inquisition in her eyes, and she asked me to tell her about Luke. It occurred to me at that moment, that this was Luke's first visit to our home, and that my siblings did not actually know anything about him. I pondered on where to start as I wondered if they'd ever get to get out of here to truly know their brother in-law.

Of course, they had met him during their visits to the States. But it was sparingly so because we spent most of our summers as a family at our vacation home, which Luke visited scarcely.

Chapter 33

July 19, 2005

I am sitting back in my therapist's office, and today I do not talk much. She wonders why, and I explain the difficulty of going back to the dismay she wishes me to divulge to her. I ask her for an easy day; to talk about something, anything that wouldn't cause me to cry or wish that I woke up with different memories than I was captive to revivify.

"Okay," she gives, "... tell me about Luke. He seems to be an important character, being that he is Sydney's fiancé, but how does he become part of your families' history."

"Sydney and I met Luke when we were fourteen years old. He was Rhys's football teammate. They were both juniors in high school at the time."

"Did they like each other immediately?"

"Sydney did not really fancy him."

"Why not?"

"Because he was... hot."

"Really? I thought girl's your age liked that in men."

"Do women your age not like that in men?"

"In my time, we did not really define boys as 'hot'"

I laughed in spite of myself, thinking of the woman's choice of words. "In her time" made it seem like she had died to her youth and was someone who resided not in that person any longer. My parents always taught me and my siblings that "your time" was still in play as long as you were still alive.

"Sydney thought that 'hot' boys were aware of it, and thus played on it at girls. Luke was a junior, and so an upperclassman. That made him the prime rib. Girls threw themselves shamelessly at him, and Sydney thought he reveled in that."

"Did he?"

I shook my head going back to that time, when the greatest problems we had had to deal with were so juvenile. Luke was very shy and sweet by nature; it made him very uncomfortable, the attention he would get from the shameless hags at school. It fascinated him that

Sydney did not give in with them to (what he would later describe as...) torment him.

Luke was sweet and kind in nature. He had a quietness that did not make us uneasy around him; in fact, it made us like him all the more. It was a quietness that did not even call attention to him for being quiet; and the more we liked him, the more it discouraged Sydney from being apprehensive of him.

It did not take long though for Sydney to like Luke. While he did not display his charm on her, he did not surrender to her playing hard to get either. He gave her as much attention as she gave him. At first. When we had completely become sold to Luke, Sydney dropped her guard; as much of it as she could drop for a boy she was a little over acquainted with. Several dinners with my family had acquired for Luke, my parents adoration as well, so Sydney, trusting my parents' judgment, not only cared for Luke as a friend, but as something more. There was a slight problem though. We were not allowed to date in high school.

When our American parents had told us of their arrival to this decision, that we could not date in high school, Rhys, Sydney, and I had decided to go to school in Uganda. Our parents, however, had this (what we considered) inconvenient habit of consulting each other on any decision we discussed with them. My parents agreed with their decision, and so we stayed put. Sydney, who was going to ask my parents what they thought of her dating Luke, withdrew her wonder forthwith.

That, however, did not stop Luke. It started with him leaving little presents in the form of chocolates, coupons for a free scoop of ice-cream, and my personal favorite, a shoulder padding for her school bag strap.

Sydney began to look forward to seeing Luke everyday at school, and even though she knew she could not date Luke, she anticipated his attention to her with unconcealed glee waiting patiently for the time that she could.

"No one if possible was happier for Sydney to care for Luke's advances more than me." I said coming back to the present day that found me sitting across from a soft-spoken therapist.

"What do you mean?" she asks me.

"I wanted Sydney to like Luke. It was important to me."

"Why was that important to you? Why was it important that Sydney be interested in Luke?"

"Because in my head, I had Rhys, and I knew he could like me too. I mean, we'd never talked about it, but... I do not know how to explain it; we lived together, and so emotions were plainer..."

"And you wanted Sydney to have Luke? Why?"

"It wasn't really that I wanted Sydney to have Luke as much as it was that I wanted her to have somebody."

I think back onto that time, and I am ashamed of myself because that was not a noble enough reason to coax Sydney into affection for someone else. She was neither lonely, nor was she an old maid.

I thought far into my fantastical world that inhabited Rhys and I, and in the corner, I saw Sydney, who would be left alone by the sister she was so close with; a sister who now had someone just as close to her, leaving Sydney to herself.

I am greatly indebted to Luke for removing any worth from any shame or guilt I may feel. When Sydney became a junior, and Luke a college freshman, the halls and lobby of our school still saw his presence waiting for Sydney with a bouquet of flowers on Valentine's Day, or for lunch when we became seniors and were allowed out of school grounds for a period.

"What happened to your parent's rules about dating?" My therapist asks.

"They did not know."

"You did not tell them?"

"No"

"Why not?"

"Because we understood the reason for their rule, but we thought that Sydney and Luke were too exceptional to interrupt. We did not know if our parents would be as accommodating as Rhys and I, so we did not tell them. It was harmless enough to trust."

On the day we graduated high school, Luke told our parents that he loved Sydney and needed their blessing to formally ask her on a date. My dad asked Luke why he felt this was an appropriate time to ask him. Unbeknownst to us, our parents knew all along what had been going on between Luke and Sydney, and I suppose in retrospect, that did not come altogether as a surprise to us. Nevertheless, Luke was granted permission to formally date Sydney; and beautiful was the day I watched Sydney for the first time saunter across the driveway into Luke's car as he drove her away into their first date.

Chapter 34

To err, they say, is human, and to forgive, divine. Personally, I have come to believe that to err is human, to forgive, divine, and to forget, celestial.

When Augustina had turned eleven years of age, she had begun to discuss with my parents her desire to leave home. Isaiah's and my absence from home though very much hailed by my parents caused them some longing that always seemed to tug at them. They were not keen on letting go of any more of their children. When Augustina raised her anxiety concerning the present situation arising even worse with every passing year, my parents had decided to move the family to Kenya until there was some steadier form of peace. My father, however, would travel back and forth to Hosanna, away from the family more frequently as it was a task that had to be done.

Augustina unbeknownst to me between when they had moved to Kenya and when I had returned home – about a six month lapse – had begun to grow in indignation towards me.

I worried that Augustina was seeing the easy part of America that was fleeting, and freshly painted. It did not help her desire that every year, she came to the U.S. to partake of its 'milk and honey' lifestyle. She was attracted to a simpler life she saw in the summer vacations she enjoyed with us. I was worried that she did not ponder beyond escaping the hardships of war into escaping the hardships of not only being black in America, but being a black African in America. There would be frustrations that would build from the assumptions made about a land that even though it frustrated her, tied her heart devotedly to it. There was the difference of school schedules, expectations, and the weather. More so, there were the difficulties of going through all of that with parents who lived thousands of miles across the waters.

According to my sister, whose letters to me never indicated it, she was angry with me for not supporting her desire (I would later find out) to come and stay with us in the U.S. I did not know that she felt deserted by me. When I had come home after their move to Kenya, I apologized to Augustina for any way in which she may have felt that I erred terribly toward her, and she forgave me, which was divine. Forgetting, on the other hand, I never actually felt that Augustina necessarily trusted me again after that. It wasn't an obvious apprehension that I necessarily felt all the time, but I knew that even to the minutest extent, it was there.

I know that no matter how much I had hurt Augustina by not being there during the important times of her life, she would always forgive me because that was what we did in my family. We forgave each other and showed love, because we were family. When Augustina started to show signs of her frustrations towards me, my siblings in some subtle ways expressed how much they wish they did not have to tell me aspects of their lives that one should assume their sister was there to witness. My brothers seemed to convey almost successfully that they had forgotten any hardening of the heart they may have ever felt at me. Sometimes though, when they would tell me of events that had happened in my absence, they would finish with "if you had been here." They said this so often, in fact, that if I had trouble understanding that part of the bible where Martha says it to Jesus, I no longer did now. I could have overlooked the fact my childhood friends were now letting me have whatever I wanted 'so that I wouldn't leave'. I was also informed by my friends that one of them refused to come to the house for a visit because I had failed to attend her graduation from primary school to secondary school. Another friend was upset that I was not at her wedding. Angela did not really let me know what her problem with me was, but I rationed that if everybody had a beef with me, then so must she.

Augustina, I never quite understood what her matter truly was with me. I could understand my siblings wanting to be selfish with their older sister who went from giving them all the attention in the world, to suddenly being completely physically gone from them. Augustina was only four years younger than me, and it was not in her nature to be petty. I suppose that I expected a maturity from her than her age and the situation in which she was faced with could afford her.

My parents were a little tricky for me. I knew that they would not let me stay home even if they or I wanted it so; but I also knew they missed me terribly and wished the current state of affairs was different. I had posed to them the question as to why they would not let Augustina come to the U.S., to which they had replied that their reasons soared above missing her. My parents put it very plainly with me: Isaiah and I were the savers of our family. If anything were to happen to them, Isaiah and I were to make sure that the legacy of our family lived on forevermore. It was not about the best schools or the best of anything; after all, my siblings went to the best American school in Kenya. It was about what they deemed important, and necessary. Isaiah and I weren't given the high life and freedom to go away from the worst to the best. We were handed an ancestry to preserve. We were handed a responsibility.

The person who took away any tension between my siblings and I, was my grandfather. I had actually come back home for a visit a few months before because he was on his deathbed, and my parents wanted him to bless me before he died. He summoned me and my siblings to him, to tell us the most important thing that we must believe for the rest of our lives, that there was nothing that was more important than the person who comes for you when the billows start to roll.

"You wanted Calista to come home; here she is like she has always been as often as she can. It does not matter when she comes, when you wake up in the morning, she's here, and not gallivanting in town bars and the streets. You all need each other now more than ever."

We all fell very silent.

"Do not fight any longer please" he asked us with a weak voice but with a very commandingly strong heart.

"Yes Papa" we all replied. I looked around the room into the faces of my sisters and brothers, and I saw inside their hearts that they had forgiven me. I had always known they will. Things started to get even better after that, Augustina wasn't distant any longer, and there wasn't an apprehension there anymore. The most important thing was that my family knew that I loved them, and that I always thought about them.

I returned to the U.S shortly after my grandfather died, and my family returned to Uganda to bury him. They would not return to Kenya again before I would join them with Rhys, Sydney, and Luke to celebrate our engagement.

I come back to the place where my sister is holding on to me on the bench in the backyard in the dark. I feel her warm breath on my arm as she sleeps almost soundly on my lap. I think about the years between then and now, the pride I feel in the woman I am gently rocking, and I envy a strength I knew at that age, I never possessed. Most of all, I found just a pocket of joy in the knowledge that my sister and I, were close; and every day with these children of my mother, I am handed a trust that I hope I aspire passionately to.

Chapter 35

November 3, 2004

I struck the match to light the kerosene lamp. The wick flickers and I am once again delivered from the black night and its stronghold reaching far deeper into me than the present darkness.

David came into the kitchen and stood by the door and knowing very well that it was him, I did not look up, but allowed him to stand there watching my movements. My sisters looked at him, then at me, catching the corner of my eye. He walked over to where I was squatted giving the rice a second washing, He gently brushed my hair to the side. I took my face from him and shifted my chair a few inches away from where he was stooped too close to me. I had always imagined that I could forgive David for his many indiscretions towards me, including taking away his friendship from me just because I did not return his affection in the gravity he would have preferred, but for David to facilitate a plot to destroy my family, that, I could never forgive. In my many plans to set me and my siblings free, I would take David's life without a second thought, if it presented itself as the only way out.

He heaved a great sigh before walking out of the kitchen, stopping at the door just long enough to tell me that he had no choice in bringing me here, although, it was not difficult when all he had to do was tap as frequently as possible to the bitterness in his soul toward my dissolution of his love for me.

I purse my lips as I reach for the pot, and begin to dump the wet rice from the basin into it. Augustina was blowing furiously at the embers alight in the hearth, while patiently I waited for the flames to erupt to match the one in my chest against whatever situation that suddenly had Augustina in a kitchen with me cooking for a husband whom she did not love.

Angela drew close to me on a three-legged stool and put her head on my shoulder. She raised it up again looking me in the eye.

"Cali? What is love?" She asks with such expectance in her innocent eyes. I looked up quickly to gaze in her face before she sat down on the low stool with a timid smile on her face, as if she already knew something that I did not know but may very well intelligently suspect. With a very firm voice, and raise of my eyebrow, I answered my sister that love was that very dangerous emotion that was severely forbidden in this death camp that was presently our place.

"I know," she replied, "but I still want to know."

"You want to know what love is?" I asked looking at her, and when she nodded, I relented.

"Okay..." I started and I reached for the hem of my skirt to the tiny slit I had made into it, folded it over, and hidden my ring inside of. I turned the ring in my hands; the ring I received while promising to love forever the one who had asked me to marry him.

I told my sisters about the day that Rhys had asked me to be his wife, to spend the rest of my life with him.

"Why did you say yes?" Augustina whispered still overcome by the same awe that had seized me when Rhys had proposed.

"Because, Rhys and I were created for each other. I don't believe that there is only one person for everybody, but if I do not love Rhys, I'm never going to love anybody else. I have known that since I was thirteen years old.

"What made you know? Angela asked with her hands clasped together, and her eyes closed in wonderment.

Augustina and I both look at each other in confusion as to where Angela had to be in her mind, we then looked at her with a suspicious glint in our eyes.

"What are you thinking about?" Augustina asks her accusatorily.

"I'm making up a romantic comedy in my head."

"Because...?" I asked her.

"Because I'm in a death camp here, I am going to try to squeeze as much of a romantic movie in my head as I can out of this, there is no point correcting me here."

Augustina and I snicker, and I, in spite of myself, acquiesce to my sister's imagination.

Rhys and I did not really fall in love the conventional way, I suppose, so it is difficult to pin point when exactly I did fall in love with him, or if it happened at a particular time. Our love was not traipsing past us in the air and then caught like a bug that bit us into passion. Our love was usual, obvious, and a matter of time, not just in one place. I fell in love with Rhys over and over again whether it was on Christmas day under the mistletoe in the courtyard where Rhys kissed me under the snow that fell against the eaves, or the times when he silently would sit listening to my rant about yet another frustration. Rhys and I were not always good at keeping our affections for each other as private as we imagined we were because our parents did raise up their notice of our obviousness about each other, and wanted us to make them aware of our decisions, after of course, I graduated high school.

Because Rhys and I spent a lot of time together covering the tracks of Sydney and Luke's yet disallowed relationship, we spent a lot of time fostering ours as well.

I stopped in my story to inquire of my sister more sternly as to what had their curiosity about love, and why they could not bypass that curiosity in a place where it would be most dangerous to attempt such an affair.

Angela looks at Augustina, who looks back at her, then at me, and then down to the hem of her skirt which she nervously is pinching.

"There was a boy I never got to show you. His name is Wilson." Augustina tells me shyly.

"You have a Wilson?" I asked her with a surprised raise of my eyebrows.

Angela nods to me with a sly glint in her eye. "She has a Wilson."

"I didn't talk about him sooner because I didn't see the use. I have tried to forget about him because I wonder if he even thinks about me; if he will forgive me for all the things that I have done wrong here; if he will believe me that I thought about him no matter where I was or what I was doing. I wonder whether he will marry me, or if he will think I am a bush girl, and therefore, irredeemable. I did not tell you because I think about him all the time, but I was hoping it will go away because it does me no good here. "

"So why are you telling me now?"

"Because I want to know if this is love, as I hope desperately that it is not. Because if it is love, it will never go away; if he does not love me back, I am doomed. This camp is heartbreak enough. If we get out of here… when we get out of here, I am ready to be happy again. So tell me, sister, is this love?"

My head goes swimming as I mull my sister's tragedy in my mind. I hopelessly search between the truth she wants it to be, the truth that it actually might be, and if I even know what that truth might be. I don't want to hurt my sister, so I find a palatable answer that allows the truth to remain the truth at the same time as reality sits indissolubly in my sister's stomach.

"Who is Wilson?"

"Wilson was a former child soldier I met at Hosanna when we all returned from Kenya last year. I was the first one he spoke to, and the only one he would tell his story, so Papa wanted me to work with him all the time. That is why I am afraid, Cali; I am afraid that he knows exactly what I will have to do, and he has given up that there is hope for me because of how hopeless he was."

"Did you two ever talk about him possibly being captured again?"

"He told me once that he was afraid of falling for me because if they capture him, I will forget."

"What'd you say?"

"I asked him if he would forget me if I ever got abducted. He said that he would come looking for me. Tell me Cali; am I in love with Wilson?"

I breathe out aloud, and I ask my sister what she wants me to say.

"I want you to say that I'm in love with Wilson, and that he is in love with me too, and that he is waiting for me to come out of here."

"You're in love with Wilson; he is in love with you too, and he is looking for you." I answered relieved that the truth, and the reality are both the same this time.

Chapter 36

November 4, 2004

I was out in a corner of the square beside the storehouse
beating the rice that we had without permission harvested
from fields that belonged to the villagers who worked hard
to plant the only sustenance for most. We were sieving
the grains from the chaff when we heard them coming
back – the children and commanders who had gone to
fight the Ugandan army for territory so that we did not
have to move even closer to the border of Sudan. I had
told my brothers to fight as hard as they could because as
much as I disliked telling them shooting at other human
beings, we needed desperately to stay away from
Khartoum, and if we kept getting the threats of an
impending government army, we were going to be
uprooted, and sent further toward the border.

I first saw my brother, Samuel running towards us. I
dropped my rice beater running to him, concern written
boldly over my face, checking him from a distance to see if
there was red water running from anywhere on him. We
reached each other where he informed me that the

General had ordered the presence of two of the senior wives along with me at the middle square immediately. I informed my sisters, as those women had come to be such to me due to the amount of time we had grown to spend together, and the secrets of freedom we ached for that we divulged to one another. Those girls helped me learn the customary expectations of the commanders in that camp when my siblings and I first came. They washed the blood from my body when I was beaten, they found the funniest anecdotes to settle any anxieties I may feel, even when they carried so much more than I knew I did in my heart. I worried for these girls as I wished I could take them home. I wished they had the kind of parents I had. The ones who were actively looking for their children wherever they were and finding no solace until all their children had been found. I wished they had the kind of community that would see the strength in the escape they so cautiously conspired to make. I wished they had the kind of people who saw the glory in the bullets that so unforgiving still sat in their shoulders, in their legs, and in the nape of their necks. I wished that the men who may love them until they heard the story of their bush lives and then desert them, would be patient to help them extract the thorns that were hidden in the soles of their feet. To give medicine to the aches they had become so adapted to that when it goes away, it almost feels like heaven. I cry for these women when they cannot see because I know that if they saw, they wouldn't let me. I wonder what I could possibly do to repay them for a kindness they should have been too deficient of emotions to supply me. I cry because I do not know which of them I could lose tomorrow, and that was the worst of it all. I could not help loving these sisters of mine, which was dangerous in this unpredictable hell fire. I was putting it all on the line knowing that nothing was guaranteed for us. I did the only thing that I could for these women in telling them stories of a world they have never been to, capturing their minds by delivering them to fantasies of sky scrapers, and Times Square. I would take them to Mall of America, and Niagara falls; show them ice cream sundaes and carnivals. I walked them through the halls of school, teaching them things about Western Civilizations, Napoleon Bonaparte, and the Titanic. I acted my favorite scenes from my favorite shows as I tried my best to be to them - all the people I used to watch with my family, sitting under blankets cuddling with one another. In the secret places of the dark, I sat with them to draw mathematics into the ground, teaching them the things that our evil lords discouraged. Knowing it was the officials' worst nightmare, and that with that knowledge, they one day would grow in the courage to disbelieve, to challenge, to wage a war against a pathless battle, I taught them about government, the qualities of a good leader, the makings of a worthy master, the purpose of society and the qualities that make anyone a worthy candidate to govern a people. I told them that a man, who claims to be committing these atrocities for the good of his people, faces another enemy. What kind of leader robs, mutilates, murders his own people who he is claiming to fight for? He is not fighting for the Acholi, he is fighting the Acholi. Our President is not getting whatever message he is trying to send because he has no message. He is an inadequate and ineffectual leader who may have had a good passion to bring good to his people. That passion, if there ever were any, was clouded at the first raid where he was presented with the reaping of other people's hard work. He commanded armies that were inspired by fear and terror. Driven by his own drivel, he has no consistent mission, no constant plan, and no righteous agenda as he preaches to have. I taught them to clean their minds of the lies they had been told because it was done to manipulate their minds to believe that anyone out there, if they did escape, who told them that they were anything less than fearfully and wonderfully made was telling them lies. I told them that places like Hosanna were there, and that one day we would defeat a spineless society full of stigmas placed on warriors such as ourselves. I told them that when they do get home, never to slump or depend on the acceptance on the society, but to carry their heads up so to inspire the people around them to believe that victory is what separates the fearless that ran through with thorns and bullets, from a village of cowards. I loved those women, and feared greatly the adoration I had for them, because they were me, and I, them.

As I ran with them to the square where we had been called to, I prayed to the Almighty God that none of these women would be used for target practice today for a reason that was not good enough to extinguish a human life, or really any reason for that matter. There, lying on the ground was David in the center of a group of boys who were looking him over. I looked at the boys who had come back from their overnight mission, then at my brothers who were covered in dirt and blood. Samuel looked at me with dead eyes, and Jacob just kept staring at David on the ground with his mouth open, blood dripping from his neck. I composed myself at a sight I was expected to have become acquainted with by now, staring coldly at the General, who had ordered for me.

"David was injured in battle today." He barked, mostly to everyone than he did precisely to me.

"You are not kidding" I thought to myself.

To say that David was injured was a glorified way of describing the boy whose labored breathing and the infrequent rise and fall of his chest were the only signs of life in him. He was bleeding from his legs, and the back of his shoulder. He was also bleeding from behind his head where a bullet had just grazed through the side and come out the other leaving a gaping wound. David was in an un-medicated, mind numbing, consciousness-stripping pain. And I enjoyed it.

David, despite all I had been through in this camp, all the horrors I was made privy to, all the sins I committed against souls who songs I had no right to withdraw; David's betrayal was the absolute worst. It seared my heart when I thought about how a boy I grew up playing with could be the filth lying before me. A boy I once called a friend, who now would not only deny me, but sell me to a commander for a status in the ranks of malevolence. I am saddened deeply in my heart that I must admit that as I watched him there, I hoped the commander had called to ask me to keep him alive as long as possible with no alleviation to his pain.

I watched him squirming on the ground, and I wanted him to see my face. I wanted him to see that I was the only one standing over his head, waiting for thumbs-up to gut him slowly, to sever his limbs from him with a shaving razor. I want him to see me rise above him.

That, however, is not what the General commands me to do. After praising the mighty man of valor that was the filth lying on the ground, after proclaiming of his great service to our group of rebels, he ordered me and the other wives to tend to David as princely as we were afforded to do so. His life depended on us, and it would be one of our lives for his, if he were to die.

The other wives carried him to the tent I used to share with my siblings before we were issued into separate quarters. We were never to leave him alone, so, three women were nominated to stay with him until the morrow. Since it was not my turn to be of service to the General that night, I volunteered as well.

~~~~~~~~~~~~~~~~~

"Why?" My therapist asks me as she sets out a chess game. "Do you play chess?" She asks me, throwing my pieces to me and arranging hers on her side.

"No. I have never played."

"Me neither," she replies with a smile ever so sly in delivery.

"So why are you setting up for a game that you do not know how to play?"

"Because it is as fun pretending to know how to play."

"What sense does that make?"

"About as much sense as volunteering to watch a boy for whom all you wanted was death."

I am quiet, and heave a labored sigh swallowing through the dryness in my throat.

"Why?" She asks again, moving a pawn.

"Because, I wanted to kill him" I answer emphatically. She motions for me to move one of my chess pieces. I do. She continues:

"But you were ordered to make sure he did not die." She moves another pawn.

"I found it ironic; an enraging irony, that I was being ordered to preserve the one life I wanted to take. The one life! When it came to the people whose lives I thought were to be preserved, David's did not even grace the shadow of that list." I moved a piece at her beckoning.

"Did you kill him?"

"I did not get a chance to."

"No?"

I shake my head.

"The other women stopped you?"

I smile.

"No, no they didn't."

I move my queen.

Chapter 37

The three other women were sitting on the other corner of the tent when I came back with a bowl of water, and scraps of cloth. Next to the scraps of cloth, I set down a small package wrapped with a small banana leaf which I open to reveal the mixture of salt, and ground sweet fire peppers. I look over David's near naked body laying on the mat bleeding from a hundred open bloody scars. I dip my hand into the water in the bowl, then into the mixture in my hand, and then gently I rub it into an open wound.

The women run toward me in the second before it takes David to feel the awful sting, and to send a scream tearing into the dense evening air across the square. They stuff the scraps of cloth into his mouth muffling his screams before I continue in my wickedness. With every muffled scream, I am played scenes in my mind of the evils that were David's deeds towards me. I remember the day I had begun to refuse to ever forgive David for orchestrating our abduction.

The group of soldiers who were chosen for a mission would further be divided into sub-groups. Each group had a task assigned them to carry out when they reached the frontlines or the districts they were to raid, molest, and loot. I prayed fervently to God, to keep my brothers from being put in whatever groups did the killing, the mutilating, or burning houses with family members still inside. I offered Thanksgiving that they were not expected so far to take as many lives as each member of their troop usually did.

David never allowed my brothers to kill, which naturally would seem saintly of him. However, my brothers were reported to the Chief Commander and the General as to have gone astray from the duties they were assigned. David knew this would always be my brothers' plight; that they would come back to camp, be reported for their disregard of orders, and be sentenced to unspeakable cruelties. David, on the other hand, got constant praises for taking their responsibilities onto himself, garnering promotions to even higher ranks. While my brothers suffered punishments of starvation, whipped with acid coated canes, and caged with their hands suspended by ropes from the ceiling, David got a choice of a girl for his service at his leisure. Angela was always his victim, to the point that it happened so often to my little sister that after their missions, and David and his co-officials were granted any maiden who was not wedded to any other at the camp, Angela would walk to David's tent. He would look at me with dancing eyes of victory as he walked proudly in to join Angela.

I remembered him beating me unconscious on that first day of training. I remember him forcing us to kill people who did us no wrong. I think about the delusions that suffered my brain even up onto the day of our abduction. The day I stared the Satan in David straight in the eye.

~~~~~~~~~~~~~~~~~

"What do you mean by delusions?" Asked my therapist as she packs up the chess game we had wrongly played.

"I was packing... I was packing to leave for my last trip to Gulu, when Sydney came into the room. She sat cross-legged on her bed resting her elbow on her lap, her chin in her palm. She sat quietly watching me pack. It is hard for most to believe, but as chatty with other people as Sydney and I can be, we can be very quiet with each other. I think we are that comfortable not having to fill the silence and still hearing everything. Sydney and I can have almost an entire conversation wordlessly. When we returned from captivity, Sydney would tell me that she recited letters to me in the wind. I would tell her that I knew, and that I heard them. We seldom needed words – Sydney and I.

However, that evening, as she sat on the bed and watched I knew that words were essential to something I already knew was troubling her."

"Was there something troubling her?"

April 29, 2004

"My, my, what nuisant mind you have there, sissy." I say jokingly to my best friend and sister without turning to look at her.

"Is nuisant a word? Anyway, the better to be concerned my dear," she sighs.

"Yeah? What are you concerned about?" I asked sitting on the edge of my bed.

"David."

I do not respond right away as my eyes dart to both sides to figure of which David she spoke, and what he had done that was so concerning to Sydney to bring her down at a rather exciting time of our lives.

"What about David?" I ask, hoping that with that her reply I should very well know "What about David."

"When was the last time you talked to him?" She asks me, the wrinkles still obstinately remaining on her face.

Oh. That David.

"Two years ago, after we had returned from our last visit, he had written me a letter about how angry he was that I was with Rhys. He thought Rhys tricked me into being with him."

"Tricked you?"

"I tried to tell him that I could not keep receiving letters from him that were so hateful and mean. I told him that if his next letter made me feel guilty for loving someone else other than him, I would stop reading the letters he sent me."

Sydney walked over to my dresser and opened the middle small one to pull out a stack of letters that were yet unopened.

"I am supposing that his next letter held the same bitterness as it always did because you did not read these," she says flipping through the letter still bound by the rubber band I had secured them with.

"Nope" I answer emphatically pursing my lips in protest to any furtherance of concerns with David."

"What if we see him? What if he comes by and… do we just act normal?" Sydney asks ignoring my desire to quell this particular conversation.

"I will try to talk to him if he comes by, but he has not been coming by that much since we were sixteen. I doubt he will come by now."

"David was our friend. We all kind of grew up together. How do you leave that? How do you let that go?"

"I don't know Sydney. I have never had to before."

"Me neither."

Chapter 38

I was beating furiously at a pathetically wincing David, who coughed into the cloth being held over his mouth by the other women when my brothers came running into the tent. They rushed at me and tried to pull me away from David, but I freed myself from their grip and proceeded with my blinding rage exerting itself on an already severely wounded David.

My brothers at that time employed another tactic, which involved some verbal threats about getting the Chief Commander who would not care what amount of money was on my head.

"He can always lie!" they tried to scream some sense into me that my presence is not needed to get any monies from my parents.

"They do not need you. Not in his place they don't!"

I realize what they are saying to me, and I agree; however, my hands with a mind of their own continue their ferocious attack on David, who by now is making no movement save for reflexive jerks at the punches that land over him.

Angela and Augustina rush in because, as I found out later, Joshua had been beckoned upon by my brothers to summon some reinforcements.

"Cali!" they call in their loudest whispers. "Stop!"

"He saved our lives!" Angela says a little louder this time.

I stopped beating David long enough to listen for an explanation to the absolutely impossible.

"How did he save our lives?" I ask breathlessly searching for the hope to believe their words. "He knocked me out on the first day of training!"

Augustina reached for the cloth that was hanging on David's face, and dipped it in the water.

"That is because his overzealous behavior took center stage to your insolence. The Chief Commander would have killed you. David just used you as an example of a beating, which evidently pacified his loathed highness!"

"He molested Angela!" I hissed, still refusing that there was any semblance of good in David.

"He did not..." Angela started, taking off David's shoes from him. "He took me to his room so that the other boys would not touch me. He didn't do anything to me."

"He got the boys in trouble. He caused them to be beaten almost every time that they came back from a mission."

"We would rather have been beaten..." started Samuel, "...than have to take a life. David knew that we did not want blood on our hands, and so he made sure that we did not get blood on our hands."

"Did you know that all along? Did you know that was his plan all along?" I asked them.

"Yes." They answered quietly.

"Why didn't you tell me?! Why did you let me continue to hate him for things I didn't know weren't the ways they seemed?" I asked them as shame crept up my face pinching my cheeks.

"Because..." Jacob answered washing a bloody rag in another bucket that one of the girls who had been in the tent with me brought in, "... David had to be hard so that he wouldn't get in trouble for having emotions for anyone in this camp, which it would have seemed like he did because you would have been nicer to him than to any other of the junior commanders, and that would have caused suspicions."

I thought for a moment about what my brothers had said to me, and even though I knew deep in my heart that they meant well, I could not help thinking that was their most ludicrous idea to date.

"You should have told me!" I hissed at them in my loudest whisper. "I would have known how to pretend that I did not have any care for him. I do it with these ladies all the time!"

Samuel looked at me and then walked over to the entryway of the tent to pour out the water with which the girls had been cleaning up David. "Do you really think that you could have pretended to be as unforgiving and hateful towards David if you had any idea that there was some soul left in him?" He asked me.

"I'm sorry Cali," Jacob said, "I submit that you're a woman of many talents, but 'actress' is not one of them."

I chuckled softly at first, and then it continued unstoppably to grow inside of me until I started to laugh. This must have been much to the relief of everyone in the tent with me because they all started to laugh along with me in a way we had not done since we had come to the bush. I had my siblings say good-bye to David before they went into their tents, leaving me and the other ladies who were to watch him that night.

The next morning, I was on my way to aid the other women in tending to the morning meal when David called for me. He asked me to bring him the Chief Commander, and the General before I asked the other women who were to tend to him that morning to come in. I was standing at the mouth of the tent when David refused the offer of the Camp's highest officials to take him to another place for treatment. I was standing there when he informed them that he did not have the strength to make it past that morning. I was there when David asked for permission from his commanders to peacefully leave a life they had no rights to give or take.

I returned to that tent after they had left me with instructions to grant him everything he needed on his way home. I figured it was the least I could do.

~~~~~~~~~~~~~~~~~~

"Did you say anything to him?" My therapist asked me.

"No. I did not know what to say to him after beating him up. I was scared that if I had not beaten him, maybe he wouldn't have been too exhausted to live."

"Did he say anything to you?"

"He told me that I did not beat him to the point of death. He told me he was sorry for everything. He asked me to tell my friends and family that he was sorry. He wanted me to tell Rhys and Sydney that they did not do anything wrong to him, except care about feelings he had long lost for himself."

~~~~~~~~~~~~~~~~~~

I couldn't say anything to David in return for his words. I was no longer angry at him, but I did not know what to do with all the new things I had learned about someone I had hated for so long. I alone looked after him through that because I decided that would be the only way I knew how to show my remorse for beating him. At night, David's breathing became more labored in expense, and I realized he was nearing that time when we would see him no longer. I sat down next to him searching for anything to say to him.

"How do you get here? How do you get to boil a boy in a kettle over a fire you made his own mother set, and then force her to eat him? How do you cut off somebody's hands that you did not give to him? How do you stare into the white of a child's eyes, into the pools of black longing for a compassion they just know has to be there, and you want for their blood? The pleasure of intercourse is the unbridled willingness of passion between two souls. There is no pleasure in force. How do you get to where you burn a baby alive? How do you get to where you cut open the stomach of a pregnant woman? How do you starve children like you do not remember what it was like to be one? How did you get to where all this, all of this becomes the regular, the un-repulsive, the normal? How do you get here?

David struggles to talk, but his words are hard to come out past the breaths he can barely make. I watch his mouth make out the words of his apologies to me as tears formed in his eyes, spilling from the sides. I take his hand in both of mine to bring it to my cheek.

"You have saved my life David, I know now, so many times. For that, to you, I remain grateful. But for hundreds of others, you have trespassed unforgivably against them.

"Pray for my soul Cali." He answers a little louder this time, "Pray for my soul, because if God judges me like you, I am done for."

I kiss his hand as it begins to grow limp in mine.

"God is not man, old friend. God is not man."

I put his hand by his side slowly, and I kiss his cheeks; after which, I go to tell the General that they have lost another rebel soldier to a war he did not have to fight.

Chapter 39

November 14, 2004

It was seven days before it would become six months since we had been gone from our parents that Samuel became a junior commander. It was also on that day that I decided that it was time for us to put our escape plan into high gear. Samuel becoming a junior commander meant that he would be in charge of missions, which in turn meant that his presence was not one likely to be released anytime soon. I was supposed to be chanting along with the children who stood around the bonfire in the square, but I was far too troubled to sing in any semblance of joy or merriment. The usual rites followed his initiation, including "Holy water" which was sprinkled over his head and over his face soaking the red singlet he was wearing. I watched his face for the pride that was supposed to be associated with this office, but found none. He just stood there without emotion, except for a vacancy in his bloodshot eyes. A string of shells was put around his neck meant to protect him from bullets and other enemy arms. A looted goat was slaughtered and hanging in the middle of the fire, its blood dripping into a bowl then rubbed onto my brother's skin in the sign of a cross.

The merriment continued well into the evening, the sound of boys with full bellies playing soccer in the square, riddling the air. I sat with the other girls in front of the tent behind the fire that was beginning to die down to watch Joshua play. Something about his little legs trying to keep up with those of the older boys gladdened my heart; giving me hope that maybe he could play that game again with his father, and his brother, Isaiah; away from fear, away from pain, away from worry, away from here. My joy was dampened with the reminder that Joshua would be accompanying Samuel on his first mission as a junior commander. Samuel was in charge of leading a team of children into the village mostly to loot homes because we were beginning to run out of supplies. It was a far more daring mission because the villages were becoming deserted, so our troops had to press farther into the more populated areas of the town. Going into better populated areas meant, being in greater danger of the bullets, and bombs of government soldiers. I worried for Samuel and Jacob. I worried for Joshua, because he was small. I always worry for Joshua, because he is small. I worry that everybody would get back on the truck, and he would be standing there like he was standing there when his parents were killed; alone, vulnerable, and afraid. I do not want my littlest brother to go, but there is nothing I can do to stop it.

A young girl who was sitting next to me got up and brushing the dirt from her dress, she informed us that she was going to my brothers' tent.

"Why?" I asked her.

"I am tonight's consolation prize;' she answered shrugging her shoulders rather dejectedly.

"He is not going to do anything to you." I told her smiling reassuringly.

"I know," she replied smiling; "Never has being prostituted sounded like music to my ears." She leaves us walking to the opposite side of the fading embers. She stopped a bit later, turned around and said:

"You know, if Samuel were to ask me though, I would, with my heart. With my whole heart."

~~~~~~~~~~~~~~~~~

"Did she have a crush on your brother?" My therapist asked me, watering the flowers by the window in her office.

"I don't know. I never asked. I would imagine she did. Who wouldn't?"

"Did any girls like your brothers?"

"Yes. Several of them. I, however, did not encourage it. It was not an appropriate time for anyone to develop an interest in anyone else."

"Did your brothers have crushes that you know of?"

"They were very nice to the girls. Samuel was very nice to the girl who was sent to him that night. This is why I think she was chosen; because they thought he fancied her, or something."

"What did they do then, if he wasn't going to be with her?"

"I went toward their tent, not because I did not trust my brother; I was curious as to what they would do instead."

"What were they doing?"

"He was teaching her "Self Defense.""

~~~~~~~~~~~~~~~~~~

I stood by my tent watching my brothers march off into the bush slowly becoming blackened by the impending night sky. I issue from the deepest of my heart, a prayer to God for their protection and safe return home so that I could breathe once again. To remove my mind from wondering, I began to sew some new underwear for some of the boys in the camp letting my thoughts go to my friends in the U.S. I wondered as I often did what they were doing at that moment, if they knew that I was gone. I wondered how they were doing with me being gone the way I was.

~~~~~~~~~~~~~~~~~

"Did you find out?" My therapist asks me, sitting across from me and crossing her legs in front of her.

"Find out what?"

"What they were doing."

"Yes." I smiled sadly, even though the thought of my findings of what my friends were up to while I was gone was nothing short of heartening.

"One morning, my friends got up at four in the morning to along the highway. They sewed numbers next to a name of a missing child soldier, and in big block letters on posters they carried with them was written:

"CAN YOU SEE US NOW? WILL YOU HEAR US NOW?"

They raised twenty thousand dollars to set us free. They sent the money to my parents explicitly requesting that they use it to bribe the police, to come for us." My voice catches in a sob, and I don't necessarily care to stop it, but continue to speak through my tears.

"They did not care about the moral of bribing anyone, or about getting in trouble. I have to get better. I need to get better. I need to show my friends that what they did was worth it; that I was worth the bother. I need to thank them. I need to thank them well."

"Cali, you will get better." She assures me nodding with an empathetic smile.

"How do you know?" I ask her quietly, almost in a whisper.

"Because you want to. You are more passionate about getting rid of this pain than this pain is passionate about staying in. You are committed, and essentially, that is the most important component of this process."

I smile a rather cheesy smile because I cannot help the joy that promise brings. She mocks me for my smile laughing out loud herself. She inquired further into what happened on Samuel's first day as a junior commander.

~ ~ ~ ~ ~ ~ ~ ~ ~ ~ ~ ~ ~ ~ ~ ~

I was washing clothes in the backyard when Jacob came running up to me. I was not expecting to see him because he was not accompanied by the usual victorious chants of the returning soldiers. My heart somersaulted into my stomach as I waited for the words that were stuck on his lips and would not come out. He made out the word "Joshua", and before he could finish any sentences that he may have had within him, my feet grew a mind of their own. I was tearing down the path through the bush toward a destination I did not know, hoping that my ears would guide me to a noise I desperately hoped Joshua was joyfully making. Not too far from camp, I saw a group of boys standing around in a semi-circle, and a boy lying in the grass. I ran blinded by tears to the body that was not moving, with a struggling rise and fall of his chest. I, wailing, begged my brother to hold on because I did not know how to tell his mother that I did not return her son to her alive.

I promised him that it was getting better soon. I promised Joshua that he could have anything in the world he wanted if he would just hold on and live. My sisters reached us not too long after that, and with their help, I carried Joshua into the boys' tent. I stripped his clothes from him, cleaning the blood from his body with the clothes that were on him. I found the source of the unstoppable red liquid all over my brother's body. There was a bullet hole under his right chest that I knew still contained the bullet rigidly lodged in there. I quickly cleaned up the hole and plugged it with a piece of cloth tying it around his body to hold it in place inside of him. I held the little boy in my arms, rocking him and praying over his weakening body, just like his mother would. He did not die that night, but Joshua remained unconscious for two days, with his body growing weaker, and his siblings' hearts growing with increasing fear. We feared that we would not get our brother home in time to believe us when we had told him that the best days are yet to come.

Chapter 40

Life was almost the way it used to be. By God, I was going to will everything in me to guide my past to where it belonged, and to leave it there. There were silly music videos to make with friends I trusted enough to allow their love and support that never went away. There were fires to build at the beach against sunsets as we danced to the rhythm of guitar and drums. There were slumber parties to stay awake through as we waded the mucks of relationships, laughing at our pretenses that we were better off without them. It was in one of these joys that I was introducing back to home when my mom informed me that a letter had come for me earlier that day. The letter wasn't an actual letter, she would modify. My parents had called to inform me that they had received a letter from our village elders, and that they needed a phone call from me as soon as I received their message.

August 30, 2005

I am talkative today with my therapist just two days after I returned my parents' call to find out what the letter they received had concerned.

"What did it say?"

"I hate letters. They are always bad. Even though the events of the first two led to a wonderful life, there were still such misfortunes in them."

"What did the letter say?"

"The town wanted my siblings and I to sign a petition granting the LRA commanders forgiveness, and immunity, so they would return to live peaceably among civilians."

"What was your reaction?"

I sigh deeply before I reply.

"Let's just say that I am currently heavily medicated."

"What did your parents think of the letter?"

"They said that it was up to me... that they would be supportive of whatever decision I was to make. The elders meet in thirty days to take the results of the petition to Kampala. If I chose to forgive, I may give my parents permission to sign it on my behalf. If I chose to fight it, I was to be there when the elders met, to testify as to why they should not be granted immunity."

"What are you going to do?

"My flight leaves in three weeks. You have three weeks to change my mind."

"Do you want your mind changed?"

~~~~~~~~~~~~~~~~

It occurs to me that if my parents did not have even the minutest portion of them desiring that I forgive, they wouldn't have bothered with asking me in the first place. There is something miraculous and powerful about the aftermath from the genocide that occurred in Rwanda, an occurrence people tend to point out to me whenever they heard I was from a war-torn country in Africa. It is the now peaceful existence of victims with the people who once betrayed and hunted them. Forgiveness was a concept ordinarily that I struggled with. None of the former things that ever happened in my life, however hurtful, were measurable to the unspeakable horror that was my life for six months. People hear stories like that in bulk. Like: there was a war; people died; so many bodies; shots were fired; people returned home; people were forgiven. For me, it did not happen in bulk. It was particular. It plays slowly in recesses of my mind. Those people that were read about in black print on white paper were bodies in front of me. They were lives in front of my cocked gun, souls that prayed with me under stolen stars under the raffia thatched roof of the kitchen. Nobody tells of the scales traversed to get to forgiveness, or that it takes a little longer than nine months to get there. Do they know that my sister, Angela did not speak a word for a month after our return? Do they know that the children of Acholiland die long before they enter the bush? They died when they could no longer play fearlessly in the fields, go into the bushes to fetch firewood, or plant in the fields. We died when a nation that once enjoyed a time of peace, happiness, and prosperity could only hand down to its children sorrow, helplessness, and despair. Do they think that when we come back, that the nightmare is over? In our dreams, we are running in blood-soaked clothes, brandishing guns heavier than ourselves. We are shells of ourselves, seeing poison in our foods, and monsters lurking in every corner. If we are ever fortunate enough to escape, we are treated rather like prisoners of war, than children who survived a tragedy and need love, and a promise of good. Do they know that we have lost our youth and virility? That we are afraid of our own shadows and run from a knock on the door? Do they know that traditionalist make escapees have to go through cleansing rites to rid themselves of the guilty conscience that consumes them for the lives they have taken? Girls are belittled by men who underrate them for once being wives of the enemy. These are men who have the audacity to speak to a survivor of battle when they tucked their genitals between their legs running at the sight of AK-47s.

Do they know that we have to relearn the impudence to rise up like the warriors we were, for we have been through hell and back and lived to tell of it? We stared into the barrel of a gun, got caught between enemy and safety cross fires, and still had the courage to run home. Do they know that my sister, Augustina was found by my father with her legs thrashing in midair gasping for air from the rope wrapped firmly against her neck? Augustina was admitted into the Psychiatric Hospital in London soon thereafter. Do they know that parents like mine struggle to forgive themselves from feelings of not being protective of their children enough? Everybody in my family sees a therapist. Does anybody know that?

After I received the phone call from my parents, I do not remember much else. Against the white sheets of the psychiatric unit of the hospital, I am laying now, trying at the bid of my therapist to summon the memory of my reaction to being asked to forgive the General. I remember finishing the conversation with my parents. I remember heading for my room as life proceeded as it did sometimes when I was overcome with anger since we returned. I saw everything in snapshots like in that of a camera; my eyes blinking frequently to slow down the thought shooting across my mind. I heard glass shatter; I remember falling onto the ground; I remember shaking uncontrollably. I do not remember anymore.

~~~~~~~~~~~~~~~~

"What do you think I should do?" I ask the woman sitting across from me.

"You said you leave in three weeks."

"It is as I desire it in my mind. Before I actually do it, what do you think I should do?"

"Cali, a lot of positive things can come from either. Forgiveness is necessary for healing. If you do not sign the petition, and the commanders do not surrender, more lives are at stake. If you forgive, you're not even necessarily setting them free, but you give them back the past they cast on your shoulders. You take back the power they continue to have over you, over your relationship with your family, your friends, with Rhys." She smiles to me and informs that along with her sage advice came a surprise for me. I follow her eyes to the door to see my father all the way from Uganda, standing there like a mirage on desert sands.

"Papa!!" I scream, flying out of my bed and straight into his wide-open hands. His hug is tight like it has always been even more so since the return of his children from the brutal bowels of the Northern Uganda bush.

"Your therapist tells me you'll be here a few more days. Do you think you'll be ready for home in three weeks?"

"Yes Papa." I answered, my smile growing even wider as he clenches my hand in his.

A few hours later, Rhys came in to let me know that the rest of my family was on their way to the hospital. I ask him what the chances were that the old man came just to innocently check on his daughter's well being after she'd been admitted yet again to the psychiatric unit of the hospital.

"Do you really want the answer to that question?" he asked.

I suppose I already know without verbal admittance.

When eventually the rest of my family makes their way up to my room, and all the pleasantries are done, I explain to my father that I wasn't much for beating around the bush. While I enjoyed his presence, there was still sneaking suspicion that there was an agenda to his visit. There was. My father did not think that in our fragile state, my siblings and I were in the right frame of mind to make any decisions concerning the immunity of the rebel commanders. Rhys's hand was holding tightly unto mine trying to keep the warmth creeping up to my neck from exploding out of my mouth. My parents had said that they would be supportive of whatever decision I was to come to. There wasn't enough support coming from a trip all the way across the equator to sway a decision I most likely would prefer. I told my Papa that I did not know what I was going to eventually do, but at the moment, forgiveness wasn't lining the skies of my consideration. He reiterated to me that my parents would support whatever decision I arrived at in thirty days, but that if I wanted to know how far he'd like me to have healed by then, it would be to forgive.

"Have you forgiven them?" I asked him.

"Yes." He replied.

"How could you?" I asked my father through clenched teeth. "You're supposed to be in rage. You're supposed to want to kill them. You are supposed to want to rip them apart until they feel all the pain they inflicted on your children for the rest of their lives. How could you forgive them already?"

"Cali, it wasn't easy. But we have to be good examples of the lessons we teach our children. What God requires of you..."

I do not remember the entirety of my Papa's sentence as my eyes begin to blink again, flashing snapshots of the room across my face. I cannot control my mind to finish any particular thought. My hand leaves Rhys's as I rise to my feet speaking words in sentences that barely made it to the end.

"When I was a child, before I came to Hosanna I never went to church. M... my... my father never took me, my grandmother was too sick. But every Sunday from the neighbor's radio bellowed church service, I would go and listen to them b...b... because there was a translator, so I could understand. I did what the preacher said that God wanted from me, even though as far as proof went, God had long abandoned me. In all the years since then, I have done what God wanted from me. I have never willed anybody ill. I have respected my parents. I have never put anything above God. I go to church to church on Sunday. I volunteer. I do not drink. I do not smoke. I remained a virgin even at a time when sex is like a race to the finish bed. I did it anyway, because God said that if I do... if I... if I believe in him, if I do what he says for me to do, he would watch over me. He would see me through anything; He would protect me from the evil one. He would do the basic "God" things, like: NOT LETTING ME GET ABDUCTED... and kicked, and stabbed, and shot, and given away like a prize... and raped... and I can smell him... I can smell him... I cannot stop smelling him... I cannot ... I do not remember my former life... I do not have anything to give anybody... they took everything... where was God? I can smell him... I cannot stop... where was God... tell me... "WHERE WAS HE?!" I finish pounding at my father's chest and slumping onto the floor where I wailed in protest against promises failed. A nurse came in and courteously asked my family to exit the room until I calmed down. Right before I fall asleep from the medication she had administered into my veins, I asked her to tell my family that I would no longer be needing visitors for the remainder of the night. I woke up hours later to a nurse checking my stats at the foot of my bed. When she saw my open eyes, she smiled kindly and checked my vitals while asking some routine questions.

"What time is it?"

"It is seven a.m., dear. How did you sleep?"

"Fine, thank you."

"Should we allow visitors today?"

"Sure."

"Alright. For now, it is just a young man. He's been here all night." She said before paging a nurse to let Rhys in.

"How is she doing?" Rhys asks my nurse, just as she leaves the room.

"She'll be alright."

I hoped against hopes, she was right.

I hate letters.

Chapter 41

November 19, 2004

I lay in the General's bed wondering if this truly was the last time I was going to lay down there in his room with him. I was afraid that moment was one of the memories that I would never forget because the smell of sweat on his body, and the smell of his breath on my face seemed like it would never vacate my mind. I looked at him slowly out of the corners of my eyes as I turned my face slightly towards him, and then at the revolver that lay on his bedside. My mind went back again to the raid where we had massacred the IDP camp in Gulu. I saw myself again slip that paper under that fence and pray into the wind that help would find its way to us.

I wondered how they would save us, what they would do, when they would come. I got up from bed and began to put my clothes on. The General woke up and asked me what I was doing, and I told him that I wanted to go and tend to my sick brother. He got up and sat on the other side of the bed with his back to me. He told me in a firm and cold but calm manner that I knew the rules. My brother was given three days to get better, or he would have to be killed.

"It is a gunshot wound" I attempted to reason with the devil that sat before me. "He cannot recover in such little time."

The General turned on his side to look at my face. I saw softness come over his face in a split second, and then just in that same split, it was gone. His eyebrows creased and he informed me that it took the manpower and the resources of seven children and soldiers to supply my brother with the necessary aid to keep him alive.

He left me two options: I was to either allow my brother to be killed either by starvation, or a single gunshot to be administered by one of my other brothers or to select seven children who were to die in his stead. I stood for a few moments as if the soles of my feet had grown studs and bolted themselves to the ground. I swayed slightly absently with the wind that came into the room as I allowed it to take my spirit with it and allow the impatient numbness that wanted to occupy my senses. I turned around slowly in almost a robotic fashion, and began to leave the room. His voice, the coldest I'd ever heard them if it were possible stopped me dead in my tracks.

"I feel something wrong coming upon this camp. I feel like something is going to go very wrong."

He turned again to look at me with menacing eyes, and finished:

"I will kill you first, and the rest of your family, one by one."

He lay back down just the way he was before I had gotten up; I turned around and continued my robotic walk out the door. There was something though changed inside of me, sort of like I snapped. I wasn't afraid anymore, and I pleaded with my spirit not to return. I wanted the numbness; I wanted the absence. I wanted the recklessness that arrives with faith, which draws you to believe that in planning the absolute best, you cannot expect the absolute worst. I walked out of the door of the General's room, knowing within myself that that would be the last time I would ever spend the night with the General.

****

I heard them, as I sat with my sisters beside the entry way
of our brothers' tent. The planes approaching overhead.
We looked at each other knowing that either this was the
last fighting we would ever do until we see each other
home at the end of it, or it would be the last time that we
saw each other on this side of glory. Either way, we were
going down victoriously. We would go down refusing to
suffer any longer, and we would go down together. With
Joshua safely tucked in his hideaway, I whispered the plan
again to my sisters as if to remind them, in case they had
forgotten. I hugged them and kissed them. I could not see
my brothers' faces in the other tent, but I knew they could
see me, and they knew that I loved them, that my prayers
were in the wind which blew so softly across their beings.
They came closer, and by the time I was done ridding
myself of any other inhibitions to finally take me and my
family home, the camp was in uproar. Bullets were flying
everywhere and everybody was running helter skelter.
Children ran into the bush with their hands on their heads
in protection, and prayers were being uttered along with
the name of God as each bullet threatened so close to

each child. My siblings and I ran into the bush with the rest of everybody as the fire shot down and burned parts of the bushes in our path. My siblings as advised ran straight for the shadow over the mountain, and I ran to Joshua's hideaway to pick up my brother. I scooped him up in my arms, and though he had grown quite heavier than I remembered, I carried him and ran as fast as I could further between the big leaves that were now covered with dust and the blood of the innocent beings that were trying to make their way through. Just as it started, the noise stopped. The planes were gone, and I could hear soldiers looking through the bush for children. Two things happened then. In my mind, I had always assumed that in the event I chance an encounter with a UPDF soldier, I would turn myself in and ask for protection. But sitting and hiding in that bush, that early morning, I did not say a word. I was quiet because the second thing that came over me was fear. Fear that I could not trust that my father's betrayer was not looking for me. For some reason, I had hoped to see a familiar face like Rhys's or Sydney's. I had not anticipated that they most likely would not be allowed just like my parents to be there, especially without the assurance as to whether or not their children were there.

When the soldiers were gone, I took a deeper breath and let it out to plan my next course of action. I knew that I had to run for the soldiers so that they could save my brother. I took a cloth from the sling bag on my shoulder and put it over him. As I turned to run for redemption, I heard a click on the side of my head.

"Get up" the voice said next to me. It was the General.

There was something my mother had told me when I had written her not too far apart after Rhys had asked me to marry him. I had written her in a bit of wonder as to if I would sacrifice my own self for my children because I always feared that in the middle of a war that if I were running with my children, I would leave them. My mother wrote me back and said to me:

"Nothing prepares you for when you should save someone before yourself, nor does anyone tell you who to save."

Joshua, my little brother needed to live. I needed for him to live, and I was going to do any and everything in my power to see him live; to watch my mother scoop him up in her arms and never let him go ever again. I saw that picture. I saw the fluorescent lighting of our living room, and all of us gathered around the center table playing cards and trying to figure out far fewer stressful situations than these. In that moment, I refused to die. I knew that in order to stay alive, I had to go with the General back to camp and prepare his things for our long and painful trek to the Sudan.

"Can I bring him?" I asked the General with all the sorrow of the slippery dream that almost came true waning farther in my mind.

"You can bury him."

I looked at him, getting up to let him know that I was not going to bury my little brother alive; but he pointed out to me that the little was no longer alive. I looked at the body that lay behind me and watched in the faint light of the barely there dawn for his chest to rise and fall with the rhythm of life. He had none. I blindly reached for him as my head filled with pain, and my eyes with tears. My hands rested shakily on his head as I opened his mouth to hear or feel something... anything. He felt cold, as cold as he had felt when I had picked him up, but I did not have time to recollect that my little brother who had escaped the harrowing events that happened to his parents had arrived at the same fate.

I cried. I cried for my mother and for myself. I tried to speak to him, but no words would come out. I had intended on putting up a fight against that General until either he killed me, or I escaped. However, to hold Joshua's lifeless body against myself, I did not care any longer. I did not want to live; I did not want to go home, and I did not want to tell my mother that Joshua was dead. I told the General as I covered Joshua up that I was going to bury Joshua back at the camp, that I was not going to leave him in a blood-soaked field of the "unidentifiables". My brother had fought bravely for himself, for everyone, and for me. I was going to bury him with honor, and mourn him like he deserved.

I had always thought salvation was felt; that salvation was given in an emotional and non-physical way. I heard mine – my salvation. As I started to lift Joshua, I heard them. UPDF soldiers were in a circle around the General, my deceased brother and I and they were commanding the General to put his gun down.

All I remember, mostly because that is all I want to remember is picking up my brother, and entering into a vehicle that had made its way along a path by the bush. I had turned around after I had entered, cradling my brother on my bosom to look back on the evil that we had suffered for six months, and there was the General laying in his own blood. I remember a soldier shooting him as he attempted to seize me as his bullet proof, and means of escape.

Chapter 42

Joshua and I were taken to a UPDF barrack that I was informed in the vehicle already had my siblings who were waiting and praying I was alive making my way to them. I watched the fade farther as we made our way out of enemy territory to the safety of the friendly men who had been sent to save our lives. I saw my siblings running toward me from a slight distance, and my heart gladdened at the sight of them. I wished I did not carry pain for them in my arms as I held Joshua with me out of that car. They stopped dead in their tracks slowly peering at the body in my arms. I began to cry, and they knew in that moment that it was not to be that all my mother's children would return to her. They ran over to me as I walked toward them, then we gathered around Joshua's body, and holding onto each other, we wept.

A man slowly walked over to us, hesitantly reaching for my shoulder. He expressed his deepest condolences, and at that time, I noticed that a silence had fallen over the barracks, and the UPDF soldiers were looking at us with sympathy and moistness in their eyes. The man in uniform who tapped my shoulder bent down and whispered a music he did not have to sing, for I will never feel the redemption I felt that day in those simple words of his.

"Would you like to go home, now?"

We were taken to another civilian camp, which was a bit smaller than the one we had been at previously where we were escorted inside a shed that felt hotter inside than it was outside and were told to wait for the van that would return us to home. I, still with my little brother cradled limply in my arms, squatted to the ground to put him down. I sat down next to him and stared sadly at Joshua as tears again filled my eyes. I looked at my siblings and one by one we looked at each other with tears in our eyes and dancing in our hearts. I looked down again at my brother to see this immense peace that seemed to breeze on his face as if to send us all a message of what hope can do.

Angela screamed first summoning everyone to follow her eyes to the figure standing next to a van that had parked a bit away from the shed. There was Isaiah walking towards us in a sort of a daze, as if not sure it was us, and trying not to get his hopes up in the event that, in fact, we would just turn out to be this beautiful mirage standing in front of him. We ran to the outside of our tent but not directly to him because we did not know if our brother would love us, or care that we were home. We did not even know he was alive. Angela moved a bit ahead of us, and he continued to walk closer to us. We all followed her who had begun to walk now with only a slim hesitation. We followed until we all stopped, because he stopped, because we did not know what else to do.

I knew that UPDF soldiers off standing in the corners of the compound were looking at us, some of them had begun to disperse when Isaiah had gotten there, but most of them still stood around. Augustina broke the awkwardness of not knowing whether or not to hug our brother and unleash the familiar blood that would pulse our hearts with his alike. To hear the rhythm of our mother play again in that unison we'd always known.

"Are you here in anger or in love?" Augustina asked him with her voice shaking and tears coursing down her cheeks.

Isaiah heaved a heavy sigh mixed with sorrow and relief. "In love..." he said with a catch in his throat. "In love."

He knelt to the ground, letting us throw ourselves at him, crying without fearing that we would wake up, and this blessed reunion would have been just a dream. We took him into the shed to tell him what had happened during our escape. He cried even more for the little boy who laid there not being able to see this glorious sight that was taking place right before him. Eventually, we all went into the van, and headed for home. We had two escort cars go in front of us, and two behind us to ensure our safe delivery home.

I sat back and watched the shadow start to disappear beside us until it was behind us, never to be seen from the side we had for the past six months ever again. I relaxed when it was gone and thought about what would become of us when we got home. In the midst of my excitement for home, a new worry settled in; a worry I had not anticipated to rear its ugly head. I worried of how many people back home would blame us for the misfortunes they had encountered in the wake of our abduction. I wondered if my parents could love us like they did long before we were stolen from them. If they would love us not because the seminars they had organized prescribed that they do, but because they wanted to love us and care for us. I wondered what would become of us; how many nightmares we would have until our family would tire of us and liken it to just the norm. I wondered how many times we would react violently to people who would even attempt to love us and maybe envision the idea that we came back in peace and could not abduct children from the camp. Most of all, I worried that we would not entertain any love or affection that anyone in our lives would dare to lavish upon us. I worried about the future of Rhys with me, about how everyone in the U.S. would react to the horrific experience I had gone through with my siblings. My siblings looked out the windows, and silently we rode through town watching people pass by and peer into the car, not understanding the children who rode among the soldiers.

* * * * * * * * * * * * * * *

The first face I saw was my mother's as we pulled into Hosanna. To me the car could not have stopped fast enough. It was as if my eyes were watching her in slow motion, but it was in a flash that my fingers reached for the handle on the inside of the van. The door swung open and in that moment, I realized the van had not actually stopped, and we were still ways from my family who were walking toward us in the distance. The dust that settled into the air from all the vehicles clouded the space between us and our family.

"You are home." Isaiah spoke quietly to us as we stood rigidly to the ground waiting for our unbelief to take its leave as the figures behind the dawn's fog. We ran toward them. They ran toward us. I stopped to let my siblings reach my parents first and fall into their arms. My mother cried pitifully with the same kind of tears that unabashed spilled from my father's eyes as he looked up from kissing his young children. He stood up, and I ran into the arms that I knew had been waiting so longingly for me. When we were all welcomed, my parents drove us to Hosanna where Sydney and Luke were waiting. From the distance, I could see a fidgety Sydney see our van and begin to jump wildly for joy. Again, I opened the car door before it stopped, running wildly for my best friend in laughter and tears at the same time. My siblings rushed at Luke, who held them so dear to him. Sydney kissed them all as Luke held me in an embrace. We both watched Sydney love on the god siblings she sorely missed.

"It is like you were dead, and now you're alive…" Sydney cried. "… Someone could literally break through a coffin and say 'Praise God! I'm alive', and I wouldn't be any more shock than I am right now."

I laughed in spite of myself and could easily have died right then and there, and known the completion of what it means to be undeniably and uninhibitedly happy. I looked around for Rhys but could not see him anywhere. Sydney saw the anticipation for something beyond the crowd and knew what I carried in my mind.

"He had to stay in the house. We got a threat from the rebels which said that anybody who sights Rhys and does not kill him, the LRA will find out, and that they will kill that person. It is not true, we know, and the likelihood is very small, but fear is powerful and can make anyone do anything. He was told to stay in the house which is heavily guarded now in case anything happens."

"He really wanted to be here," Luke added for my assurance.

"I know," I answered knowingly.

We left for home after we all had said hello to everyone and had cried and laughed in spite of pain together. As we pulled up to the house, I got the same butterflies in my stomach I had gotten when I arrived home in the U.S. It was as I never allowed myself in captivity to forget. With a candle burning on every window, it stood majestically waiting for its inhabitants who brought joy, and laughter into it to return, and would never let those candles die until we returned to its solace. In front of its giant front doors stood my prince, my love, my breath, my life, everything I had ever deemed worthy of all things honorable in my life. Rhys was standing in front of the door waiting for me. The car stopped, and I jumped out of it shooting straight for his arms. I realized then just how I had actually not believed I would ever see him even up to that point. I held on to him, and I refused to let go. Wrapping my arms around his neck, I kissed him with the release of everything that had been within me dying to tell him, to feel him, to love him. My godparents had arrived in our absence and had waited patiently behind me after greeting my siblings to welcome me home. We hugged, thanking God for our safe return, and weeping on one another's shoulders for the brother, son and godson we were to be with no more.

Isaiah, standing in the doorway with tears still streaming down his face welcomed us home, asking us to enter and to stay forever. We entered with silence that fell without prompting of everyone; letting us breathe in the familiar scent of home, and the warmth that came whenever one walked into our home. There was rejoicing. There was laughter and tears as we all celebrated our homecoming with music that played all night, and food that we were all too full from gratefulness to eat.

Chapter 43

September 7, 2005

I wake up in the morning the day after I told my therapist of our return home to our families. I look around me in the room I cannot believe that I have called home for the month. It has been ten months since we were rescued from the bush, and thirty days since I have been in the hospital. The longest I have been here from a psychotic break in the duration of my recovery. An orderly comes into my room to put my fresh clean laundry on the dresser that sits beside a window. She informs me that my therapist was expecting to see me later that morning. I thank her, stuff the clean laundry into my packed suitcase and leave the room for my morning medication. I walk tentatively toward the pharmacy station to take my pills. I put my head back as the medicines slide down to my throat, and I could almost feel them drop inside my empty stomach. I thank the nurse and walk over to the window like I always did every day, to see the granite sign that stands majestically all of five feet toward the courtyard of the building. It reads:

Richard J. Camelot II

Mental Rehabilitation Center

Newport Beach, CA.

It gleams despite the rain clouds that hover threateningly over the town. My therapist was in the room by the time I returned. When I entered, it was no longer like I remembered left it. There was a frilly comforter on the floor with a bowl of candy in the middle, candied apples on one side, cheesecake on the other. She asked me to take a seat on the floor beside the food, and I saw a game of scrabble laid in the middle of the feast in front of me. We sat and ate together talking about nothing in particular, but of life's other trivial matters. We played the scrabble on the floor, and though I was glad to be there, I could not help but miss her already, knowing that it was going to be a while until I saw her again being gone to Uganda.

The journey to the end of the story of the girl who along with her siblings had been betrayed by a trusted caretaker and sold into slavery to child abductors in a Northern Ugandan bush was one I am almost certain my therapist did not expect such unhinging particulars of. But so it was, even to the very end. A knock at the door interrupts our meeting, and at her beckoning, the knocker opens the door. Sydney comes walking into the room, and I smile up to her in great appreciation that she was there.

It was not in the brightest of airs that we had said goodbyes when she came to visit the day before when I had become unfairly short with her.

"You do not understand what it is like Sydney!" I had shouted as I stormed from my room carrying some clothes down the staircase to the launderer.

"I know that Calista! I get that, okay? I get that I probably never will! But help me at least try!" She said, standing at my doorway not coming after me.

She always came after me; but that day, she stood at my doorway watching me walk down the stairs to the laundry room. I sat down at the last step and cried into the clothes

I carried in my arms hoping that I would never succeed at ridding myself of everyone because of this fear that they would discover the ugliness my heart finds it difficult to scrape away. I walked back upstairs and went into my room to a Sydney, who was picking up her bag to leave.

"Sydney, it's not that I don't want you to understand; it's not that I do not think you understand. I have no idea how you can want to be anywhere near me right now. I do not deserve your attention. I cannot help myself understand talk less of helping someone else understand"

Sydney comes and sits next to me on the floor, and I hugged her with love and adoration for a care I know I have not made it easier for her to have. I thanked my therapist for seeing me, and told her that I looked forward to seeing her when I returned a month later. I was grateful for her because I knew she gave me the strength to go home.

Sydney holds the door open for me to walk through, and as I almost make my exit; I feel a sense of nostalgia for the woman I once was apprehensive of in the beginning of our sessions. A woman who patiently had extracted me from my inhibitions and listened, doing everything she had to do to remind me of the immense unpredictable fun, life could be. I run to Mrs. Garrison - you see that's her name, Mrs. Linda Garrison. I hug her tightly, and I whisper in her ear:

"Thank you."

* * * * * * * * * * * * * * * * *

Later, that evening before I would leave for Uganda to testify, for or against the immunity plea, my friends gathered in my bedroom for comedy night. In the years before the last sixteen months, we would get together more than often to watch funny videos, and stand-up comedians. The room was filled with laughter that was familiar to me in its unabridged gaiety, surfacing the desperate recesses of me that desired the joy within that comfortable circle. In the midst of switching another DVD in the player, and the stories my friends told to us reminding me of what I used to think would become like olden times to me, I asked them to tell me about Calista. The girl from what people kept saying, I used to be.

"What was Calista like? Could you tell me what Calista was like?"

Carrie mutes the TV as the room falls silent with my friends stealing glances between one another. Carrie sits right across from me, with the rest of my inching their ways closer to her.

"No. We cannot tell you what Calista was like. However, we can tell you what she is like; who she is right now." Carrie starts:

"Calista loves to play soccer. She drives her coach crazy because he would finish assigning all these drills for the field to everyone, and Calista would go out there, and just play the game. She just loved to play the game."

"Yeah, she drove the coach crazy and made him complain about how she did not fully understand the concept of "competition." Allyson chimed in.

"Calista would like to think she knows how to swim, but she really does not. Whenever we are in the pool, one of us would stay in there just to make sure she does not drown."

"I can too swim!" I interjected mocking offense.

"Cali, treading the water for five seconds while your head bobs in and out of the surface is not "knowing how to swim"."

"Cali volunteers in almost everything. If anybody needs help, Cali always helps them, even if they were mean to her."

"Cali doesn't ever say "no" to people. She always explains why something may be a good idea, or a bad idea. She only says no to being forced to do something."

"Cali is really energetic and silly. We think it might have something to do with the fact that she eats entirely too much candy."

"Is there such a thing as too much candy?" I interject.

"YES!" Came the resounding reply from all of them.

"Even though Cali puts everybody's feelings first, she is very aware of her worth." Danielle said resuming their answers.

"Cali can be impatient."

"I am not impatient; people are just really stupid lately. It is like the world's getting dumber." I interrupted.

"She's got a bit of road rage."

"Californians cannot drive!" I exclaim animatedly.

"Cali can be pretty timid about defending herself, but when it comes to her friends, if you hurt them, you might want to steer clear of any dark alleys."

A solemn spirit came over the room as my friends continued to tell me about this person I knew because she was me fighting through the murk of despair. I am reminded with the tears in their eyes that I encourage my friends to love life and appreciate every day. That a good day must consist of no more than six hours of sleep, and two cups of coffee – give or take five. Well… give anyway. I learn that I love company, from the ones my parents invite frequently for dinners to the ones of just my girls any time of any day. That besides Rhys, I thought Tom Welling was the hottest man who ever walked the planet earth. I learned that I enjoy the wonderful invention that was the television screen, and everything is usually done in front of one, a habit my parents desperately hoped Law School would break in me.

I stood up from my friends walking over to the window where below in the backyard, I watched the moon's reflection float on the pool's dark water. There are uniformed sniffles with Sydney's closer beside me where she stood taking my hand in hers.

"You know something else about Calista? It is kind of sad really." Sydney said staring at the dark outside that window, "She got abducted, kidnapped from so much love from family, friends, the sisterhood. She prayed and begged God to take her home, but He didn't. Calista never came back to even more love than before she was stolen. She wasn't missed from hearts that felt like someone poked a hole in it, and... and all the air is being let out, and you're trying... you're trying to breathe. Calista's prayers were never answered, because you see, she died there... in the bush."

I turned with furrowed brows to my sister who is still staring at nothing in particular, and tell her the story I remember differently.

"No she did not… she did not die."

"Hmm… how 'bout that? I suppose she didn't."

The air warms behind me as silhouettes of my friends, crowd my once sole figure against the window pane. With the next day in my mind, I ask my friends what they think I should do about forgiving. Allyson stands on the other side of me and says:

"Before the last sixteen months, if one of us were having a bad hair day, one of us could fix it. We fail an exam, a night of sugar binge highs and secrets, with minutes of actual studying fitted in, solved it. We break up with a boy or get in a fight with someone, even though some may take time, we could make it go away. When we got news that you were gone, time stopped. Every minute took an eternity to pass by. We didn't eat; we went to school because we had to, but we were never really there. We just existed silently in each other's company not knowing what to do. We fixed everything; we used to know how to make everything better. The not knowing where you were; the not knowing what to do; the not knowing if you were alive or dead. That was the unbearable part."

Allyson could not finish because her shaking body is breaking up the words she is trying to say. I put my arm around her as Carrie takes over the rest of the story.

"Eventually time started to move fast enough for us to attempt anything. We did not know whether you were alive or dead, but we knew that we needed to tell people to remember you. We wanted to always remember why we loved you, why we missed you."

I turned to the sound by the television were Sydney is putting a DVD in which my friends are going to all the centers where I used to volunteer, they went to our school, our church, where I worked, other people's schools, other people's churches. My girls made the Cassidy Estate their headquarters where anyone could come and leave words of encouragement for their missing friend. Every night, they lit a candle on every window of the house, and kept a vigil with what became over seven hundred people, who by candlelight on each hand, kept vigil until word was received that my siblings and I were safely home. I cried with my friends in my room that night during a video they had not been able before that night, to bring themselves to watch. A video they made never knowing for certain whether or not I would return that sisterhood that had guaranteed so much for all of us. My friends after the video told me that they were not willing to tell me whether or not I should forgive because it was a concept even they were battling with toward the whole ordeal. They wished I would heal. That I would allow the days which were to come, and the love they would never take away, to remind me of brave I truly was, and resurrect me from the dead. I walk to the window again where my imagination plays the mirage of candle flames floating the wind in the fields by the pool house. I look backward to my suitcases that were waiting for the last few things that would take me back, and then I look to that pool house where Sydney and I were supposed to be right now. I walk across the room, close the suitcases, take it downstairs with me past the back courtyard and into the home where there were pictures of my friends on the walls and tables; where there was nail polish on the bathroom vanity next to crack in the mirror that was caused by one of the girls missing when another tossed her the blow dryer. I opened the door to white sheets that kept the dust from the couch from where several movies were watched and stories told; covering the kitchen counter where we watched cooking channels, making the dishes we were learning from them. Those counters had been bathed with more flour than was ever actually used. I take off the white sheets from the histories they hid; returning time to the abandoned abode where waking up was the first part of the most beautiful life. My friends are standing by the doorway when I turn around to their faces registering a mixture of shocks and joys. I laugh with tear filled eyes, and press "resume" to what it used to be.

"I'm home."

Afterward

I see them, my parents and siblings, coming toward us from across the airport. My feet are almost flying, and yet not moving fast enough. Sydney and I crash into them, bringing them, and their luggage along with us to the ground with laughter that caused a spectacle that held captive even for a few seconds, every passerby's attention. The laughter in the airport resonates into my therapist's office where I am sitting now a month later telling her about the several acts of mischief my siblings and I already got into. I tell her about their recovery, and how resilient and faster at it, they are than I am.

"I hear you've gotten some letters as well; encouragement from the community, and even from your home."

"Yeah. My friends had hidden the ones that came while I was still in the bush because they were all very well aware that I did not enjoy letters. However, I did open those ones as well."

"Have you read them all?"

"Not yet. There are so many of them that it is quite overwhelming."

"Do you think that you may be over your fear of letters?"

"I wouldn't call it fear. It was more like… disdain."

I told my therapist about a letter to my siblings and myself, received from a fellow soldier with whom we'd been in the halfway camp. He had escaped much later after us from another camp that he had been taken to along with some other children the day before our escape. He wrote us of the events that transpired in the aftermath of our escape, and word from the other children.

＊＊＊＊＊＊＊＊＊＊＊＊＊＊＊

The girls, who had lost faith without our daily encouragement, had succumbed to their fates, willingly admitting that they would no longer attempt to escape, but stay with their husbands in the bush. They sent apologies in prayers, hoping daily that God would understand. The young boys having lost the girls they had gotten so used to their motherly love had felt the sense of home ripped away from them again. Some drowned themselves in the river; some purposefully ran into the front lines to be shot immediately, while some dutifully and with resignation to any kind of conscience took up with great agility, the task their commanders demanded of them. They were mad, the letter said; almost like their hearts were beating in a box hidden somewhere far away from them. In the letter, they especially thanked us for loving them, not as people who had come to take care of the poor and afflicted, but we had loved them as brothers, and sisters. We loved them with no reservations.

"I am happy to let you know..." he wrote, "... that instead of complete nightmare-filled dreams, it is now met with intervals of peace, and tranquil rest. I envision sitting on the rocks, and watching the sun set over the horizon bidding us adieu until the morrow brings us a new dawn, for us to try life, to love one another for one more day. Isaiah 40:30-31: Even the youths shall faint and be weary, and the young men shall utterly fall. But they that wait upon the Lord shall renew their strength. They shall mount up with wings as eagles; they shall run and not weary, and they shall walk and not faint.

So as each day passes, I find out that we have always been, and will always be, mightier than the wind, gutsier than the storm, more sprightly than the seas, and someday, someday we shall be brighter than the left side shadow of the sun."

****

She matches my smile, which even I must admit comes rather naturally now from several other joys.

"How are you and Rhys?" She asks me, smiling brightly.

"We are good." I answer with a silly grin on my face. "We get lost in the dark a lot."

After her advice for the session before I leave, my therapist asks me why I chose to stay and not go back to testify against the commanders.

I tell her the same thing my sister said to me when I asked her why she didn't. It was a similar reason as was in my heart, but my sister was better with words in our family. She told me that we had consistently cared about the affairs of people. We'd always made a judgment with that being the principle. The elders were not necessarily asking that we let go of the hurt. They wanted us to save the children of the village by letting the people who would otherwise take them captive out of the bush. Forgiveness, my sister would say, will come with time, and we deserve all the time in the world to get there.

"She's a smart girl – your sister." My therapist observes.

"That she is" I agree.

I get up to leave, give my therapist an embrace, and an invitation to a party celebrating Sydney and my 21st birthday.

"I suppose my story is finished now." I say to her before heading out the door.

"Calista, not nearly." She answers, with a promise that she'll be at the party.

I hope she does come. I hope she'll see my siblings. I hope she sees a family can love one another through the changes that tried to sway it and lost. I hope she can see my friends who will dance the night away with their friend who was once dead, but is now alive. I hope she will meet Luke, who loves Sydney, and will tell her so one month after her birthday in another ceremony, in front of God and man. I hope she will see me as happy as I truly am with my Rhys, to whom I am thankful for fixing me; although, he says, I was never really that broken. However, before he is finished being humble as he always is, I am going to kiss him, and let him put his ring back on my finger. I hope she stays well into the night; and before she drives away, I hope she looks back one more time to see through the window the family that is where they ever were to be. Home.

Acknowledgments

I am thankful to God, for the gift of words. I am grateful for the wisdom of knowing how, and when to use that gift.

My world is filled with beautiful people. I forget that sometimes; and then those people remind me in their special ways, that they are still here, and they are still beautiful.

Thank you all for walking miles with me, and for me. Thank you all for believing far too much of me, and for me. Thank you for allowing me, more times than I can remember, to borrow your faith.

Mathias J. Seiwert, Sarah Seiwert, David Brooks, Kerry Brooks, Njoki Mutua, Dr. C. Fyne, Elizabeth Fyne-Nsofor, Chioma Nzewodo, Chino Nzewodo, Ginika Onedibe, Sabrina Ahmed, Donald Nwankwo, Becky Nwankwo, Cyndi Morris Fusek, John Fyne-Nsofor.

And the most beautiful ones of them all, my godchildren:

Sabrina, Jasmine, Autumn, an Elijah, Madison, Sophia, and Zara.

I am so eternally grateful to all the children whose stories I told. Whose realities I shared with the world. Whose lives forever have changed mine. Thank you.

About the Author

Ife Fyne-Nsofor was born in Anambra State, Nigeria on September 10, 1985 to a Seminary professor, and a schoolteacher. Her family moved to the U.S when she was 14 years old.

Ife currently lives in Southern California where she attends University for Biochemistry, raises awareness about social injustices around the world, and volunteers her time at nonprofit organizations.

Made in the USA
Lexington, KY
11 June 2012